TETHERED FATE

BLOOD FATE SERIES
BOOK II

GRACIE STONE

WILLOW
HOUSE
Publishing

For every reader ...
May you find the
love of your life.
May it be eternal,
ethereal and
all consuming.

The heart is an extraordinary vessel that can expand exponentially when called for. And when needed, can endure the worst.

— GRACIE STONE

Tethered Fate

My grandmother's pearls are heavy around my neck, stealing the air from my shallow lungs. Tonight, I will be initiated into our coven. At six and ten, only yesterday, it is time. Mother has been restless all day, making preparations, checking, insisting I scrub clean twice in the bathing tub. I smell like petals and lavender and probably will for days to come.

The candle on my wooden dresser flickers, and my reflection ripples along the aged mirror. The dark wood paneling in my room is musty with the damp weather. Straightening the lace down my chest, I tuck a stray dark strand of hair back into the intricate styling mother spent over an hour on. This is important to her. To me.

I pinch both cheeks, and a dusty rose color blooms in each. In the dim light, brown eyes stare back at me in the mirror. Prominent cheekbones and plump, pink lips define my oval face, all features Mother assures me are to the liking of the gentry men.

With my father long passed, it is imperative I marry well, and being sworn into our coven on the eastern outskirts of the great city of London is the first step to a better life for mother and me. I am certain being of magical breeding will be to my benefit in securing a husband of the wealthy kind.

"Serena, time to go." Mother's voice echoes from the hallway. I give the sides of my hair one last sweep with the ivory brush and set it down with trembling hands.

"Let's go, girl!"

I close my eyes against the harshness in her voice and walk into the hall, not meeting her gaze. Everything must go smoothly tonight.

"The carriage is waiting ma'am," Joseph says from the foot of the stairs, as I follow Mother down. The last of our house staff after Father's passing. He does the heavy lifting, so to speak, and drives our carriage. His graying hair and blue eyes crinkled at the edges are as familiar as the back of my hand.

He offers me a meek smile of encouragement, holding the front door open. I follow Mother to our carriage and wait while she barks orders to the driver before ascending the few treads, disappearing into the midst of the curtained space.

"Say hello to your Theo for me, will you, Miss?" Joseph

extends his hand. I take it and lift my skirts, ascending the steps precariously in the full gown.

"Thank you, Joseph." I smile, and he tips his hat, releasing my hand. I draw my own from his weathered but sturdy grip. I sit opposite Mother, straightening my skirts and meeting her piercing gaze.

"You look fine tonight, Serena. Don't befuddle the initiation, so much rides on this one event."

Drawing a breath, so soft the corset barely shifts, I steel my words and hold my tongue. A forced smile is the only response I receive as she takes to looking out the window. The illuminated homes of eastern London float past, before we make our way through the more industrial areas and onto the outskirts of the magnificent city.

I couldn't imagine living elsewhere. London is my heart, my home. And I wish it to remain so. Even at the age of six and ten, I am all too aware of the fate of unmarried women. Mother is right, so much rides on my match. I say a small prayer that everything goes well this evening.

Joseph hollers, and the carriage sways to a stop. I pull back the curtain, taking in the large hall surrounded by parkland and nestled beside the cemetery. Deciding to suppress the unease of being too close to the dead in this place, I gather my skirts and follow her from the carriage. We cross the sprawling lawn and wander toward the double doors of the community hall our coven has used for decades.

Children run around, playing stick and ball, tag and whatnot. Glad to be apart from the silly childish frenzy, I track my attention to the entrance once more. Theo stands by the left door, hands clasped in front of him, waiting for me. In his best attire, a navy double-breasted coat with tails and dark trousers and brown leather riding boots, a carafe snug around his neck, he stands tall with eyes trained on me. His brown hair is combed to one side, his green eyes lit with excitement.

His square jaw moves, and he runs a hand over it. At eight and ten, he is already part of the coven, his father our leader. We have been friends since I was five and I can't imagine a day in my life without him. I let a smile bloom on my lips, and he turns on his heels, pushing out his elbow to offer an escort.

I spot coarse black hair on his sleeves. He has been playing with Rufus. His giant of a dog, a black long-haired Newfoundland. His constant companion.

"Theo," Mother snaps, heading inside briskly.

His face pales as he looks at me. Something resembling terror mixes with amusement across his face as he stands for me to link my arm in his. He pats my hand, and I look away, heat rising to my cheeks. Heavens above. Why does my face always do that when he is near? He pulls me forward and we cross into the hall.

Inside, candles adorn every flat surface. The air is heavy with molten wax and herbs. My head sways.

"Serena?" Theo's low rumble brings me from my musings, and I turn to look at him.

"Theo?"

He nods his head to the middle of the hall. A five-point star made of salt lines the floor, petals scattered around it, white candles at each point. The pentagram. Tens of coven members line the walls of the hall, all in white. Theo releases my arm. "This is you."

"Oh."

He walks and stands behind his father, Bartholomeus, before donning a white robe.

Every person in the hall picks up a candle and holds it in front of them, eyes on me. Bartholomeus raises both hands above his head. "Step into the center of the coven circle, Serena."

I step over the salt and stand in the center of the pentagram. His loving eyes drop to the floor as our leader unrolls an ancient parchment spiraled around two oak rods with rounded ends and recites the initiating words.

From hence forward, we, the coven of light, welcome our sister, Serena.

She is our blood.

Our flesh.

One with us in every way.

With this chalice, we consecrate each witch here to protect, guide and empower this child with the Wiccan ways.

May the Reed protect you.

May you carry out your life, living by the creed we uphold,

to ensure the safety and property of each and every family
of this here coven.
With the chalice of everlasting life, we offer our blood and
life to Serena.

Bartholomeus rolls up the parchment. My heart thunders in my chest. He draws a small silver athame to his palm, sinking it into the flesh ever so slightly. Crimson swells in his cupped palm, and he holds it over the silver chalice in Theo's hands, letting three drops of blood spill into its womb. Theo takes the knife from his father, doing the same.

His blood slips down his turned palm and joins his father's. When each person has let into the vessel, it is handed to me, along with herbs I recognize as patchouli, for protection and prosperity, sandalwood for purification to keep me in the light, to help me from straying to dark magic, and lastly, lavender for happiness and knowledge. Each one of them is what our coven stands for.

Bartholomeus moves toward where I stand. "May I enter the circle?"

"Yes," I whisper, nodding.

He stirs the contents in the chalice with the athame six times, clockwise, uttering an enchantment with each revolution.

"Give me your hand, child," he asks softly.

I extend a shaking hand to him, and he takes it up, pressing the blade into my palm. He makes a small, shallow line across the lifeline of my palm. Blood beads to the surface, the sting burns across every inch. He dips the athame into the pool of red and runs it along the cut, melding the life force of every person here with mine.

"Welcome to the coven, Miss Serena. We are so proud to call you ours."

"Thank you," I breathe past the stone lodged in my throat. I look up and meet Theo's gaze. Pride and happiness fill it. I smile at him and look back at our leader.

He steps away from me, and I stare at the reddened wound in my palm.

"I invoke the right for my daughter to be bound." Mother's words are sharp, the fire lining her eyes worse.

Bartholomeus hesitates, not leaving the circle. Every set of eyes alternates between Mother and our coven leader. What are they talking about?

"That hasn't been invoked for decades, Anjelica. It's an outdated practice." Bartholomeus shifts on his feet but squares his shoulders.

"As second in the order, I insist." Mother moves forward, not sparing a glance.

"But there is no proper consensus."

"It is my daughter's birthright and my duty as your second to ensure all obligations are met by leadership, Bart."

With a sigh, the leader turns back to me. A moment

later, Mother and he flank my sides. She holds her hand out, and he presses the blade into it. She slices a small cut on her wrist, an inch long, and passes the blade back to him. He does the same.

"We are going to hold your hands now, but first, we need to make a small incision on each wrist." Bart meets my gaze. His soft, a hint of concern washing through it.

I nod. This wasn't part of the plan, but if Mother thinks it is worth it to secure our future, I will do it. She snatches the blade from his grip and grabs my hand, turning it over. She cuts a line into the soft flesh of my left wrist and drops it. Plucking up the right one, she does the same to it. Not bothering to return the blade to its owner, she grabs my hand, pressing her wrist into mine. The cuts burn. Bartholomeus does the same and closes his eyes, hanging his head. "Close your eyes, Serena."

I let my lids droop until closed and hang my head.

I call on the power of the four elements to bind this child.
From now and forever, may these three souls be entwined.
Three hearts beating as one.
Three minds thinking as one.
Three bodies connected.
And shall one be taken to the afterlife, this child may take
the rightful place as successor, if no other brother or sister
of blood remains.
And so, mote it be.

. . .

The crowd chants the words. "So, mote it be."

"You can open your eyes now, Miss Serena," Bartholomeus says.

Mother drops my hand abruptly and wanders into the crowd. Tears burn behind my eyes. What just happened?

Before I have time to gather my thoughts, Theo appears, albeit blurry, in front of me. The women of the coven sweep the salt and petals away toward the door. Theo's large, warm hand slips around mine and he tugs me outside into the cool, fresh night air.

"That was intense." He deposits me against the outside wall of the old hall. I pull my gaze from the ground to his face. "You alright, Seri?" His hands wrap around my wrists, and I curl my cut palm closed. The sting on each wrist disappears as his healing light tingles through my skin. I offer him a small smile of thanks. Theo's brows are drawn, his mouth twisted.

"What is it, Thee?"

"Your wounds are not healing as fast as I would like. There's too much magic in one place. I'm afraid it will take a little longer, Seri."

Dizziness washes over me as I look down to where his hands cover my now shaking wrists.

"I'm—"

"Just breathe, only another minute, I promise."

As he said, the tingle stops a moment later. The dizziness evaporates, leaving me stronger than I was before the ceremony. What did he give me? Laughter splits the night air, and Theo jerks, as if he has been almost asleep. His eyes are hooded, his face paled a little. The women walk toward us, holding skirts off the ground, conversation flowing excitedly.

He takes a small step out of my space and the women of the coven spill from the hall, chatting about what just happened. One of the older girls brings a candle, handing it to Theo before wandering off with the younger children. He raises a hand around the flame, watching it as it dances in the threatening breeze.

We lean against the old hall; the wood is sturdy against my back. Theo closes his eyes for a moment, candle still in hand.

"Your undermining actions of tonight have not gone unnoticed, Anjelica." Bartholomeus's voice is stifled through the wall but mostly audible.

"Your days of running this coven are fast coming to an end," Mother says.

I straighten and turn slightly, pressing my ear to the weathered wood.

"You have no idea what it takes to run a peaceful coven. You would have the members practicing for your own gain. Over my dead body that will happen, Madam."

"Suit yourself, you uncivilized ingrate."

My gut plummets. Mother has used dark magic more times than I can count, especially in the months after father's death. She told me sometimes we do hard things because it is necessary for our survival, and to count the costs later. I glance at Theo, only to find he is staring at the trees. His eyes are moving as if he is processing what he is hearing also. Good.

"There has been evidence of you using dark magic, Anjelica. Reports have come to light of the many ways you manipulated your earthly talents to your own benefit, in direct conflict with the Wiccan Reed. If anyone should be concerned about their place in this coven, it is you."

Theo's gaze drops to mine. I offer a sad smile. Confirming what his father is saying is true.

"Seri, do you still feel safe at home?"

"Yes." The word slips without hesitation but seems off. Mostly, I do.

"The second that changes, send Joseph to fetch me. Please."

I nod, warmth rising in my chest. He pushes off the wall and grabs my hand, leading me into the park's forest. I lift my skirts with my free hand and stride along to keep up. Once we are deep into the heart of the dim lit forest, surrounded by oaks, he stops and turns back. His eyes meet mine and he drops my hand, placing the candle on the mossy ground.

"Theo?"

He stares between the trees, his jaw feathers, and he swallows before turning back to me.

"Are you alright?" I ask softly, raising a hand to touch

his, now twisting in the lapel of his double-breasted coat. He tugs at the material over his neck briefly and steels himself with a harsh breath.

"Serena," he starts. Why does he look anxious?

I shuffle a little closer. "Yes? What is it, Thee? You can tell me anything, we have been friends for years, there is nothing you could possibly say that would find you in my ill-favor."

He chuckles, low and strained.

My heart picks up pace, my face bunching with worry. The corset around my chest tightens with every deep breath I take.

"I want to marry you, Seri."

I jerk back, as if slapped.

"What?"

"Not right now, obviously. When you are of age, of course. I can't imagine any other in my life but you."

"Thee—"

He shakes his head and presses a finger over my lips. My breath shallows out almost completely. I have thought about marriage. But it was always strategic and in the distant future. A decision made akin to one of business, feelings and love not deserving a mention. That is only for stories, fairytales. I never considered I would have the choice of who I married. Let alone the splendid opportunity to marry for love.

His finger drops from my lips, and I feel its absence immediately. "You don't have to, Seri. I mean, if that is not what you want. I will bow out gracefully when the time comes."

"You are going to wait for me to decide? What about you, Theo?"

"I have from this day to the minute you turn of age to spend with you either way. Please, don't worry about me."

"Serena!" Mother's harsh tone is all but dimmed by the ancient woody forest, but reverberates through me nonetheless. I pull in a breath and step back from Theo. He watches every breath I take, every movement I make.

"I have to go."

"Remember what I said about Joseph. If you ever need me, please send word."

"I will." I dart forward and press a peck of a kiss to his cheek, heat flooding my own before I have pulled away.

He huffs a laugh, green eyes darkening, lips parted. He runs a hand through his hair, and I stare at him.

"Serena! The carriage is here. Now, please!"

"Go, Seri. I'll see you in town, maybe next week."

I smile, but it's all wobbly. Grabbing up my skirts with both hands, I turn away from his gorgeous stare and sprint through the trees. Happiness floods every inch of me. I shut my eyes briefly, striding across the green mossy forest floor. A moment later, eyes open, I slow my pace and stop mere feet from my mother. Her face is pinched in distaste.

"Honestly, child, how are you ever going to attract suitors, running around like a wild heathen? Have I taught you nothing of elegance and grace? Your match with a wealthy suitor is your only option. I trust you will adjust your behavior thus forth. As an official member of one of the largest, most prestigious covens in London, you ought to start considering this. Now, get in. I have a migraine coming on."

She snaps her focus between the trees as Theo wanders from their depths carrying the candle. I step into the carriage, holding his gaze. Mother studies us, her eyes alternating between her daughter and her leader's son, before narrowing. Her mouth twists with hate. I duck into the carriage, not wanting to cause Theo any of her undesirable attention.

A heartbeat later, she steps inside, lowering to the bench and adjusting her skirts. The coach pulls out of the hall's iron-gated yard and sways toward home.

"You are an intelligent girl, Serena. Make sure you remember your obligation to this family before considering any offers that come your way."

Her fiery stare pins me to the velvet seat. I swallow. She controls everything I do. Who I marry will be no different. I suspect the likelihood of her allowing me to marry for love, marrying Theo, is infinitely dismal. An ache grows in my chest at the thought of spending a life with someone else. At living totally separate lives. Tears prickle behind my eyes.

I track my focus to the glowing moon overhead. At her apex now, she shines, sending her light and energy around the world. If we could harness that kind of energy, the possibilities in this life would be endless. I think of Theo, of the life we could live together. Moonlight pierces the carriage, bending around the velvet drapes, spilling over my lap. I lay my hands, palms up, willing her to offer me what I cannot attain for myself.

Freewill.

CHAPTER 2

SAMMIE

CASTLETON, VERMONT 2024

I mourn the loss of Grandma's touch the moment my eyes open. Her touch, gone. Her kind eyes, gone. Her knowing words and guidance are now only an echo. White walls and soft linen swaddle me. The aromas of sandalwood and spice tangle with leather. Soft voices drift through the open bedroom door.

Lewis's bedroom.

I sit up, and instantly, my head feels set to split. Pressing my hand to my temple, I moan through the fierce pain. With a few long, slow breaths, the pain eases and I toss the covers back. One of Lewis's T-shirts hangs loose over my bare chest, the hem just shy of my mid-thigh. And panties, but nothing else. I pad toward the door. Serena and Lewis whisper softly about timing and choice.

The past few moments before I woke up slam into me. Grandma. Lewis's curse. Anjelica.

I died.

Holy shit. I was dead?

I grip the doorframe and sink to my knees, bile rising up my throat. I groan, swallowing it back, and the burn tracks all the way down to my stomach. I shake my head and push up to my feet. I survived Anjelica, broke the curse, died, and still managed to live. I curl both palms in front of me and flames hiss to life.

And I still have my magic. Shit, Sammie. Nailed it.

I close both palms, snuffing out the cool flame. I look up as Lewis stops in front of me. Instantly, I rush to him, wrapping my arms around his neck, burying my head. He chokes through ragged breaths before losing a low, painful groan. His arms fold around me, tight.

"I guess this is my cue. Good to have you back, girl." Serena's soft words from behind are lined with happiness, but wobble still.

I push out of Lewis's hold and meet her gaze. "Thank you!"

"What for, babe? You did all the work."

Moving closer, I take her at arm's length and fight my face that twists, threatening to burst into a sobbing, ugly mess. She wipes my tears with her thumbs and forces a smile. "I'm just glad you're still here, Williams. We can't let that stupid mother of mine win every time."

I huff a pained laugh. Serena runs her gaze down and up my frame. "Go back to bed, Sammie."

"I'm not tired."

Lewis moves in behind me, wrapping his arms around me.

"Oh, I know. Go back to bed, girl." She winks and waves as she walks down the hall and through the living room.

"You should listen to your friend, Sunshine."

I raise my arms and spin in his embrace. His eyes are pained, torn between desire, happiness and grief, stealing my breath. "Lewis."

"Sammie." The word is no more than a soft growl. He pulls me onto his hips and walks back into the bedroom, depositing me on the mattress and turns back, walking toward the door.

"Please, don't leave. I need to tell you something. And ask you a few things."

He studies my face before walking back to where I lie. I shuffle backward, sitting at the bedhead, and pat the spot beside me. Lewis obeys, sitting on his side, his gaze not straying from my face.

"While I was gone, I saw my grandma." I want Lewis to know I know, and that I don't blame him for what happened to her. To see if he realized the connection between me and her.

He leans against the bedhead and his eyes fall shut, sighing. "I never—"

I turn to face him, legs crossed, and grab his face with my hands. "I know. You never meant for her to get hurt. She knows it too."

He opens his eyes, pain and regret lacing them entirely.

"She promised me, if she thought it wasn't going to work, if she didn't think she was strong enough, she would stop."

"She wanted to help you so much. I guess, in the end, she did."

"What are you talking about?"

"I saw her, we talked . . . about everything. About you."

He forces a small smile. "She wasn't worried that a good-for-nothing blood sucker was defiling her granddaughter?"

I slap his arm and snuggle into his side. "Of course not. And you are far from either of those things, good for nothing or a blood sucker, Lewis."

He folds me into his chest with an arm, kissing the top of my head.

"What else happened while you were gone?" he asks. His heart rate speeds up.

"I made a choice. I could go either way. Stay with her and severe the mating bond and live in peace or come back. To you."

He turns, loosening his hold, eyes widened, and lips parted. "You choose me? I mean, the mating bond, you don't get a choice with that. But you came back, so you chose me despite it?"

I rise to my knees and lift one leg over before settling on his lap. I slide my hands around his neck and his eyes darken. My blood thunders through my veins, heat pooling in my core.

"Of course I chose you. Bond or no stupid bond, you are

stuck with me, for as long as you still want me. I will always choose you, Lewis Sullivan."

He closes his eyes and grips my hips, the groan that leaves his mouth rattles all the way down to my bones, in the best way possible. Wetness lines my panties, and he shifts underneath me, hardness growing thick between my legs. I wriggle on his lap, knowing exactly how torturous that will be for him.

He opens his eyes, grabbing my face with his hands and claims my mouth with his. I part my lips, and his tongue plunders my mouth. I moan softly, and he pulls back. His eyes study my face, as if watching for any sign of damage. With one swift movement, he deposits me back onto my side of the bed. I huff, my eyes narrowing, slamming my gaping mouth shut.

"I don't want to hurt you, Sunshine. You've been through enough."

"That wasn't a 'you're hurting me' sound. Besides, you can't hurt me, Lewis. How many times do we have to cover this?"

"You died!" He bolts up from the bed. "And it's my fault. You think choosing me is a good thing, Sunshine. It isn't. You should have stayed with her."

The second the words hit, hurt rips me apart. My breath stops. Did he honestly just say I am better off dead than with him?

What the actual hell?

"That didn't come out right." He rolls his head back.

"It sure as hell did not!" I jump off the bed and stalk to where he stands. "You cannot possibly believe that?"

He turns on his heels and walks toward the door. Where is he going?

"I'll be in the kitchen if you need anything."

My mouth hangs agape. "I'm not hungry."

"You should eat. It's been days."

"How long was I out for?"

He stops, turning back. "A week."

A whole week?

"I'll get you some food. You need to regain your strength."

"I feel fine," I grind out.

He shakes his head and leaves. Truly, I do. I'm not sure what a person is supposed to feel after dying and coming alive again, but I feel normal. It's like nothing happened. I push off the bed and walk to the dresser, opening the top drawer. Some of my clothes sit alongside his. I pluck out a pair of jeans and slip them on. That's better, more human. Or should I say, more me. I am far from human.

Not bothering with a bra, I pad to the kitchen to where Lewis stands in front of the refrigerator. He doesn't look back as I enter the room, lost in thought. Everything looks the way it was before. There's no sign of Denver anywhere. I round the kitchen bench and slide in next to Lewis, lacing my hand in his. He stiffens, not looking at me. The fridge is almost bare, as if he hasn't left the house for the entire week I was asleep.

"Lewis?"

"Mhmm."

"You have been stuck in this house the whole time I was asleep?"

He turns to me. "Yes."

I imagine him, worried sick, pacing the floors. Denver trying to talk him out of the dark place he goes when he feels guilt. I don't know what to say. So, I stand, mouth agape, staring at my mate. My stomach grumbles, as if contesting the lack of food as well.

His brows draw down, and he walks from the kitchen, grabbing his car keys from the bowl by the front door. "I'll be back in half an hour. Pizza okay?"

"Sure," I manage to say, watching his back as he leaves.

I wander toward the door as he crosses the threshold and walks over the porch and down the stairs toward the garage housing his mustang. Something low in my gut twinges. I rub a hand over my belly and pull in a long breath. The rumble of the car echoes as he backs out of the garage and turns onto the driveway.

Reaching for my pendant, I am relieved to find the warm metal snug between my breasts. Conscious not to rub it between my fingers anymore, I pull out and twist the chain around my index finger, eyes tracking Lewis as he shoves the car into drive and pulls away. My phone pings, and I turn back to see it on the entry table.

The screen is lit up with a text. Serena.

> Hey, you okay? My pendant warmed up
> for a moment.

I swipe the screen to reply.

Gravel crunches under the Mustang's tires as Lewis drives away. I grip the doorframe, and the pain low in my belly twists to an ache.

I start typing. "No. I'm—"

The pain in my stomach rises to behind my ribs, and I force breath in and out of my lungs and hug my arms tight around myself. The car disappears around the first bend. As the pain intensifies, my legs give way as I slide down the doorframe and hit the porch.

What is happening?

The phone slips from my hand, hitting the patio floor.

I hear the Mustang come to a crunching halt, the engine still rumbling. I try to cry out, but my body won't move, my voice is nowhere to be found. It's all I can do to keep my eyes open and breath entering my lungs. I reach for the pendant. This time, I grip it tight until it warms in my hold.

Lewis is screaming my name.

"Sammy! Sammy! Sunshine, answer me, answer me!" His words float closer and closer, and I force my eyes to stay open. The pain lessens the closer he gets, but I have nothing left.

Nothing at all.

A beat later, soft, light footsteps rush up the steps and

onto the porch. Through a haze, I recognize Serena's shoes beside me. She crouches, resting her hand on my shoulder.

"Sammy, Sammy, can you hear me? Jesus Mary, mother of Joseph, what's she done now?"

Thumping, heavy footsteps move up the steps, and Serena turns away from me, for a second. Lewis flounders, doubled over, moving incredibly slow, his arms wrapped around his stomach, his face pale and drawn. He collapses on the porch beside me.

Darkness swallows me whole.

)·)·)·◐·(·(·(

Serena's face drifts into focus as I squint and sit up. A blanket falls from my chest, settling in my lap. The living room is dark, the fireplace fully lit and warming the room. Instantly, I remember the moment on the porch.

Where's Lewis?

I dart my gaze around the room, but he isn't here. Releasing my feet to the floor, I go to rise. "Where is he?"

Serena rests a hand on my shoulder, holding me to the sofa. "Lewis is fine. He's in bed. It took a larger toll on him. He hasn't eaten for the entire week you were asleep. I guess his reserves are low. Denver's gone out to get some animal blood as quickly as he can."

I stand on wobbly feet and pad toward his room. Serena follows behind, as if monitoring me. Hold up. What just happened? It? She said 'it', like she knew what just took the two of us out. I spin back to her.

"What happened, Rena?"

Her mouth flattens to a thin line, and her eyes crinkle with worry. "You need to hear this together, Sammy. It's not something I can tell you until Lewis wakes."

"What are you talking about?"

"It affects you both, profoundly, if it is what I think it is."

A shiver runs up my spine. Nothing in what she is saying sounds good. I wish I had brought the blanket with me now. I turn back and pick up the pace, desperate to see Lewis. My heart rate soars when I cross the threshold and take in his limp form on the bed.

He's pale, more than usual. His breaths are too quick. I scramble beside him, picking up his hand. The leather bracelet around his wrists slips down a little way. I swaddle his hand in both of mine, kissing his fingers. He's so still. The only movement is his too shallow breaths.

What have I done?

CHAPTER 3

LEWIS

The first face I see is that of my brother. His usual clean face is covered in a few days' worth of stubble. That's how I know things are not what they ought to be. The next dead giveaway is the woman sitting next to him, her pretty face crumpled into a frown.

Serena.

I jerk upward, wobbling to an awkward sitting position.

Sammie.

"Where is she?" I rasp. The desperation in my voice shows on my brother's face. My gut plummets.

Serena stands and walks closer to where I sit. Instantly, I lean away from the witch. She tilts her head, giving me a disbelieving frown.

I clear my throat and lean back toward her. "Sorry, habit."

She folds her arms over her chest and turns to glance at

Denver. What is going on here? Have these two teamed up or something?

"Where is Samantha?" I force out.

"She's in the living room, actually. We wanted to make sure you fed before you got up." Denver hands me a bag of blood.

Human blood.

Whatever happened must have been bad if he thinks I am going to drink this shit. I haven't touched human blood, apart from biting Sammie briefly, for decades. I hand it back to him and he frowns. "You need to regain strength, brother, this is the fastest way."

"Then I'll hunt. I'm not eating that."

Serena catches my gaze. "Hunting could be a problem."

"Why?"

"Come on, we should have this conversation with Sammie," Denver says, standing and holding out a hand. I grip it and push off the bed.

But the rise to my feet is slow, and my footsteps are unsteady. When I'm certain I won't collapse, I wave him off. He releases me, walking behind me.

Serena leads the way to the living room. Sammie is curled up on the sofa, mug in hand, staring in the flames of a roaring fire. I hobble at a rush to where she sits, and she whelps, slamming the mug onto the coffee table and flying into my arms. I falter backward and she grabs my shoulders. "No." The word is all but a whisper.

I steady my leg against the sofa and pull her back into

my chest. She winds her arms around my waist, nuzzling closer.

"Sunshine."

"God, Lewis. I was so scared."

"You're okay, Sunshine."

She pushes away a little. "I'm not worried about me."

Denver clears his throat. "You two should sit down for this."

We sink onto the sofa, still holding tight. Sammie is so close she's almost in my lap. I shunt the image of her straddling my lap away.

"Serena has something to tell you. And I don't think you're going to like it."

I open my eyes to see Denver's bothered stare.

Serena glances at him before returning her attention to Sammie and me. "When our girl here broke the curse, it triggered a kind of backup enchantment."

"What are you talking about, Rena?" Sammie says, leaning forward.

"Lewis and you are—" Denver starts.

I whip my focus to him. So, he knows already. I grind my jaw shut. "Spit it out, witch." The words are harsher than I intended, but my patience is thinning. My attention wanes as a blinding headache floats over the front of my forehead like a storm cloud.

"You're tethered." Serena looks between us, as if making sure we both heard her.

"Wha—what does that mean, exactly?" Sammie asks.

"When you broke the curse, to punish you, Mother had an enchantment that tethers the person who lifted the curse to the now, un-cursed."

"You're tethered, but as far as we can see, not bound. But it's hard to gauge so early," Denver offers. I guess years of research into the supernatural have taught him a thing or two.

"Bound?" I ask.

"When two people are bound, when one bleeds, so does the other," Serena answers for my brother, as if they have been working together, tag teaming the guardianship of our existence.

"How do you know we are not bound?" Sammie asks.

"We don't, for sure. But when you died, nothing happened to Lewis. Physically, at least."

All eyes land on me. Sammie's are tight with worry.

"There have been cases of the bindings triggering later on, sometimes months after the event that caused it. But so far, so good." Denver leans across the gaps between the sofas, across the coffee table and pinches Sammie's arm.

She lets out a small yelp. "Hey, what's that for?"

"Lewis?"

"I didn't feel it."

Serena sighs. "Good, so far, so good."

"Back to the tether," I say, shifting on the sofa, pulling Sammie back into my chest. "What are the restrictions of the two people tethered?" My voice is low, almost guttered. Sammie turns on my lap and meets my gaze. The air all but vanishes from my lungs. I did this to her. Her kindness saw her save my life, and this is how I repay her.

"Hey." Her hands rest around my face. "I know what you are thinking. And don't you dare."

I pull in a burning breath.

How do I tell her how much I regret she felt obligated to do this for me? How do I tell her I wish she'd let me die? If only to save her life.

"You should have let me go, Sunshine." The words are gravel.

She drops her hands, mouth gaping. A moment later, she moves from my lap and stands. "I can't be here."

The three of us watch as she pads to the front door and leaves. Nothing pangs in my gut, and I realize she's only gone outside to the porch.

Serena's frown finds mine. "I'll go."

She rises and walks out after her friend. Denver moves to sit beside me, sitting aside to face me. I slump back on the sofa and rub my hands over my face. This is the last thing I wanted for her. The last thing she deserved.

"Lew?"

I groan into my hands, before pushing them into my eyes, hard. Pinpoints of light flicker across the dark space of my vision. My brother's tight grip wraps around my wrist and tugs my hand from my face.

"This is the last thing she deserved, Den."

I can't look at my brother. How selfish can one man be? I hate myself right now. Not only is she tethered to me with a mating bond and risked her life to save me . . . Now, she's literally tethered to my sorry existence.

Fuck me.

"You remember the day I met Zahli?" Denver says softly.

"Like I could ever forget," I utter, half lost in my own miserable thoughts.

"She told me life always gives us what we need, not what we want. In your case, little brother, you got both."

"I got both. Sammie got nothing she wants. She wants an education, freedom, to travel, to grow old with someone who does all those things with her. And now she's weighed down by me. All because I thought I knew what's best for her. If she hadn't gone to the cabin with me, this thing between us wouldn't have snapped. She would still be free to choose. Now, she's done the only thing she knows how to —put everyone else before herself. As a result, she's stuck with me, literally."

I push out of the sofa and pace in front of the fireplace. Denver rises, and a glass clinks a moment later. He appears by the fireplace and leans on the mantle, handing me a glass of amber liquid. I stare into the swirling hues of solace, wishing I could take back the last few weeks. Like retracing our steps and somehow erasing them, until the bond is wiped away and Sammie is free.

Free of me.

"You know, Zahli was right," Denver says. He gulps the whiskey back in one quick mouthful. "Life doesn't pick and choose who gets their happy ending and who doesn't. You both needed this. Not just you, Lewis. Sammie loves you, brother. She needs you. Whether you believe it or not. She wasn't upset about being in pain when the tether kicked in, she was beside herself that you had suffered while she was out of it for an entire week. Her only concerns were for, are for you. Don't you get it, Lew. It's not only the mating bond, brother. You got it all. You have her heart and her bond."

He slaps me on the shoulder and wanders toward the kitchen. I lean against the mantle, staring at the dancing flames, not seeing a thing. My chest rises and falls at an erratic rate. I tune out the sounds of life around me and focus on the two heartbeats on the porch. Both steady. Both calm. She's talking to Serena. They toss around the events of the last week, as if it's so matter of fact. Sammie doesn't seem fazed by dying, or the mating bond, or the tether. Her only words of concern are for me.

"What happens to Lewis if we are too far apart?" she asks.

"He loses any vampire abilities, speed, hearing, healing, and immortality."

"You mean if we are too far apart, he can be killed?"

I stiffen, standing taller, and the glass in my hand glints in the fire's hue.

"Yes, if you are too far apart, he wouldn't survive a targeted attack on his life. But Sammie . . ." Serena trails off.

"What is it?"

"If he's without you for too long, like more than a couple

of days, he will die. Between the mating bond and the tether, he would suffer immensely, and eventually, after being alive for much longer than any human lifespan, he would die. Marbleized and then shatter, like any other vampire death."

"Oh my god, Rena."

"It's okay, we'll find a way to break the tether. It's going to take a while. Like the curse, there are specifics, but it's not infallible."

"Can I break it? I broke the curse?"

"You're part of the tether. I don't think it works that way. I'll keep looking, okay."

So, Sammie doesn't want to be tethered to me. Why would she? I slam the last of the whiskey down and move to my bedroom. I slide to the floor and lean against the bed, shoving my hands in my head. Another mess I have gotten us into.

For fuck's sake, Lewis.

))) ● (((

The sun is fading on the western horizon by the time my bedroom door cracks and soft footsteps pad toward where I sit on the floor still. For hours, I have been going over all the ways I can try to get Sammie out of this fucking mess. But everything that comes to mind is either useless or too risky.

"Lewis?"

She stands beside me, and her big blue eyes are wide with worry. Her curly blonde hair drapes over her shoulders, framing her beautiful face. Lips so red, I could lose myself and drag them through my teeth before swallowing her whole.

She kneels between my legs and shuffles closer until her chest touches mine. Her hands run through my hair and the air vanishes from my lungs, replaced by a stone in my airway. I lay my head back on the bed and slam my eyes shut.

"Are you okay?" she whispers.

I resist the urge to hack out a sarcastic laugh. It's not me she should be worried about.

"Look at me, Lew."

I don't.

Her hands trail down my neck to rest over my heart. "Please, look at me." Her voice trembles.

I lift my head from the bed and meet her gaze. "What is it, Sunshine?"

A small, sad smile lifts one corner of her mouth. "I won't let anything happen to you."

"God, Sammie. I'm the last person you should be worried about." I shake my head.

"You are the only person I worry about," she says, kissing me, letting her teeth drag over my bottom lip.

I growl and grip her hips. "You know I'm no good for you, right?"

"I will be the judge of that. Besides, you're stuck with me." Her eyes light up. Who am I to rain on her parade?

For now, we seem to fit.

I lay my legs on the floor, and with one lightning-fast move have her straddling my lap. She giggles, tossing her head back. God save me, it's the most beautiful sound I will ever hear.

Recovering from her laughter, her eyes find mine, darkening by the second. "I could really use a bath."

"Agreed."

Laughter consumes her pretty face again, and she slaps my shoulder. Her hands find my hair before her mouth covers mine. I kiss her back, deepening the movements. Her hands find the hem of my shirt and she lifts it from my back, throwing it on the floor.

"Lewis," she breathes.

"Yeah, Sunshine?"

"I need you closer."

"You have me."

She runs kisses down my neck, fingers curling into my skin. Heat and hardness grow under her, and she leans back and smiles with a small wriggle. I groan.

A smile splits her face. "I love that sound."

A second later, I am walking to the bathroom, Sammie wrapped around my waist. Her blue eyes trap my own, while her breaths cycle deep and heavy.

"Don't make me wait, please," she pleads, hands around my neck. We slide to a halt in the bathroom, and I kick the door shut behind me. I deposit her on the vanity and turn on the taps, letting the steaming water fill the bath. Next heartbeat, I am standing between her legs, her shirt in my hands as I lift it over her head.

Her red lace bra is almost overflowing. She pulls my mouth to hers. I undo the button on her jeans, and she wriggles as I slide them off. Her hands find the buckle on my belt, and she tugs it from its loops, tossing it aside. A few moments later, my jeans slip to the floor with hers.

I step back. She sits on the vanity in her red lacy underwear. She's stunning. How the hell am I going to control myself? Air burns through my lungs with every erratic breath.

"Come here," she rasps.

Need springs to life and I do as I am told, stepping between her legs. "Sunshine, you're going to have to hold me back."

Her eyes are hooded with need. "I will, I promise."

She rotates her wrists, making a small wind to buffer me backward as if making good on her promise. I release the clasp on her bra, and she whimpers as my hands find her breasts. Lord above, how did I get so lucky?

Fuck me.

My hardness aches painfully. I need her wrapped around me. I rub my thumbs over each peak, eliciting a breathy moan from her. I catch them between my teeth a second later and she cries out. "Lewis."

I grab her hips and slide her to the edge of the vanity

before trailing kisses down her stomach to where red lace meets skin below her belly button. Her hands sink into my hair instantly. I know where she needs my mouth, by the way her hands work frantically.

"Is this okay?" I ask, knowing it will get her more riled up, having to wait for pleasantries.

"Lewis," she growls, low.

I rise back up and kiss my way around each breast. If she has to be stuck with me, I intend on making her time with me worthwhile. I trace a finger over the top of the panties, sucking and kissing each soft, gorgeous breast, slowly. She arches into me, hips wriggling with impatience.

"Sunshine?"

"Uh-huh . . ."

"Tell me what you want."

"You."

"No, specifically, what you want."

Her eyes open, finding mine. "I want you inside me."

Her hand finds my aching hardness, wrapping around tight before tugging. I all but collapse onto her. Slamming fists onto the vanity either side of her. The marble cracks. The bench groans with my weight and force added to hers.

"You promise you will hold me back, Sammie?"

"I promise. Please."

Right now, she's happy. If that changes, I will let her go.

Even if it ruins me.

CHAPTER 4

SAMMIE

Lewis trails his finger across the skin above my panties. The heat pools in my center, and the wetness soaking the red lace between my legs is driving me insane. I swear if he doesn't do something soon, I may internally combust. "Please, Lewis."

His finger slips under the material, his mouth still sucking and tugging my peaks between his teeth. Each breath comes fast and shallow. His gorgeous blond hair pulls through my fingers. I whimper and he lifts his head.

His dark eyes smolder. His square jaw slackens as he watches me, lowering his hand to find the wetness right where I need him. His thumb finds my throbbing apex, and another whimper spills from my parted lips. He holds his gaze to mine as he sinks two fingers inside me.

With a growl, he closes his eyes, his chest now heaving

with choppy, needy breaths. His grip on my breast tightens. I summon my wind, readying for his inevitable loss of control. His eyes darken further.

Steam has long since flooded the bathroom, fogging up everything around us when I remember the bath. The water is still running. "Lewis."

"Mhmm," he breathes.

"The bath."

With my legs wrapped around his waist, he lowers himself into the water, shutting the tap off with one hand, and hugs me close. I shudder as we descend into the hot water until he is sitting at one end of the tub with me in his lap. It sinks into my skin, sending tingles through my body. I run my wet hands through his hair, slicking it back, accentuating his gorgeous face. I will never tire of him.

I run a finger down his chest, over his hard stomach, and find his hardness. I run a thumb over the bell softly. This time, it's his turn to feel loved. I wriggle backward off his lap.

"Where do you think you're going, Sunshine?"

"Diving."

He holds his arms out, as if to pull me back.

"Nope. You stay where you are. Tell me if it gets too much, okay?"

"Okay?" He drops his arms into the water.

I submerge. The shape of him beneath me fills the floor of the tub. His muscular body is still rigid in the steaming water. My curls float around my face as I grab his length with one hand. He stiffens and his hands rise from the water. I imagine them gripping the sides of the bathtub.

I flick a finger over the bell of his swollen cock before slipping into my mouth. He groans and, even under the water, I feel the rumble. I can imagine the look on his face. Happiness warms my chest, spiraling lower to my belly. An ache grows in my core with every movement I make up and down.

He tastes amazing.

For a second, I'm tempted to keep going until he explodes down my throat. But I need him, the heat and stretch only Lewis can give me. His hand slips from the tub, his hand taps my shoulder roughly. I rise from the water, dragging in a long breath as I push the hair from my face.

Instantly, his body hits mine. And I'm reeling backward as he pins me to the other end of the bath. Water spills over, pooling on the marble. His eyes are completely black. I summon the wind to buffer between us.

"Now, Lewis."

I wrap my legs around his waist and guide him to my aching center with one hand. He growls, low and loud. His hand slams over my throat. I push my air between us, trying to pry his hand from my neck. His grip loosens, and he slams into me.

The stretch is overwhelming. My mouth waters as pleasure coils in low in my belly. He slams into me again. Over and over. Heat and tingling rise with each thrust. His fingers dig into my throat as his movements turn harsher, each more devoted than the last. When the air leaves my lungs and doesn't return, my eyes widen. I channel everything into keeping him at bay.

"Lewis," I choke.

He hesitates for a second, eyes losing the total blackout he usually has when we are this far gone.

He heard me.

"Lew."

Pleasure grows in my core. I moan, unable to stop myself from spiraling higher with every thundering thrust. He slips back into his darkness, eyes blackened again. Sweet agony spirals to bliss and I cry out, losing my hold on my power. This time, Lewis reigns his instincts in, and his brown eyes meet mine before he roars with release.

Oh, my god.

We did it.

We came without him losing it.

I slacken against the side of the bath, letting my head loll to the side and closing my eyes. Large hands find my face, and a soft kiss presses to my lips. "I love you, Sunshine."

I open my eyes, mouth parted, breaths all too short again. Stunned, I study his gorgeous face. "What did you say?"

"I love you, Sammie." His forehead rests on mine, and he closes his eyes, breathing heavy. Sobs tumble up my throat and my trembling hands find his, my fingers curling around.

"I love you, Lewis."

"I can't lose you, Sunshine."

"You won't."

He pushes back, hands still encased in my own. I lower them to my chest. He sits in the center of the bath and pulls me over his lap, my aching core straddling his lap again.

"If how you feel about me ever changes, please tell me. I will le—"

"It won't." I smash my mouth to his, as the heat rises in my core again.

He hardens under me but holds me at arm's length. "I mean it. The minute this all gets too much for you, you walk away. Please promise me you'll do that for yourself."

I sit on his lap, burning for him again. No words come. I wouldn't even know how to reply to that kind of selflessness. Instead, I run a hand over his jaw. "I want to do this with you for the rest of my days. However many, that is. Maybe one day we can do it without the wind between us?"

"I think with enough practice, we could get to that point."

He smiles, and it takes my breath away. His brown eyes lit up, his wet hair hanging over his face.

I drop my hand between us in the water and playfully tug at his hard length. He tilts his head; the smile dropping away. "Are you sure? I don't want to hurt you."

"I think we need more practice." I chuckle and nip his bottom lip. Then, rising, I guide him to my aching entrance.

"I almost had it before. Hearing you makes it easier to stay present and not be pulled into the instinct of lust and thoughts of blood."

"Oh? I like it when you bite me, Lew."

"Sammie," he warns.

"What, I do. Please, do it again."

"No."

"But you need it. Denver said you're weak. I want you to bite me."

"If I do, it's too hard to fight off the instinct. Almost impossible to stay here with you."

"Well, I'll have to make lots of noise then." I giggle, and he tweaks each breast with his fingers. Instantly, heat plummets to my core.

Oh, my god.

"Don't do that," I utter, but my eyes fall closed and my head tilts back almost of its own accord.

"Do what? This?" He lowers his head and sucks on each peak, one after the other.

"Yes . . . oh God." I arch into him again.

"You can call me God if you want to," he says with a chuckle that reverberates through my chest, sending me higher.

I sink onto his lap, the stretch warming every inch of me. I am completely filled. It's heaven. Lewis groans and his hands cup my face. "You really will be the death of me,

Sunshine." I hold his gaze and rise on my knees until the tip almost pops from my entrance before slamming back down.

His face turns feral.

"Your turn," I rasp with heaving breaths.

I push him to the end of the bath and press his shoulders against the wall of the tub with my wind. The water I send around the tub in a whirlpool torrent. I rise to the tip again and he groans. I send my hands through his hair, and his mouth finds my peaks. Whimpering through every move his tongue makes, fire builds low in my belly.

His hands slam over the edge of the bath, gripping with until they turn white. The iron groans. Cracks appear under his hands, splitting toward the base of the tub. He rides out the current. His eyes snap to black. I moan and rise on my knees again. The black fades.

"Sunshine."

"I'm here, don't you dare leave me."

He groans and the tub shudders. I feel every inch of him as I move up and sink, ever so slowly. His tip stretches me so deliciously my mouth waters.

"Oh, Lew."

"Now, Sunshine. Now."

I let go, and the water sloshes, slowing. The wind between us falls away, and he grips my hips, so tight I whimper. But his eyes are brown, although hooded. He roars through his release, and I follow him over the edge.

Holy shit, we did it.

I can't flatten the smile on my face. We actually did it. I

dot kisses over every angle of his gorgeous, sweet, exhausted face as his eyes drift shut, a smile pulling at his lips as he leans his head on the bath.

"You are absolute fire, my love," I whisper into his neck.

Lewis chuckles, opening his eyes. Our gazes stray to the broken tub a second later. "Denver is going kill me, this lump of cast iron is an heirloom." He pulls the plug, and I lay against his chest, listening to the water swirl away underneath us.

My body aches, but my heart is full.

)))·◐·(((

My phone buzzes in my pocket. I toss the notebook from the bed in what used to be my room at the Sullivan house into my satchel before tapping out a reply to Serena.

Be there in twenty, just waiting for Lewis.

Okies.

I pull the bag strap onto my shoulder and wander toward the front door. Denver is leaning against the door, scanning me up and down as if a protective father double checking an outfit before his daughter leaves the house. "Denver?"

"You warm enough?"

"Yes, Dad." I roll my eyes at him. Footsteps thud behind

me, and I smell Lewis before his arms wind around my waist. He dips his head into my neck, letting the sharpness of his teeth graze the skin.

"Remember, no further than fifty feet. Or you will both end up in the college nurse's room."

I groan and move my head to the side, pressing a kiss to Lewis's temple. "We remember, Denver."

"I'm sure you won't make it further than five inches apart after yesterday, but just in case. Remember the risks. Lewis?"

"Yeah, brother. I remember."

He unfolds me from his warmth and steps around to open the door. Denver smiles as we walk onto the patio and down the steps. He closes the door when we reach the garage. Lewis watches his brother's silhouette disappear into the house before he pins me against the Mustang.

Without having to worry about hurting me, he's insatiable. I'm undecided if it is the mating bond, or what he said to me in the bath yesterday. Either way, I'm loving every second of his constant need for me. I need him just as much. He nips his way down my neck, a hand sliding under my sweater. My breasts ache with the need to feel his fingers push and play with them.

"Sunshine, how the hell am I supposed to teach a theater full of students with you anywhere near me?"

His thumb brushes over my nipple and I whimper into his neck. He grinds me into the car. All I can think about is his hardness stretching me every which way. My panties are beyond damp at this point.

"Lewis." His name is a prayer, a plea.

He grabs my bottom, throwing me up onto his hips, and wanders to the bonnet of the car and lays me on it. With one swift motion, my jeans are on the cold ground, his hands roughly pushing back my inner thighs and his tongue finds my aching apex.

"God, you are so wet, Sunshine."

I moan as he suckles and kisses the throbbing. A growl rumbles from him, vibrating through my wet heat. Bliss coils low, hot and fast. I'm so close. "Lewis, please, don't stop."

"I wouldn't dream of it."

"Ahh. Oh . . ."

He slides two fingers into my center, and I arch off the bonnet. With slow, delicious movements, he pumps his fingers, and I tighten around them further each time.

My phone pings.

Shit.

Serena.

I move to look at my phone.

"Don't you dare, Sunshine."

He sucks hard on my apex and all thoughts of my best friend waiting patiently for me fly from my mind.

"You have no idea how insane you are driving me, Sammie." The gravel in his voice confirms his words.

"Come for me, Sunshine."

"No," I pant.

"No?"

He slides a third finger in, stretching me and I lose all self-control. His tongue flicks over and over my throbbing apex, sending me spiraling.

"God, Lewis." I grab his hair, lifting off the bonnet. I want to see him wreck me. See how he destroys into a million tiny little pieces so damn easily. His eyes flick to mine. Darkened but not black like so many times before, he has control. His hand moves to my nipple, tweaking it almost painfully and instantly I spill over the edge of the precipice I was hovering. I cry out with every wave of beautiful agony.

He stays on his knees as a cheeky smile lights up his face.

I bend forward and cup his face, crushing my mouth to his. He tastes like me. My core aches to have him inside me.

"We are going to be late, Sunshine."

"I don't care."

He rises to his feet. A second later, I am jostled on the car and my jeans are on, Lewis fingering the button closed.

What? No!

"Hey, no fair," I moan.

"I have been wanting to do that all morning." He winks at me and opens the car door, gesturing for me to hop in. This is a new level of self-control for Lewis. I know exactly how hard it is for him to fight off the vampiric instinct when we are intimate. Perhaps he's testing himself. To see if he can be selfless as well as in control.

I move to where he stands and peck a kiss on his lips. "Full marks, Professor. Your best effort yet."

He chuckles and closes the door as I sink into the leather passenger's seat. I cannot wait for the day to be over. The second we get home, it is my turn to test his theory. Self-control test number two. Let's see how riled up this vampire can get without breaking any more furniture.

CHAPTER 5

LEWIS

Every second of this ridiculous day drags. My attention span for anything is non-existent and there is no hope of trying to wrangle a semblance of concentration. Damn mating bond. The only thing my brain—my body—can focus on is Sammie. This morning in the garage I held off the instincts easily. But every torturous sound she made reminded me what's at stake if I lose control.

Her.

I lose her if I snap and try to drain her like I've done before. She takes notes while I speak to the entire class. Her eyes drifting to the slides on the screen above me. I hear her heartbeat, and every steady breath she takes. The student behind her, a guy, leans down and whispers something to her, his eyes lingering over her chest. Heat floods my core, and I all but tamper the snarl creeping up my throat.

"Mr. Sullivan?"

What?

Someone's calling my name.

"Mr. Sullivan? You okay? You look like you're having a stroke or something." A girl in the front row waves a hand as if landing a plane.

I jerk my gaze from Sammie to the girl speaking and clear my throat.

"Yes, I'm fine. Sorry, where was I?"

"Something about relics and language?" A smug-faced guy crosses his arms before huffing an indignant laugh.

I turn on him, hands curling into fists. His eyes widen and he pushes back in his seat.

"Professor?" Sammie's voice snaps me out of the riled-up state.

A frown puckers her face as she looks between me and the boy in the front row.

"Don't be rude, son. I hand out your grades. Remember that."

He rolls his eyes but looks away and I move back to my laptop and change slides, before picking up where I left off. I'm going to have to get Denver onto this mating bond thing, because it is messing with my mind.

Thirty minutes later, all but one student files from the theater chatting about lunch plans, study sessions, and midterms. Sammie appears at my side as I pack away my things. "Hey."

I turn, and she studies my face. "What was going on before with you?"

I run my hand through my hair, it's as unkempt as I am scattered today. "Nothing, I'm just distracted from this morning."

A sweet smile blooms over her lips. "I could see how the hood of my car would be a distraction."

"Hungry? I don't have another class until midafternoon."

"Starving. Can we meet Serena at the cafeteria? She has some new info for us. She just texted."

She waves her phone between us.

"Sure, lead the way."

It is all I can do to not lead her to the car and drive home at a crazy rate of knots and barricade the two of us in my bedroom. Denver and Zahli got through this initial mating bond period, Sammie and I can do this. Like two civilized, consenting adults.

The cold wintery breeze crackles through the amber leaves around campus, scattering them across the footpath as we make our way to the hub of student life. Shivers wash over my body. That's strange, I haven't felt cold in centuries. Sammie hugs her coat around her, tucking her head into her upturned collar.

"It's freezing out here," she says, picking up the pace.

"Maybe snow later today." I wish I had a more substantial coat now. Not the same sweater I always wear for show.

Can't have people thinking I don't feel the cold. Not here, in Castleton, where the temperatures can drop to almost freezing.

We approach the double-glazed glass doors to the common area. Serena is waiting outside, huffing warmth into her hands with breath that turns to cloud every time. I'm shivering hard by the time we reach her, and Sammie's shoulders are shaking with the cold.

"You two look half frozen. Let's go inside. They better have an endless supply of coffee ready." Serena opens the door, letting us walk in first. The warmth that hits my face from the central heating is something akin to heaven. I unfold my arms from my torso and drop my satchel beside the closest table for three. The extensive area is full of mingling students, also desperate to escape the frigid outdoors.

"I'll get us some coffee and something warm to fill us up." Sammie drops her bag with Serena's. If we were home, I would peck her cheek in thanks, or wrap a hand around her waist, nuzzling into her hair while she prepares the food. Or better still, prepare it for her and feed it to her on the bed before—

Ugh. Unbelievable . . .

"Mr. Sullivan?" a voice says from behind. I spin around to find two of the first-year students I teach standing, waiting with lit up eyes and nervous expressions, trays loaded with food in their hands.

"What's up, girls?" I shove my hands in my pockets.

"Ah, we have some questions about the last class. Is it okay if we sit with you?" the brunette says, her gaze dropping to the floor as her neck turns crimson.

"Actually, I am already here with some second-years, you are welcome to join us, you will need to grab some chairs."

They move quickly, plucking two chairs from other tables and squeezing them around the table with the other three. Sammie and Serena return with the trays and Sammie gives me a quizzical smile. I train my face to no response and simply nod to the two girls. "Some more students to join our linguistics discussion."

My mate fights to tamper her amusement, lips flattening as she clears her throat. Serena huffs a laugh but sits next to the brunette, saying hello.

"What topic are you covering this semester?" Sammie asks the second girl. Her round brown eyes widen through her black glasses, and she glances at me before reciting the topics we have covered so far in the first-year sessions.

"Nice," Sammie says, "Mr. Sullivan was my favorite first-year professor. You're lucky to have him."

I try to ignore the less than subtle compliment as the brunette stares at me with mouth slightly agape before staring at Sammie. Did she pick up we're together from one sentence?

Fuck.

"What she means to say is that most of the professors here are old and set in their ways. Mr. Sullivan mixes it up and most students appreciate the variety," Serena says, pouring sugar into her coffee cup and stirring it with a disposable wooden spoon.

"Oh, okay. Yeah, I have a few other professors. None of them drive a Mustang. My name is Jenna, by the way." The brunette finishes and stabs a fork into her salad. Her friend does the same.

"Which major are you thinking of doing?" I ask Jenna.

"Um, I have no idea yet. I was thinking of archaeology, but my parents say Indiana Jones jobs don't exist." She glances at her friend.

"That's too bad." I take a bite of the food Sammie brought for me.

"Jen, there're those guys from yesterday, we should ask about the party," her friend offers. I'm not sure whether we're too boring, or they feel uncomfortable, but they excuse themselves and make for a table with girls and guys, trays in hand.

"Well, that was awkward," Sammie says.

"Looks like Lewis, sorry professor Sullivan, has a fan club."

Sammie's face slackens, and she drops her fork, the curry and rice she bought back for the both of us splatters back into the bowl. Glad I am not the only one whose head is a mess from this mating bond. Her breathing quickens, the lapels of her navy wool coat ride the sharp rise and fall. "I need some air." She pushes out from the table and stalks out the double doors into the cold.

My hands tingle, my breaths now too shallow. As if my body is imitating hers. A moment later, I'm cold, as she would be now. Serena studies me carefully. One eyebrow is raised as her gaze alternates between Sammie and me. Heat, something like rage, floods my system. I shut my eyes and tilt my head to one side, trying to drown it out. Instead, I shiver.

Sammie.

This is what Sammie is feeling after those girls were just talking to me.

"Lewis?" Serena utters.

I force my eyes open. She is staring at me, mouth agape. Well, that isn't a good look. What the fuck now?

"Holy shit. You two are bound."

Air leaves my lungs and doesn't return. Bound? Like as in life and death. And every emotion, memory, experience, type of bound?

"Are you sure?" I growl out, but I know the answer. Denver's been researching it continuously since the tether kicked in. We've been hoping it isn't the case. Sammie shouldn't have to be burdened with my life.

"You two are bound. Just like I said. I was afraid my sadistic mother would do this. It's her style. Taking away freewill. It's like her go-to magic when screwing people over. I should know." The last part is almost a whisper. I can't possibly imagine what Anjelica has inflicted upon her own daughter.

"Serena," I utter, meeting her tortured gaze.

"You and Sammie have a much bigger problem now. With you weakened by her being apart from you and her feeling everything you do. Nobody can know about this. If the council gets wind of it—"

"Find out about what?" Sammie says from behind me.

I feel her.

Her heartbeat is slower than a minute ago and the heat I felt is gone. Her hands land on my shoulders and I glance around the cafeteria. If someone notices us together, we both lose our places at this college. I won't let her lose a scholarship she worked her ass off for.

I stand almost too fast and she jerks backward. Shit. I pluck my bag from the floor and storm out the door. My head is a torrent of must dos, don't dos and overwhelming need. I flip my collar up and duck my head, making my way through the frigid wind as fast as possible.

I make it thirty feet before the twinge in my stomach reminds me why Sammie's been in proximity all day. "Ah, fuck."

I stop and will myself to breathe through the growing ache. Sammie must be feeling the same pain. I turn back and watch as she and Serena talk, still eating. Sammie doesn't seem to have noticed the tether. If she has, she's doing well to hide it. I walk a little further away, backward. The pain grows, and I press my forearms over my stomach. I take another ten strides back.

Fire tears through my core, stealing my breath. I sit on

the park bench on the side of the footpath and take steadying breaths. Sammie bursts through the door, clutching her stomach. Her legs falter as she wraps her coat around her body, tight.

Cold infiltrates the places in my body fire hasn't claimed, and I sit waiting for her. This is so fucked up. How are we supposed to live like this? We are barely fifty feet apart and look like the zombie apocalypse has claimed us. It would be funny if it wasn't so fucking ridiculous. She sinks into the seat beside me.

"I'm sorry, Lew."

I huff a laugh and run a hand through my hair. The fire peters out, and she takes long slow breaths, her pain must be fading too. "For what, Sunshine? You didn't do this to us, Anjelica did."

"Ugh. Serena just told me. How in seven hells are we supposed to live like this? I mean, at home, it's not a problem. But we have lives, you have a job. I have school. There has to be a way to break this binding, the tether too."

"Maybe with Denver and Serena's help." I have no idea how to even start to fix this.

"I broke your curse, surely this I can undo as well."

"Possibly." The stone lodged in my gut disagrees. I highly doubt Anjelica would have worked the spell to let the victims simply undo her work. She is much too maleficent for that. Much too convoluted. I growl and rise from the bench. "Right now, all I want to do is get out of this freezing air. Library?"

"Since when do you feel the cold?"

I raise an eyebrow.

"Are you serious? Can you feel everything I do?"

"It appears so."

She bites her lip. "So, like this morning on your car?"

"It only seemed to kick in when you went outside before."

She laughs with relief but stalls out. "Hang on, so from now on, you'll feel everything I feel?"

"I have no idea. I don't make the rules, Sammie."

"Just when I think things are looking up."

"I don't know, I wouldn't mind feeling how I make you feel when you—"

She slaps my arm as three students walk past.

Fuck.

"We have a hands-off policy, Miss Williams," I drone.

They giggle amongst themselves, and Sammie rolls her eyes at me. Annoyance and amusement bloom in my chest. Is that what she is feeling right now? I wait until the students are out of earshot before continuing.

"So, whatever you feel. I feel. Does it go the other way, Sunshine?"

"I don't think so," she says, sadness lining the words.

"Ah, okay. Well, at least I'll be able to read your mind now," I joke and start walking toward the library.

"Oh yeah, being female is such an amazing experience. You wait until I get my period. You'll be really rocking that sensation, Professor."

She winks at me and walks ahead, her perfect ass strutting in front. My cock hardens, swallowed by throbbing with every sway her hips make. Right now, I am glad this thing only goes one way. I growl and shift my satchel to cover my bulge. Hopefully, I can get into the library without embarrassing myself or losing my job. For fuck's sake, this mating bond is inconvenient, to say the least, and downright inappropriate at most.

Sammie stops at the doors and drags her gaze up and down my body. As if sensing the coiled up want, she lets her hand brush mine as I walk past her into the warm embrace of the musty library. Her gasp makes me turn around. Her eyes widened and mouth curled up on one side. Heat pools low in my belly.

And I realize it's not mine.

It's hers.

She pads to where I have stopped just inside the library.

"That's not very professional, Professor."

Her eyes are level to my own. The pretty blue hues are lit up with hunger and excitement.

"You can feel it too?"

"When I touched you." She leans closer, lips brushing my ear. "There's a fire in your pants. We should probably go home."

The clerical lady clears her throat behind us, and I take Sammie's hand and lead her out of the library. Once outside, I release her and try to suppress the smile stretching my face. "Lead the way, Sunshine."

I follow her gorgeous ass, growing harder by the second. She groans and throws her head back. The Mustang passenger door slams and I plant my foot, sending it back.

We will be lucky if we make it home.

Lewis's hand moves as fast as possible over the keyboard of his laptop as humanly possible while he keeps his speed in check. I sit on the lower floor, with books spread over a large study table. Between a few weeks in the cabin in Alaska and dying, I'm behind, to say the least. The tether makes sure we can't be out of sight of each other, and it is the hardest thing to concentrate when all I want is mere feet from me.

Gone is the academically driven girl here on a scholarship. All my stupid mated brain can dwell on is that gorgeous man in his favorite navy sweater, the faded jean, leather watch, sharp jaw, and deep brown eyes. Wetness lines my panties, and I moan, dropping my head to my books.

I am ridiculous.

I drag my fingers across the textbook, alternating my

focus between the online resources and the old, timeworn books that hold treasures the internet can't possibly fathom. The crackle of the yellowed page, the musty smell they carry, the ink, somewhat faded from years of use and thousands of fingers run past their beat lines. I skim over ancient artifacts, drawing and photos of lost things, worshiped things, and languages from a millennium ago, hunting for the link between something lost to history and current meaning.

Jotting down notes, I slip into the zone. Aspects of relics and human behavior connected as if by a fine gold thread. I toss around the idea of belief and reality. Fiction and fantasy. Humans and those who are not. Time has not documented the latter well. We are the minority. They fear us. They have tried to cull us out.

No wonder Lewis lived a life of quiet days and academic pursuits only. Blend in. Fade into society to save yourself from prejudice. Even with his superior abilities and immortality, he lives in the shadows. His human life was taken from him, but it wasn't replaced by something better. Instead, he's had a half-life.

Something plops onto the page of the old tome under my hand. I look down to see a tear soak into the page. I press my palm to my cheek. It's wet.

Oh Lew.

An ache blooms in my chest for him. For Denver. For Serena, having to live the last two centuries, afraid of her only family. With the next heartbeat, I understand how incredibly lucky I have been to grow up in a loving family and live a normal life.

Magic is a choice.

When I chose not to use it, I was human. When I used it to my advantage, I saved a life. Both thoughts collide and the impact is profound. My gift is for others. Not my own. I pull in a steadying breath and close the books.

I track my gaze to the higher level.

Lewis is gone.

Quickly, I shove my notepads and laptop into my satchel and walk toward the entrance, leaving the old books on the study table. He must be waiting outside for me. I burst through the double doors and hug my coat around me instantly. The cold still finds its way in.

He's not here.

I pull out my phone and the screen lights up. Nothing. That's odd. He's been my constant companion since I woke up after Anjelica.

Something doesn't add up.

I tap out a text.

> Hey, where are you?

I wait.

No reply.

I wander back inside and take the stairs to the level he was on. Three study rooms sit each side of the hallway, the side that's closest to me is all glass walls. From here, I can see the table and books I left out clearly. The rows of wooden stacks lining the library floor stand like soldiers, bearing witness to late night, spilled coffee, and a million ah-hah moments. I walk to the glass overlooking the lower level.

Something hits my shoe.

Lewis's phone sits on the bright blue carpet. My message lights up the screen again.

I sweep it up and scan what I can see of the library from here. His things are gone, the table where he sat is bare. I turn and walk down the stairs to the clerk at the desk in the foyer. "Did Mr. Sullivan come past? He left his phone," I say.

She looks up, slim gold glasses resting halfway down her nose, and her hazel eyes find mine. "He left about ten minutes ago with a young man. Although, I don't think he's a student. He wasn't carrying a backpack and had some sort of frantic look about him."

"Frantic look?"

"Like he was in trouble or something. Perhaps he came to Mr. Sullivan for help?" She offers a half smile and returns to her keyboard, punching in words, letter by letter with two fingers. I push out the doors and look around. He couldn't have gone far with the tether. I am surprised he left without me at all. I pull my phone from my back pocket and swipe up.

Have you seen Lewis?

I send the message to Serena.

Ah, no. Have you?

> We were in the library, and he left with some guy.

Okay . . . Well, he can't have gone far, tether and all.

> I will check the park benches by here. If I don't find him, can you come?

Sure, babes.

I slide my phone back into my pocket and pace around the building. He has to be here somewhere. Why would he be out in the cold? And why leave without telling me? Fear warms my gut, and I pick up the pace. I reach the last park bench that would be in range.

It's empty.

I sink onto it and scan between the trees. Students mill about, some huddled together by the notice board. Most are moving quickly between classes, trying to stay out of the cold.

I check my phone again.

Nothing.

A hard tug snaps in my gut.

Oh no.

He must be moving further away. I can't exactly call out to him. Student-professor etiquette and all.

I tap the phone and open messages.

Help.

I send it to Serena and drop it into my bag. The tug turns to agony, much quicker than it has before, and I double over, clutching my stomach. I reach for my pendant and grip it tight. It warms against my palm, and I moan. Fire grows in my core now.

Wherever Lewis is, he is still moving further and further out of range. Nausea crawls up my throat, the bile burning the air from my lungs. A figure hovers at my side. A guy, his backpack slung over his shoulder. His scruffy brown hair hangs in his eyes.

"Do you want me to call someone for you?"

"Yes," I gasp.

I slide from the bench, knees slamming onto the pavement.

"Oh fuck, okay. Where's your phone?"

I try to nod toward my bag.

He picks up the phone. "Who do I call?"

"Serena," I bite out.

He murmurs something into the phone and tosses it back to the bag. "She's coming."

A heartbeat later, Serena walks over from the park. She could have been anywhere. My pendant cools in my hand.

"Sammie! Dammit, is it Lewis?"

"Yes," I rasp.

"I don't understand," the guy says, stepping back.

"It's fine. I can take it from here." Serena guides me to my feet, and the guy nods and walks off, checking back every few strides.

"Why would he leave? Fuck, Sullivan, you idiot."

We make it to the parking lot. The Mustang is still here. Parked where we left it this morning. If he didn't take his car, he didn't leave on his own free will.

"Rena." The word is almost torture as it passes through my lips.

"I see it, babe. Is there a spare key?"

"What? No, I mean. I don't have one."

"Shit."

She looks around as if trying to size up which car to pinch.

"How did you get here?" I manage.

"Um, you know, I kind of popped up. In the girls' toilets. Gas is so expensive." She bites her lip and offers me a sorry face.

"Can you get me to Lewis's the same way?"

"I think so. But we have to go somewhere else. Not here."

"Hurry."

She helps me to behind the nearest lecture theater. Checking nobody is coming, she takes my hand and grabs her pendant. Four words of Latin later, I stand on Lewis's porch on wobbly feet. The agony intensifies.

"He's not here, is he?" Serena says, her face stunned with fear.

"No," I choke and stagger to the love seat on the porch.

She pulls my phone from my bag and calls Lewis. It rings. And rings out. He doesn't answer.

"What the hell, Sullivan." She tosses my phone back into my bag before dialing someone on hers. "Denver, it's Serena. We have a problem."

)))·◐·(((

enver's hands are white around the wheel. Serena sits in the truck with us, me sandwiched in the middle. After a spell and some educated guesswork, Denver and Serena located a rough location for Lewis. Fifty miles north, toward Burlington, just north of Ferrisburgh. The truck sails along the highway, every mile closer feels longer. I try to subdue the pain with my magic, nothing works, my head is so fuzzy. Like I am half unconscious.

Nothing makes sense.

Serena grabs my arm as Denver slams on the brakes, pulling into a gas station. Her hand releases me and she unfolds a map, lines of blood scatter from a point like cobwebs. She waves her hand over it and the crimson lines move. They sway east on the map. The many lines from before converging to one point. Northeast, in the center of the Ferrisburgh Municipal Forest. He is in the middle of a forest. Why?

Denver slams the truck into gear, and the tires scream as they leave the blacktop. Denver's face is hard. Serena focuses a worried gaze on him. "Why would they do this?"

Denver shoots her a look before his eyes find mine. "Most likely the mating bond. It's the only thing I can think of that would compromise my brother."

So, this is my fault?

"What do you mean?" I push up from the seat. Pinpricks of light waiver at my peripherals.

"The council will not allow your union. They must have found out you're still bonded." He tracks his attention to Serena, but she's staring out the window, hands gripping the map in her lap. The lofty pines of the forest appear ahead and Denver speeds up.

"Can you get me to where Lewis is?" I ask Serena.

"You don't want to walk into whatever is going on, Sammie. You need to find somewhere to wait while I go in and bring him out," Denver says.

I turn to face him. "I'm going with you."

Serena's hand rests on my shoulder. "He's right, Sammie, if you go, they have both of you. Let us get him out, babes."

I whimper a cry and shake my head. How did this go so wrong so quickly?

Denver parks the truck at the start of the hiking trail. He and Serena get out and talk quietly as I pull myself out the passenger door and over to them. Still clutching my stomach, I come to stand by Serena's side.

"I'll be back in a moment, wait here." Denver disappears through the trees in a blur.

"We will get him back, Sammie, but you have to stay out of it. Promise me you will stay out of sight."

I nod, silver lining my eyes. The agony has settled into the depths of my core, and I take shallow breaths. Now, my entire body hurts. It burns.

Denver reappears from the tree line and gravel flies from under his shoes when he slides to a halt beside us. "Demons, not scouts, at least I don't think so. Four of them. He's unconscious."

"Shit. He's out because of the tether. That confirms it for them." Serena paces in a circle.

"Right, element of surprise. I can drop us into the middle of the room. You finish them in a few heartbeats, you carry Lewis out, I'll take care of any surprises," Serena says.

"Let's go. Be back in a moment, Sammie. Wait in the truck."

I nod and pad to the truck, sinking to the footstep, and hang my head between my knees. I count to sixty. One minute passed, no Lewis.

I count another minute.

Voices come from the depths of the forest.

Serena.

A male voice I don't recognize.

A scream.

I push off the truck and walk into the forest.

Needles, twigs, and amber leaves crunch under my boots. I pull my coat around me again. If I am feeling the cold, Lewis will too. The pain eases a little and I pick up the pace. I must be getting closer to him.

My skin still burns.

A few moments later, through the vast bark-covered columns, I see a small hut. Serena is fending off two males. Denver holds one by the neck. Another walks out of the hut and vanishes, appearing behind Serena with a blade to her throat.

Oh, my god.

I break into a run, swaying with the effects of the tether, but propping myself on the trunks of the trees as I go.

"Back off, man, or your woman gets it," the male holding the knife yells at Denver.

He turns and steps back, holding his hands above his head. "Drop the knife, demon."

A vicious laugh spews from the demon's mouth and Serena tenses, hand rising toward her pendant. He slaps her hand down. "Uh uh uh, not this time, witch."

They're outnumbered. I hide behind a tree, stealing a glance. The pain is all but gone. I fling my palms in front of me and flames hiss to life above them. I curl my palm over, snuffing out the flames, and push up to a tall stance. With a wave of my hand, I send a gust at the demon holding Serena.

He falters backward, his head flinging side to side, frantically searching for the source. Serena breaks away and kicks him in the chest. She grips her pendant and spins it before disappearing from sight. Denver slams his elbow into the demon beside him. I send a gust, flattening the second to the ground.

I step out from the trees and Denver watches as I rush to the hut. "Sammie, stop." He is holding out a hand. I push the door open. Serena is prying the restraints from Lewis's wrists. His head bowed, his chin rests on his chest. Blood covers his shirt, neck and face. I stop frozen at the sight of him.

Serena turns back, sadness twisting her face and lining her eyes.

I slap a hand over my mouth and lose a whimper.

Dizziness swallows me whole, and I shatter to the ground.

"No . . ."

CHAPTER 7

SERENA

LONDON, 1837

The ivory handle of my lace parasol spins in my grip. The chatter of the girls beside me does nothing to quell the unease plaguing me.

"Serena, darling, don't be rude. Offer the girls some of your cake." Mother's words pull me back to the party. My birthday luncheon on the lawns of Hyde Park, at her insistence. Gardens and the summer blooms on offer surround us. To our west, tall trees stand in formation, guarding the park from the rest of the city. The soft, cream blanket we sit on is covered in delicacies, from cake to wafers, flanked by a silver tray and teapot, teacups and saucers.

It took us hours to get here by carriage. These girls she has invited from her upper circles are far from my friends. This event, like everything else she does, is purely strategic. As she tries to cement us into upper-class society in the hopes I will marry above my station. I set the parasol down and take the silver-plated cake slide from my mother's waiting hand. Her face is plastered with a facade of grace and love.

I cut slices, placing them on the porcelain plates, and hand them around to all four of the girls, dressed up with more beads and lace than I ever imagined humanly possible. They use the dainty silver forks Mother brought and pick at the crumbling vanilla cake.

Mother clears her throat as I cut myself a slice and finish half. I look from my plate to her gaze. Setting the plate down, I offer her a saccharine smile. Knowing flickers through her eyes.

To get away from her will almost be worth marrying for wealth. But I would be marrying someone I hardly know, and do not love. My heart aches at the thought. If the choice was mine, it would be Theo. And I would get to make my own decisions in this matter.

My fate and Theo's would not be left to the ill-intended mind of my mother. Maybe when she understands he is serious, she will give us her blessing. I wish it to be true.

My heart belongs to no other.

After the sun has thoroughly baked our skins through, the girls fidget on the blanket. Their proper upbringing fading with the slightest of discomforts.

"Well, happy birthday, my darling. Hasn't this been the quaintest little morning sup, girls?"

"Oh, simply lovely." One smiles, the upturn of her lips not reaching her eyes.

"I really must be going. Thank you so much for the invitation, Serena. Shall I see you in town?" another says.

"Yes, of course."

"We will see you lovely ladies at the ball next month," Mother says, rising to see them off. I pluck the parasol from the blanket and follow. Good manners overriding the urge to wander off entirely. Mother walks the girls to their carriages and bids them good day.

Joseph waits patiently in ours, at the front of the line. Tender, the gray mare who he has pulled it for many years is asleep, one leg bent to the tip of her hoof, tail swishing every so often. I wander behind, lost in thoughts of what leaving my mother's household will mean.

She waves as the last of the carriages rolls away. I offer a small wave and start tidying the picnic lunch back into the basket for Joseph. I walk the basket to the carriage, leaving the blanket for Jo to fold up. He jumps down from the driver's seat, taking the basket from me.

"Did you enjoy your birthday picnic, Miss Serena?"

"I did, Jo."

He raises an eyebrow and looks to where mother is standing, straightening her skirts. "You can tell me the truth, little one."

He has called me that my entire life.

I smile and touch his shoulder. He winks at me and turns back to stow the basket under his seat. I move to Tender's head and rub her forehead. She nickers and nudges me with her muzzle. "Hey girl. You had about as much fun here as I did."

Joseph chuckles behind me, folding the blanket and placing it with the basket before lowering the seat and fastening the brass latch. "Don't you let on Tender, or both our heads will roll."

I press my forehead to Tender's and huff a laugh. The mare leans into my embrace, chewing her bit. I rub a hand over her cheek, and she nickers again.

"Oh Serena, must you touch that filthy animal at every opportunity?" Mother chides.

I step away from Tender.

She steps onto the first rung of the carriage lift. "Come, I have preparations to attend to before the full moon. I will need your help."

"Yes, Mother."

Jo rounds the mare and catches my gaze, nodding toward the trees. I turn, searching for his meaning.

I see it a second later.

Theo.

A smile splits my face, and I lift my skirts, handing the parasol to Jo. I walk so fast, my shins ache, before taking off at a run toward the trees. Behind me, Jo talks to Tender. The clink of buckles and the snap of straps, he is double checking the rigging to buy me a handful of moments.

I slow my pace and Theo walks out from beside the tree, flowers in hand. His dark coat and tails and top hat make him look taller, and more handsome than ever. Breath catches as butterflies take flight in my stomach. His green eyes are lit up, a wide smile stretching his lips. Electricity flows through my veins, a grin covering my face.

"Theo!" I fly into his arms. He huffs a raw sound, and I wrap myself around him. I don't care who sees us. Or what the proper thing to do is.

"Happy birthday, Seri," he whispers into my ear, a tremble carries the words.

"Thank you, Thee."

He holds me tight, and his scent fences me in. Sandalwood and spice. I close my eyes and wish for time to stand still. A moment later, my wish unheeded, he unfolds and holds me at arm's length.

"These are for you. I have another gift for you. But—"

"What is it? Is everything okay?"

"Yes, I-I wanted to—" He pushes the flowers into my hand and steps back.

"Theo?"

He fiddles with the brim of his top hat, now in his hands. Ducking his head, his brown hair falls across his eyes as they drift shut, and he blows out a long breath. He moves to bend down. His knee presses into the grass, one up as he drops his hat to the ground.

My mouth gapes, heart flinging against my rib cage. I step closer, my breath turns shallow, and my hands shake around the stems of the flowers.

"Seri, I know we have been friends forever, and you are—"

"Get up, boy!" Heat floods my face at the sound of my mother's voice.

I suppress the sobs choking up my throat. Theo stands up, fire laces his eyes, and I close mine.

No, Mother, please don't do this.

When I open my eyes, she is glaring at Theo. His knuckles are white around the brim of his hat. His chest heaves, his jaw set.

"How dare you tarnish my daughter's chances of a wealthy match with your boyish infatuations!" Mother steps between us.

"With all due respect, ma'am, my affections toward your daughter are far from boyish infatuation."

"What is that supposed to mean? If you have laid a finger on her—"

"Mother! Stop!"

She grabs my hand, then rips the flowers from my grip and tosses them at Theo's feet.

"No," I gasp.

"You would do well to hold your tongue, my girl. You better pray nobody of good breeding saw this charade! We are leaving."

Theo's pained eyes meet mine. "I'm sorry, Seri."

I stagger sideways as Mother pulls me from where he stands. Theo's throat works.

I sob my way back to the carriage, wiping tears from my flushed cheeks. Mother's iron-clad grasp on my wrist sends pains up my arm. Jo meets us by the steps. "Miss Serena, are you alright?"

"She is fine! If you had something to do with this, Joseph, you will live to regret it, finding yourself swiftly unemployed."

She stalks up the steps and takes her seat, shifting her skirts, before fanning her face with a black hand fan. I keep my head up and meet Jo's gaze. He offers a sad smile, something in the way of an apology. It's not his fault. None of this is. I rest a hand on his shoulder and climb the stairs into the carriage. I sit, staring out the window, as if my mother isn't merely feet from me.

"This is for the good of our family. You will thank me one day when you are not living in poverty and shame. Mark my words, Theo and his family will be magical outcasts in this city, it is only a matter of time."

I ignore her monologue as she continues to outline all the ways a wealthy match will instill our family of two into proper society. I don't hear the words, only the sentiments. My heart is breaking with every clip and clop Tender makes further from Theo.

Never before today did I hate my mother. How could she be so shallow, so cruel? The carriage sways as we cross London, traveling home to the eastern suburbs. I imagine Theo having to ride all the way home. It will take him longer, as they live in the outer eastern area.

Letting my eyes shutter against the moving portrait of the city landscape, I grab the pendant around my neck, the one Theo gave me on my fifteenth birthday. Tears burn behind my eyes and my throat closes over. Hot tears run down my cheeks. If she notices, she doesn't let on.

The carriage sways. My heart cracks clean in two. The air from my lungs is non-existent. Every angle of his handsome face, the curve of his lips, his green eyes and cheeky smile play over and over in my mind. The warmth of his hands around mine. An ache grows in my heart, spreading as it intensifies.

I hold myself together as the carriage rolls to a stop. As Jo opens the door. As I ascend the steps. As I cross the threshold into our home. As I climb the stairs to my bedroom. As I shut the door behind me. And when I slide down it and hit the floor . . .

My chest caves under the weight of losing Theo.

I rock back and forward, hugging my knees to my body.

I don't want to live without him.

How can I?

)·)·)·❂·(·(·(

The dried herbs assault my senses with every grind of pestle into mortar. The cream linen apron tied around my waist is too tight. My breaths are all too shallow. My mind is lost to heartbreak. I send the pestle around to muddle the desiccated grayed herb as per Mother's instructions. She wants it fine.

Fine enough for an elixir of some sort. I pray my ministrations are not contributing to her plans of taking over the coven. She stands chopping more dried herbs, readying them for the mortar. She hasn't said it outright to me, but from the way she talks about Theo's father and the rest of his family, I know that is what she wants. The hatred that lines her words when she talks about them, and the condescending tone she takes, worries me.

"Finer, Serena. It must be unpalatable."

"Yes, Mother."

I want to slam the mortar over her head and flee this morbid entrapment of mine.

But I can't do it.

I can't bring myself to leave the one person I have left who is family. With Father gone, I am sure she does everything in her power to keep our position in society, to keep us from falling further down the ranks of prosperity to the pit of despair. Why else would she be so insistent on my marrying well? What other reason than to help us both would she need to break my heart in two by denying me the one thing I need?

Theo.

"What is all this for again, Mother?"

"Serena, some days I fear your ears are painted on, child. This is the elixir I intend to offer our dear coven leader on his annual foray. Everyone must bring a gift, remember? I intend on giving each person in his family this healing elixir. If taken at a full moon, it will keep them in good health for a full year."

"Oh . . ." She is paying them a kindness? Her words say so, but my stomach flips.

"Mother, if Theo's family were to rise socially, would you accept his proposal to me?"

Her hands still over the board. She sighs and puts the knife down. Her hand lifts my chin as she steps into my space. "My dear girl. Everything I do for you, for us, is to better this life we have. Theo, I am afraid, is not part of that."

I swallow.

My throat is thick with emotion. I was hoping against this very thing. She has discounted him from our lives. Any chance we could have had is gone. Short of running off together and causing her great shame, Theo and I are doomed. I fight to guard against the burning that swells behind my eyes. She studies me for a moment before releasing my face and returning to her chopping. I breathe through the pain twisting its way through my aching heart and turn to the mortar and pestle in a daze.

All I want to do, in this moment, is see Theo. To hear his voice. Hear his laughter. Feel his warm hands on mine. His breath against my ear. His eyes lit up before they darken as he steps into my space. To be completely surrounded by him. My next breath chokes out.

I shake my head. His love may as well be unobtainable now. Mother will have me married off to the highest-ranking socialite she can find in a matter of months now that I am eight and ten. My chin wobbles at the thought.

I send every ebb of heartbreak down into the mortar through the pestle. The old stone groans with each muddle I make. Tears drip from my chin, hitting the wooden kitchen bench.

"Chin up, child. He is merely a boy. There are plenty more. Many better options will come your way. Of this I am certain."

I can't respond.

Every word tears at the hole in my heart.

Sending it wider and wider.

CHAPTER 8

SAMMIE

It's been three days since we brought Lewis home.

He is weak.

The tether rendered him defenseless against the four demons, and they did their worst. Inside the pocket of one was a paper with the order to find and bring Lewis to the council by any means necessary. Denver's been analyzing it for days.

Each word.

Dates.

Timing.

Wording.

If it's on the now tattered piece of paper, he's scoured over it.

Lewis is healing, slowly, the damage done is substantial. Even his vampirism hasn't quickened the process. Only one thing can heal him quickly. The blood of his mate. My blood. I have tried to get him to take it, but he's still refusing. There is one way to get him to take it almost involuntarily.

I push from the doorframe where I have been leaning for the past half an hour, watching him breathe. He stirs, rolling in his sleep, his battered face touches the pillow, and he jerks back in his sleep. I shut the door and lock it. On silent feet, I move to the bed, pulling my top over my head.

I unhook my bra and toss it to the floor. The mere thought of him has my peaks hard and breasts heavy. I wriggle from my jeans and panties and crawl in beside him. His bare skin under the sheet is hot on mine. I snuggle in and kiss his forehead, his jaw, his lips.

He murmurs.

"Lew," I whisper, sending my fingers over his jaw, kissing his mouth. He groans against my lips. "Let me help you."

"Sammie." My name is barely a word on his lips. He rolls toward me and his eyes open slowly.

"Hi." Seeing him this way, my throat closes over. I fight back a whimper as I trace the damage on his face tenderly. "Oh, Lew."

He groans, pressing his forehead to mine. I run a hand around his neck and dot kisses to his neck, trailing downward. His breathing shallows out. I duck under the sheet and make my way down his hard stomach, tracking soft kisses as I go. He tenses, grabbing the sheet with one hand, his other searches for me. I go lower still. His hard length is warm in my hand. I lick the tip and plunge it deep into my mouth.

Lewis groans, his body rigid, the hand on the sheets turns white, his other finds my hair. I smile around him and make slow, steady, long movements. My apex throbs at the taste of him in my mouth.

"Sunshine," he growls.

He's awake.

Good.

If I can get him to the point where his instincts kick in, I should be able to have him take what he needs. He needs it. I need him to be okay.

I need him, period.

I swirl my tongue around his bell, and he moans, hard, fisting my hair. I can imagine his eyes darkening.

"Sunshine, stop."

I keep going.

With long, languid strokes, I pull him higher and higher. He growls and tosses the sheet off me. His eyes are near black. He's close. I take him deeper, still.

"No!"

He pulls me up under the arms, fast, and I use the momentum to settle over his hips, straddling him. His breaths are erratic.

"Sunshine, stop, I don't want to hurt you."

Those words from his broken face wrench a sob from me.

"I am not stopping Lew, you need this."

I move, setting his tip at my now wet and aching entrance.

"No, what if I can't control it?"

"We'll be fine." I sink onto his hard length and moan with every inch I take of him. God, he is everything. I bend down and smash my mouth to his. His hand wanders, tweaking each hard peak before trailing down my stomach to where we are joined.

"Hold me, Sunshine." His voice is gravel.

I summon wind and keep him at bay as he flips us over, pressing me into the bed. Lewis's eyes are black. I raise my hips to meet his movements and whimper. I can barely restrain a moan as he slams into me. I make sure to stay as quiet as I can, so he falls over the edge into his instinct.

He grabs my wrists, pushing them into the pillow beside my head. Something coils low in my belly. I'm so close. I want to touch his face, kiss his mouth. But I don't want to distract him from the instinct.

Instead, I raise my hips to his again, driving him wilder, higher. His canines descend and his movements become harder, more erratic. I summon more wind, keeping him from crushing me through the mattress.

He tilts his head to the side, and a groan spills from his lips.

Low and feral.

Bite me, Lew. Do it.

He lowers his gaze to mine. A second passes and his teeth pierce my neck. I can't help the whimper escaping my lips. Fire sears across my neck. He sucks, hard. I channel wind between us. His hips slam into mine, and I come harder than I ever have. I cry out, oblivion stealing my soul with every wave of gorgeous pleasure.

Lewis releases his hold on my neck, and his eyes search my face. Black orbs stare at me before fading to brown. My blood drips from his canines. His gorgeous face, now healed, stares back at me. I did that for him. And it worked so fast. The magic of the mating bond, I guess. A ragged sound of elation splits past the smile stretching my face.

"Do it again, Lew, please."

"You like that, Sunshine?"

"God, yes."

He takes longer, slower strokes now, and nuzzles the other side of my neck.

"Hold on," he whispers. I grip his shoulders and wrap my legs around him. A momentary blur and we're against the wall. I shake my head with a light chuckle, and he smiles at me.

Next second, we are in the study, his office at the front of the house. Dizziness from the impossible movement washes over me for a second. I steady myself, sliding my hands behind me on the desk. Papers and books crash to the floor.

"This better?" he asks.

"Yes," I breathe. "Much better."

I flick my wrist, slamming the door shut with wind. The papers on the floor stir up in a flurry. Lewis chuckles and stands between my legs, studying every curve, every part of me. "Fuck, you're beautiful, Sunshine."

"Take whatever you need, Lewis. Please, bite me again."

I know he needs more. He's been out for days. Part of me, a selfish part, wants to crash into oblivion with him joined to me in every way.

Lewis grips my legs, opening them wide. He rubs his thumb over my throbbing apex, and I arch off the desk toward him. He growls and claims my mouth with his. My chest heaves against his. Peaks aching for his mouth. His tongue parts my mouth and I widen for him. He slams into me, and I tighten around him instantly.

"Do it, Lewis."

His brown eyes drop to my neck, the undamaged side. "Are you sure?"

"Yes."

He closes his eyes, and his canines come down again. When he opens his eyes, they're still brown, darkened but still brown.

He can do it on command?

I arch up and tilt my head to one side. "Will you do something for me, Sammie?"

"Whatever you need."

He pulls out, slamming into me hard.

"Come for me, beautiful."

Oh God.

I nod, unable to speak.

His thumb circles my apex. His hard length fills and

stretches me with every delicious stroke. Beautiful agony grows in my center and I cry out. Lewis bites down and I explode around him. He growls and I completely lose it.

"Lewis!" Pure, precious pleasure rips through me. Lewis sinks his bite deeper, and I squirm under him. He roars to his climax a moment later. The tortured face he pulls sends warmth through my chest as my blood trickles from his mouth and down his chin.

Before I have a second to recover, I am scooped up and we're in Lewis's ensuite. He sets me down on the tile and turns on the shower. His body is clean, all of the damage from the demons is healed.

He's perfect again.

My legs shake, my body aches in the best way possible. Clouds of steam rise around us and Lewis folds himself around me.

"Thank you, Sunshine."

·)·)·)·●·(·(·(·(·

The piney breeze carries the scent of deer. I walk behind Lewis, huddled in my coat. He still shivers with every step we take. If we could be more than fifty feet apart, I would have let him hunt alone, but part of me is worried about him still. And if more of those demons find him, he cannot afford to be affected by the tether. I will not let it happen again.

Breaking it has become my priority. He won't be safe

until the tether is broken. Denver's been researching along-side Serena, but so far, they've discovered nothing useful.

Lewis stops. Still shivering, he stands otherwise motion-less. The crack of debris underfoot whips his head to the left. He disappears in a blur, and I fly into a sprint to keep up, trying to minimize the distance between us.

Through the trees, he darts before breaking off to the right.

I jump bushes and dodge the old rough tree trunks the best I can at speed and slide to a halt before a clearing. He stands arms out at his side, shoulders heaving. Facing a bear. Holy hell. His eyes are black orbs, his canines descended. He snarls, and the animal rears on its feet, returning a growl.

Slowly, he stalks around the clearing, the bear turning to face him with every few steps. He rushes it. It swipes and catches his arm. Still slower than usual, Lew's balance is not what it was. I curl my hands by my sides and hold the grizzly in place with wind. Its eyes widen when it tries to move, tries to attack Lewis and can't. Lew steps back, his gaze darting to me. I offer a small smile, and his focus returns to the bear. He moves to its side, and it claws at him again.

He tries to breach its swinging arms but lands on his ass with a strong swipe from the bear. He pushes off the ground, his face taut as he rumbles a growl. He can't get close enough, quick enough. I step into the clearing and the animal spins back.

With the flick of my left wrist, my grasp on the animal tightens. I raise my hand, and it leaves the ground. Higher until it is over our heads, I fist my hands, and it drops to the ground.

Stunned, the bear lies on its back winded. Lewis flies into it, sinking his teeth into the bear's neck. His hand dives into its chest, closing around its heart. The beast jerks and goes limp. I stand by as Lewis takes what he needs. Drawing more and more blood, his urgency fades as he's finally satiated after weeks of trials. I turn and check the forest flanking every side of us.

Listening for movement.

Looking for anything bipedal.

All is still, the birds continue their twitters, the small animals rustle the undergrowth. Nothing to threaten us, for now.

Arms slide around my waist. I lay my head back on his shoulder, listening, wrapped in his warmth.

Lewis hums in my ear, and I spin in his embrace. His dark brown eyes are bright, his color much better.

"You must feel better, Lew."

He drops his forehead to mine. "I do."

I kiss his lips and slide my hands behind his neck. He deepens the kiss. Copper finds its way into my mouth.

My breath hitches.

He breaks away, frowning. "Sorry."

"Occupational hazard or something?"

He chuckles and cups my face in his hand. His skin is cold. We should go. "Something like that, Sunshine."

We start back toward home, walking through the forest in silence. "Any luck with the tether research," Lewis asks, breaking the silence and my train of thought.

"No. Den is still working on it, though."

"Den?" He smiles and meets my gaze.

"Well, I figured if he is calling me Sammie, I can call him Den."

Lewis laces his fingers in mine. "Sounds fair."

The smile turns into a grin. I'm happy his brother liking me makes him happy. I like Denver, he's solid. Grounded, although sometimes hotheaded. But Lewis is everything to him. And that means a lot to me.

"You know, you two should spend more time together. Without me, at least without me being in the same room all the time. You both love research and cooking, you could do that while I mark the thousands of papers I have piling up on my desk."

"You wouldn't mind? I mean, he's your brother, it wouldn't be weird?"

"Why would it?"

I chuckle. "Well, if you say so."

"What do you mean?"

"As long as it won't trigger some mating bond jealousy thing."

"Ah." He shoves his free hand in his pocket and stares

ahead. "It wouldn't be the first time my brother and I have shared, Sammie."

I stop dead in my tracks.

"What?"

He turns back, looking down at where our hands are joined before meeting my gaze. "I don't know what you're thinking. Is that a surprised what, or a shocked what?"

I open my mouth to say something. I close it. I guess I was . . .

"Surprised?" The word is feeble, as if the mildest forest gust could sweep it from existence.

He steps into my space. "Just you and me is okay, too. Always."

"Okay. I don't know if my heart is big enough for both of you. I mean, like that."

He breathes a laugh and cups my face with both hands. "All I want is you, mating bond or no. You are the light to my dark. Please know that, Sunshine."

I nod, tears burning as the air in my lungs vanishes. Nobody tells you loving someone this much hurts. That you are torn in a million directions about a million things when it comes to the person you love. I grab the lapels of his coat. What I know is this, even without the mating bond that tethers and ties us together, Lewis was meant to be mine.

And I his.

CHAPTER 9

LEWIS

I know she misses her family desperately. If I had to spend my days miles from Den, I would too. I tap the screen of my phone and pull up the message from Serena last night. Apart from her statement about Friday nights being her own, she came through and sent me Sammie's home address in Burlington. I rang first and checked if her family would be home, explaining to them it's a surprise trip.

I hope she loves it.

Part of me wants to make amends for the loss they endured because of me. Another bigger part wants to make Sammie happy, and I know she is desperate to go home. But the tether is preventing that. So, the next best thing, we go together. Whether she tells them who I am to her, I will leave to Sammie.

I dump an overnight bag in the Mustang's trunk. "Sammie, come on!"

"Be there in a sec."

I slide into the driver's seat and turn the ignition. The purr that follows always makes me smile. I sit, checking my phone for the address again, committing it to memory. Whately Street, South Burlington. The passenger door opens, and Sammie sinks into the seat, her perfume filling the space instantly. Her blonde curls bounce around her shoulders, brushing my cheeks as she leans over and plants a kiss to my lips.

I grip the stick and wheel. Trying to ignore the heat growing in my core. Her fingers thread through my hair before she pushes back into her seat and pulls on her belt. I shake my head, resetting the thoughts that went from excitement for our trip to cascading need for her.

"Ready?" she asks.

I clear my throat and shift the stick. "Ready when you are, Sunshine."

She laughs and punches the radio dial, scanning the channels as we roll down the drive. Twenty minutes later, we are heading north. She's quiet, and I am tempted to ask her what's on her mind. The last few weeks have been extraordinary. And not in a good way.

"Were you serious about sharing?" Sammie finally breaks the silence.

I hold my focus on the road, caught off guard by her question.

"Lewis?"

Sharing Sammie with Denver would be an intense dynamic with the mating bond. We have done it before, but never with a mate. I look from the road to meet her gaze. She's chewing her lip, hands cradling her phone. But her eyes are bright.

She's thought about this. I want to say yes. I want to be big enough to move beyond the thread of jealousy that sprang up when I first mentioned it. I want her and Den to both be happy. Instead, I turn my focus back to the road and change the subject. "We should be there in just over an hour."

She studies me for a moment. "Okay."

Hell, I'm an idiot.

Why did I bring it up? Or entertain the thought when I can't deal with it myself. Brilliant, Lewis.

Just Brilliant.

After an hour of silence drags past, we roll into Sammie's street.

"What are you doing?" she says.

"This is our destination. Our trip. Your trip."

"This is my parents' house," she says as we pull into her drive.

"I know that. Thought you might want to see your family."

Her mouth gapes, and a hand presses over her mouth. A second later, she is out the door and running up the step onto her porch. Before she can get too far from me, I kill the engine and follow.

By the time I arrive at her side, the front door opens. Sammie squeals and flies into her dad's arms. "Hello pumpkin, what are you doing home?"

She pushes from his arms; her face wrapped in a wide smile. "Just visiting for the weekend."

Her dad turns to me. "Who is this?"

"Oh, sorry, Dad, this is Lewis."

I extend a hand to shake his. He takes it cautiously, his grip firm. "Well then. Nice to meet you, Lewis. You're a student at the college also, I presume?"

"I attend the college also, yes."

Sammie rolls her eyes at me but guides her dad inside before he can ask any more questions.

I follow them inside into the foyer of their home. Her mom appears, wiping a tea towel between her hands. She tosses it onto the entrance table when she sees her daughter and pulls her into a tight hug. Mrs. Williams gives me a coy smile. She must remember me from the college open day last year. Sammie embraces her family and my heart swells. I can't keep her from them, it would be selfish and cruel. Whenever she wants to be back here, I'll willingly bring her.

"Who is it, Mom?" a boy's voice calls from upstairs.

"Jackie, come down!" Sammie calls.

Footsteps thud down the stairs. He jumps down the last four treads and sweeps her up into a hug. She giggles and holds him tight. For a little brother, he towers over her, at a solid six inches taller. He puts her back on her feet and ruffles her curls with a hand. "You got shorter, Sammie."

"Ha ha. You just grew like a weed!" She pecks him on the cheek and slaps his chest before turning back to me. "This is Lewis."

"Hey man, I remember you," Jackson says, holding out a hand. "You're the linguistics professor Sammie had last year."

"Ah, yeah, one and the same." I take his hand and shake it.

"Professor?" Sammie's dad says with a frown.

"Don't make a thing about it, Marcus," Mrs. Williams says, shooting him a warning stare. Sammie stands beside her little brother, beaming. Whatever happens here today, just for this moment, it was worth it.

"You two must be starving, come in, lunch is almost ready." Mrs. Williams waves an arm toward what I assume is the kitchen.

"Thank you, Mrs. Williams," I offer, avoiding Sammie's dad's stare.

"Oh goodness, Lewis, call me Laura." She ushers us into the kitchen to the right of the foyer hallway and Sammie slips her hand in mine. I curl my fingers around her and she leans into me, taking in the food-laden table in front of us. Laura really came through. I wasn't sure she would be receptive to my idea. By the amount of effort she's gone to, I'm guessing she's okay with Sammie and me.

"So, Lewis. What do you teach?" Marcus says, sitting at the head of the table, folding a napkin in half before setting it by his plate.

"Linguistics mostly."

"Dad, do we have to do this?" Sammie shifts in her seat, gaze alternating between me and her father.

"Do what, honey?" Marcus frowns. Again.

"The third degree. I'm not a teenager anymore."

"I'm aware," he drawls, but smiles at her. "Linguistics sound fascinating. How is it related to archeology?"

"Ancient linguistics is a first-year course at the college," I offer.

Jackson is piling food onto his plate. Sammie starts with the salad and hands it to me.

"Ah, I see. Very good, then." He winks at his daughter. A peace offering. But his face falls as soon as she looks away. His heart rate spikes the moment Jackson pointed out who I was, along with a dump of adrenaline.

Anger.

I take a small amount of salad and set the bowl down in the middle of the table. Chicken and something like meatloaf are passed around and I fill my plate. Jackson is halfway through his food already and Sammie tosses a cherry tomato at him.

"Hey," he mumbles with a mouthful.

"Slow down, Jackie, or you're gonna choke trying to swallow it whole. No wonder you have shot up and filled out." Sammie grins.

The tomato flies back toward her and she flicks her hand up, letting it hang in the air inches before her face.

Marcus drops his fork, his mouth gapes before snapping to a thin line, brows down.

"Sorry, Dad," she utters, the tomato falls to the table.

Jackson glances between her and Marcus. Who, by the looks of it, still doesn't approve of his daughter using her god-given talents. She has every right to do so. My hand whitens around my fork, and it bends. I slip it under the table before her family sees. Straightening it out with both hands, I watch as her father stands and leaves the table.

Sammie pushes up from her chair. "Dad, I'm sorry."

Laura offers her a small, sad smile. "Maybe keep that part of your life away from your father, honey. You know he doesn't cope with it. Not after—"

After what?

After her grandma?

Did something else happen?

Sammie's eyes find my own. They're lined with silver.

Jesus Christ.

"Excuse me," she says and pushes the chair back in and pads up the stairs on almost silent feet. Fuck, this is not how I planned things would go. Her family is supposed to make her happy. The smiling face from moments ago is now torn by hurt and disappointment.

"Ah, Lewis, I think that's your cue." Jackson nudges my elbow, nodding to the stairs.

"Of course, sorry."

"Don't apologize, you weren't to know," Laura says softly.

I track up the stairs, running a hand up the polished banister. Two bedroom doors flank the right of the passageway at the top. One is open, baseball and soccer posters line the walls, dirty clothes hang on the floor with books and a backpack. Jackson's room.

I try the next door, leaning against it. Sammie's heart beats on the other side. Her breath shallows through small sobs. I push the door open and step inside, closing it behind me.

She is lying on her bed, curled up in the fetal position. My gut sinks. What happened that she would fall apart with one look from her father? I walk to the bed and sit beside her. She wriggles over but does roll over to face me. Her hands cover her face, and tears soak her pillow. I rest a hand on her shoulder and another sob rattles her.

"Sammie?"

She doesn't respond.

I stand and scoop her up until she rests her head against my chest. "Do you want me to take you home, Sunshine?"

She sucks in a ragged breath. "No."

Finally, after a few moments, she lifts her tear-streaked face to meet my gaze. My heart cracks at the sight.

Fucking damn it.

"You can put me down."

"Nope. Not until you're okay."

She huffs a laugh and kisses my neck. Fire snakes, low, sending my cock against my jeans. "Sunshine, can you tell me what's wrong?"

She kisses my neck again, traveling to my jaw. Her teeth drag across my skin, and I spin and dump her on the bed. My body crushing hers. She gasps but smiles, tears pooling in her eyes, her smile wobbles. I ignore the heat she created and hover over her with my hands either side of her head, my face almost to hers, knees either side of her hips. "Tell me, Sunshine."

Her eyes drop instantly.

I brush her jaw with my knuckles. "Nothing you can say is going to change how I feel about you, Sammie."

She meets my gaze and her chin wobbles. Finally, she blows out a breath. "Fine, but can we go for a walk?"

I kiss her nose and peck each cheek, tracking my way down her neck. She arches into me. I push off the bed to my feet and pull her with me. Holding her against me for a moment, I nuzzle her hair, my lips next to her ear. "I'll get your coat."

She pushes back, searching my face. "Okay."

I wander down the step to the foyer. Marcus is waiting.

Great.

"I'm sorry, I was just surprised. So, you know our Sammie is a witch?"

"Yes, sir."

I grab the coats from the brass hooks and turn back to face him.

"It has been years since she's practiced. I-I overreacted." He shifts on his feet. Why is he telling me this? He should apologize to his daughter.

"Yes, you did. I don't know what happened that could make you think Sammie practicing her gift is a bad thing, but she's done good things. She is an incredible woman and a formidable witch."

He smiles and nods and wanders back to the kitchen table. I jog up the stairs and pull Sammie's coat around her. Her mouth meets mine. I deepen the kiss, and her hands slide against my chest. How on earth we are going to stay civilized in her parents' home, I have no idea. I break from her hungry kiss and take her hand. "Let's walk."

She smiles at me, the coy and cheekiness making my gut flip. How did I get so damn lucky?

·)))·◐·(((·

The forest near Sammie's family home teems with wildlife. The soft earth gives way underfoot as she leads me through the trees. Not too far from the house is a makeshift hut. It's too small for anything decent and she turns back, smiling before opening the small rickety door and ducking to walk inside. I follow, bending down to get inside.

It's a cubby house. A small table and two chairs sit in the center. A small bench with old pots and pans lines the back wall. She sits at the tiny table, and her knees poke above it. I do the same, easing down slowly, praying I don't smash the chair.

"This was Jackie's and mine."

"Amazing structure, you should have been an architect, not an archeologist."

She laughs, and it fills my heart. "Well, Jackson might become one yet. For the two of us, it was great. We spent a lot of time out here as kids." Her voice fades out on the last few words. What happened when they were children?

As if she read my mind, her face falls and her eyes meet mine. "The reason I stopped practicing my magic was because of something that happened when I was eight."

She fiddles with the corner of her coat on top of the table. "I was trying to control my fire, when—"

I move fast to her side. She swallows. I hold out both hands and she shakes her head. "I want to do it here."

I sit on the table and turn to the side to face her.

"He was helping me practice. Like target practice." Her chin wobbles, and a tear slides down her cheek. My insides clench. I sweep her up and deposit her on my lap.

She doesn't flinch.

Doesn't react.

Her fingers find the hollow at the base of my neck, and she traces circles around and down, like it's helping her concentrate. My body responds to hers again. I ignore it again.

"I closed my eyes. Trying to summon bigger energy to make better fireballs. He was supposed to be moving. But he stood still, and I threw the fire, then opened my eyes. Two fire balls engulfed him."

Her breath hitches and sobs come. "There wasn't anything I could do. My water magic didn't exist. I ran over and flattened him to the ground and rolled him around until the flames went out. But it was too late . . ."

I rub her back with one hand, the other cupping her jaw as my thumb caresses her cheek. "It wasn't your fault, Sunshine."

She shakes her head. "My dad blames me. I'm the oldest. I'm supposed to look out for my little brother, not set him alight."

"He looks fine to me. You did the right thing tackling him to the ground and putting the fire out."

Pain laces those beautiful eyes when she finally looks at me. "My dad will never forgive me. I won't either."

Heat lances through my veins. Why is she blaming herself for this? It wasn't her fault; he was supposed to be moving. He volunteered. She saved his life by dousing the flames. I growl and press my forehead to hers. She is the most selfless person I know. The brightest soul. Kindness runs in her blood, in her every breath.

"Look at me, Sunshine," I rasp.

She grabs my sweater under my coat and meets my gaze.

"You were eight years old. This is not your fault. Your dad overreacted. You're a grown woman now. And your gift, your talent, should not be tempered by anyone. Ever."

She forces a small smile, and gratitude lines her face.

I run a finger over her plump pink bottom lip. Her eyes

darken, and she wriggles in my lap before a cheeky smile pops over her face.

"Ugh, Sunshine. This is going to be a long two days in your parents' house."

She huffs a laugh, her fingers trail from my shirt to my belt. "It is."

CHAPTER 10

SERENA

No amount of Mr. Darcy can replace Theo. Or patch up the hole in my heart growing larger with every day I have to live without him. For almost three centuries, I've had to make my way through every day without him. And it hurts. Even when I try to ignore it.

Even on the days I'm busy, he's front of my mind every minute. Not having him beside me is devastating, and I will never stop fighting. Every week I travel back to the place where I have him hidden.

Where he's safe.

It's been easier since I no longer need to hide my time travel trips from Sammie. I'm counting down the days until I can bring him home with me. The moment we can secure Anjelica and hand her over to the council or she takes her last breath . . . Theo comes home to me.

The catch is she thinks he is dead. Or presumed dead. So if she is free, and discovers he is still alive all these decades later, she will go to great lengths to finish what she started. Especially after I helped Sammie and Lewis. What else could I do? I couldn't let my best friend lose her mate. If that was me and Theo, and I lost him, my world would shatter.

I prop my head on my hand, elbow on the study table in the library. Not my favorite place to be, but my mother, Mrs. Stewart, is right, I need a degree if I want a real chance at a life after Anjelica. Having a mother who cares about me and helps as much as she can has been the best part of the last ten years on Sammie watch. Anjelica may have planted me in Sammie's life. But she inadvertently gave me one of my own. There is always a silver lining.

Always.

His fingers trace the angles of my face as I lay on the warm grass, head in his lap. His green eyes are bright. His lips curved into a smile that warms my heart. The tips of his fingers trace the lines of my cheekbones, before lowering to brush over my lips. Breath leaves my lungs, and I open my eyes.

Theo isn't here. I stare at the lined notebook, the rowdy commotion of the unsettled class filters back in. I'm wearing jeans and sweater and boots. No lace, dresses, skirts, corset and parasol. An ache in my chest starts for those days I miss. The ones I missed with Theo. The few months we shared affections were much too short.

"Right!" A book thuds onto the bench at the front of the lecture theater. I jump and grab my notebook before it flies from the small movable table in front of me.

Lewis scans the class from behind the lecture. Sammie must be nearby. I let my gaze wander, stopping on her golden curls, front row, closest to the door. She leans back in her chair, reading. This is not her class. The tether, for all its benefits, makes their life more complicated. I would move to sit beside her, if Lewis wasn't already two slides deep into the presentation on some ancient thing nobody's seen for centuries.

I flip my notebook to the last page and sketch out Theo's face. His eyes, always full of life and happiness. His nose, broad and well proportioned. His lips, stretching into the most amazing wide smile between the edges of his square jaw. The light brown messy hair constantly falling in his face.

With his face roughly done, I flip back a page and draw his hands. I miss those hands. Broad and strong. I have imagined his hands on me time and time again over the last few centuries. The one and only time we were intimate was the day before I left. We left. The day before my mother lost her mind with revenge and the hunt for power. Now, thinking of those few days brings back bittersweet memories.

I force my focus back to Lewis. He's wrapping up the lesson.

I shift in my seat and gather my belongings. Sammie

sees me, and I wave. She waits by the door. I jog down the red carpet steps and fold her into a hug.

"What's that for?" she says with a laugh.

"Rough morning, I needed it."

"Serena." Lewis appears by my side with his bag. We stand aside as students file out the door. A brunette gives us the side eye before a scowl takes over her face. What the hell was that all about?

"Hungry?" I ask.

"Sure, but Lewis has another class."

"All good, I can grab takeaway, we can eat outside the lecture hall," I offer.

She nods and waves as I push through the door. I make my way to the cafeteria. The line is not too long, and I grab a tray. The aroma of winter stews and fresh bread torments my stomach the closer I get. I load two bowls of steaming beef stew onto the tray and grab two warm, soft bread rolls from the basket. I push the tray along the server to the end to pay.

"Dining in today?" the lady at the register asks.

"No. Takeaway today, please."

She nods and plucks two recyclable cardboard cartons with lids from the pile to her right and scrapes the stew into them, one after the other. "Careful with these now, they tend to spill. Beats me why plastic's no good."

"Thank you," I say, taking them from her hands. I tap my card with my free hand and toss the rolls on top. She hands me some wooden disposable cutlery before turning to help the student behind me. I make it to where Sammie sits outside Lewis's other lecture theater and hand her a container and a roll. She places it on her lap and lifts the lid. "Oh my god, this smells divine." She spoons some into her mouth and groans. Must be good.

I taste mine. It's divine. Heavenly. I eat, thinking about Theo, about the times we had before everything changed.

"You're quiet, Rena."

"Just thinking."

"About?"

"Theo."

"You must miss him. I don't know how you have done it all this time."

I huff a small laugh and bite into my bread. I did it because I had to. What was the alternative? Letting my mother kill the man I love? Letting him go so he would be safe, but heartbroken? We both decided what we had was worth fighting for. Long before my mother became a threat to his family. And with Joseph's help, we were able to, at least for a short while.

My phone vibrates.

Email.

I slip it from my coat pocket and swipe it open. I tap the unopened email. The college invoice. I should go pay it.

I finish my meal, and Sammie cracks open her latest fantasy novel. Another Maas tome. It's thick. It must be around eight hundred pages. Who can write about a city named after a stage of the moon cycle for so many pages?

I push to my feet. "I'll see you later girl, I got bills to pay."

"I'll be here." She smiles, looking up from her doorstop of a book.

I sling my bag back over my shoulder, dropping the empty container and cutlery into the bin by the sidewalk. A few minutes later, I walk across the threshold of the administration building, the swoosh of the automatic doors and warmth from the central heating beckon me deeper into the old building. I reach the front desk and show the receptionist my email.

"Upstairs, first door on the right is student finance, the one before the Dean's office."

"Thanks." I slide my phone into my back pocket and climb the stairs. The dark hardwood railings whine under the elegant pendant lights commandeering the center of the foyer. When I reach the top of the stairs, I find the door to the student finance office shut and voices echo down the hall.

"When did you say you noticed this development?" the Dean asks.

I lean on the wall by the finance office to wait.

"It's been going on for a couple of weeks now," a girl's voice says.

"Oh, I see," the Dean replies.

"It's not right and isn't that kind of thing illegal?" the girl says.

"I can assure you I will have this sorted very soon. Thank you for bringing this to my attention."

"By sorted, you mean fire Mr. Sullivan?" she says.

"We have protocol in place for instances like these. Please rest assured we will do everything necessary to rule out this unfortunate circumstance, should it be proven to be true."

"Proven? I saw them together. The blonde with the curly hair and Mr. Sullivan."

Oh shit.

I didn't think Sammie and Lewis were conspicuous. But if this girl noticed, others would have too. The tether is going to see both of them kicked out of this college. I know Sammie would be absolutely devastated. She worked so hard to get here.

The door opens and the brunette from earlier, who scowled at us, files out of the Dean's office. That bitch. She sees me and drops her gaze to the floor.

Huh. Not so brave now, are you?

"Hey," I call to her as she walks toward me. She looks away from me and picks up her pace. I move to the top of the stairs and block her path, folding my arms over my chest.

"Can I help you?" she says, not looking at me.

All fire and brimstone with the Dean and she can't even look at me.

"You should mind your own business, girl."

"Whatever." She shakes her head and tries to get past.

I step sideways and block her again, releasing my arms. "What's it to you what other people do?"

"It's not—" She drags her gaze up. "Fair, it's not fair, alright. If she thinks she can sail through college because one professor took a liking to her."

"Huh, you really think you're on the money here?"

"I—" She shuffles back and readjusts her backpack, studying the wall to her right.

"How about this? You stay out of my friend's business, and I let you keep your freewill."

Her mouth opens, not closing. Her brows drop and her eyes meet mine now. "What the hell?"

I step aside. "See you around, wench."

"Ah, you preppy bitches are the freakin' worst." She walks down the stairs on awkward legs.

"You have no idea, sweetie."

I turn, standing at the top of the stairs, folding my arms again. Making for the door, she looks back as it swooshes open for her. I throw her a mock smile, malice lining my eyes. Stupid girl. She should know to stay out of other people's business.

"Miss Stewart?" a lady says from behind.

"Yes." I turn back to see an older lady holding the door to the finance office open.

I walk in and take a seat. She closes the door behind her and moves to her side of the desk before sitting down. "What can I do for you today?"

"I want to pay my invoice for the year, please."

"The entire year?"

"Yup."

"Oh, okay." She types away, bringing up my name and student number. Something in my gut twinges. The talisman tied into my bracelet on my right wrist heats, irritating my skin. I swallow as sweat blooms over my forehead. I fan my face with a notebook from her desk. She shoots me a look but continues.

"Is the central too hot for you?" she asks.

"No. Just my coat, I think," I say, pulling it from my shoulders and tossing it over the back of my chair. The round penny I've used as Theo's talisman for almost two centuries heats again.

Something is wrong.

"Right, here it is. Card or cash?" she asks.

"Card."

I pluck my purse from my backpack and slip my card from its space. She holds out the machine. With no student concessions, an exorbitant figure lines the top of the machine. Almost five thousand dollars. I tap the card and enter the pin.

The lady eyes me while the machine moves through its process. I have a significant nest egg. One of the perks of being centuries old. Stocks have always been my happy place as an investor. I learned the trading game from one of my fellow supernatural acquaintances. The transaction approves, and she replaces the machine in its holder.

"I will just print you a receipt for your records."

The coin burns into my skin, and I wince. "That's okay."

I rise from the chair and snatch up my backpack and coat. I stagger from the office and down the stairs. The receptionist gives me a puzzled look as I spill through the automatic doors and run straight into Sammie.

"Rena, what happened?"

"Something is wrong." I hold my bracelet up. It's red hot. "Theo."

"Oh shit! It's burning your skin." She tugs the bracelet from my wrists before I can object. It cools in her palm. The penny going from amber back to a blackened copper.

"What does this mean?" Sammie asks.

Lewis appears behind her a moment later.

"Theo's hurt or in trouble. I spelled it to heat when he's afraid or hurt. I really have to go."

"I'll go with you," Sammie says.

"But Lewis has—"

The brunette from before is leaving again a tree on the lawn across from us. Fucking hell.

"You have to ride with me, Sammie." I grab her arm.

"What? Why?"

"I'll tell you in the car. Trust me, you and Lewis need to try to not be seen together."

"Sure. Let's go."

"Wait, don't you have classes this afternoon?" I ask Lewis.

"I can swap. You two go ahead. I'll be fifty feet behind you. Literally."

Sammie hooks an arm through mine. We walk to the car park, and she opens the passenger door of my car. I fold into the seat and hug my middle tight. The ache from before is growing to a full-on cramp.

Great.

Sammie drops into the driver's seat and starts the car, and we head toward the Sullivans.

"What can I do?" she asks, glancing between me and the road.

"Nothing. I need to go back. Now."

Her face crumples into a frown. "I wish I could go with you and help."

"That would be epic, girl. But I need to do this one on my own. Besides, trying to blend into the 1700s isn't a cakewalk, nor is it safe." I stare out the window, replaying all the times I only just made it out of scrapes, the cause purely being a woman in those times. I wouldn't subject Sammie to that. I have my persuasion to help me. She's an elemental. Witches are burned at the stake in that century. I wouldn't risk her life.

My own and Theo's are more than enough. We pull into the Sullivan estate and Sammie kills the engine before appearing at my door. She opens it and helps me out. We make it onto the porch as the Mustang rumbles past and into the garage. I clutch my stomach, padding toward the door.

It's cracked open.

Sammie notices it at the same time I do. We stop inches

from the threshold. A second later, Lewis is by her side. His eyes shutter and he growls.

I'd know the scent anywhere.

Demons.

Lewis shoves the door open. He walks in, his body racked with tension. Sammie and I stay rooted to the spot. The last time demons came around, we almost lost Lewis.

A twang of pain lances through my gut. The bracelet Sammie removed sits in my palm, the penny heats again.

I have to go.

"What do you need me to do?" Sammie asks.

"In my backpack, clothes."

She rushes to the car and returns with my bag. I pull my renaissance dress from the side pocket. A shawl from the bottom of the bag.

"Here, you can change in the front office." Sammie opens the door to Lewis's study.

She guides me into the small front room. Papers line his enormous oak desk. I slip out of my jeans and sweater and pull on the cream, lacy dress I have been wearing for the last few decades of short visits to Theo. I cover my hair with the shawl and tie it. I slip my bracelet back over my wrists and make sure my phone is in my backpack. Sammie watches from the doorway. "What if you need backup, Rena?"

"I'll be fine, girl. I'm a shadow witch. Not a mortal."

I try to offer her a smile, but this is the first time in forever the penny has heated. Something bad is happening to Theo. She walks into the room and stops inches from my face. "Please, be careful and come back."

"All clear. If they were here, they're gone now," Lewis says from outside the office door, taking in my attire. His gaze goes from intrigued to reminiscent.

I grab Sammie's hands. "I will be back in a few days, hopefully. If not, I am in the south of France, 1722."

She nods and releases my hands. I grab the pendant and delicately spin the central rings anticlockwise. "I'll see you."

My words trail off as the room around me disappears and everything blurs to gray. I slam my eyes shut, hoping to ward off the sickness that comes with time travel. As my feet hit solid ground again, I'm assaulted by the stench of burning, charred flesh, thick dark smoke fills the space around me. I make out the wooden walls of the back room of the provincial house Theo lodges in. His stretcher is empty. What the hell?

Screaming starts.

My heart flings into my ribs.

"Theo!"

CHAPTER 11
LEWIS

I f staying put wasn't our plan A, I would have quit this job three minutes ago. The Dean stands behind his desk, arms folded over his chest as I lie my way out of this latest accusation. This time, ironically, it's not life and death. But to Sammie, losing her scholarship would be pretty close.

So, I reassure the Dean, nothing's been happening between myself and Miss Williams, apart from a side project we have been working on together about ancient supernatural beings, that's it.

Not an entire lie.

I am centuries old.

She tests my boundaries on the daily. At least she did this morning in the shower. I fling the thought from my mind and draw a long breath.

"As I was saying, Lewis. If the parents or other students

suspect you are having an affair with a student, a scholarship student nonetheless, your life will get complicated very quickly. Should the rumors be accurate, the two of you will be removed from this institution. Immediately."

"You have nothing to worry about. I have no interest in any woman on this campus." The lie burns my tongue. But Sammie is safe. Her scholarship is safe.

For now.

"Fine. I will have a chat with the student who brought this to my attention and squash it. We cannot have rumors flying around campus."

"Yes, sir."

He nods and sinks into his office chair, waving a hand, indicating I am dismissed. Now, I feel like the naughty student. Which is absolutely hilarious, since I am three times his age, at least. I make my way out of the administration building and to my lecture theater. Falling snow washes out the air around the campus. Flakes settle on the shoulders of my coat.

I shiver through the frigid breeze, insistent on accompanying the falling snow. White lines the branches of the trees that flank the path to my lecture theater like dutiful soldiers. Close to my theater, walking in the opposite direction, is a trio of students. A brunette gives me a sarcastic smile. Not very subtle is she . . . Giving herself away like that.

She slams into my shoulder.

Flesh into marble.

I hope that hurt.

Sammie waits by the door with a dusting of snow on her coat. Her body pressed against the building, so the eave of the high roof offers her some protection from winter onslaught. Her pretty face pulled into a frown. She thumbs the strap on her pack, watching the trio walking away from us. The brunette turns back, hand rubbing her shoulder, and eyes Sammie before huffing and walking on.

"Hey, we should get inside before your stalker snaps a pic," I offer.

She rolls her eyes at me and then peels off the wall and pushes through the door, disappearing into the theater. I school myself to not look back, to not search the campus around us for peering eyes and lurking tittle tats. The last thing we need is to confirm their stupid, childish whims. They have no idea how life plays out in the big picture, their innocence and righteousness too fragile for anything other than mortality. She is oblivious to the game she's playing. Or who she is playing it with. Either Sammie or I could snuff out her miserable mortal existence in a heartbeat.

Stupid girl.

We wouldn't, ever.

But the thought lightens the mood.

Inside, the central warms me to the bone, and I relax slightly. I dump my satchel on the front bench and bend to pull my charger up to the top.

"Lewis." Sammie's voice is soft and lined with fear. I bolt up, hitting my head on the underside of the bench. It splinters with a loud crack. I straighten to see what Sammie does. Four scouts sit in a row of seats. She backs up closer to me. Instantly, the four men stand and filter down the aisles of stairs either side of the central seating and home in on us.

For fuck's sake.

I come to stand beside Sammie and fold my arms over my chest. "What the hell do you want?"

They stop short of Sammie and me. "Your little witch here needs to come with us," the closest and largest of the four says.

I huff an indignant laugh and glance at Sammie.

"I don't think so," she says, letting her hands fall by her side. What she does every time she is readying her magic.

"You either come willingly or we will force you." He shifts closer, glancing at her hands.

"I said, no."

"You heard her, now fuck off." I inch closer to the prick, and he snarls.

"There are four of us and one of you. You really think we are leaving without the girl?"

"Lay a finger on me and I will finish you," Sammie growls. "Lay a finger on him and I will make it slow."

That's my girl. I suppress the smile eager to stretch my face. "You can show yourselves out."

The three other witches close in on Sammie. I rush to the door and spin the lock. No innocent mortals need to see this or be involved. And students are due in three minutes.

Sammie summons fire and lets it dance in her palms. She raises both in front of her. "Leave, now!"

The man in front of her frowns and curls his fingers to fists. Her flames snuff out. Sammie's face falls with shock, her mouth agape.

I'm by her side a beat later.

"What did you do?" she utters.

"Now you are coming with us," he growls.

"No, I am not going anywhere with a pack of her scouts!"

The witch to our left steps forward, his gaze drilling into Sammie. A moment later, she hits her knees, whimpering. Shadow magic. I lunge at the witch, and he falters backward. My fangs sink into his bounding vessel. Apparently, the magic takes all of his focus. He was a sitting duck. I rip out his throat and spin back, stalking toward their ringleader. "Let her go!"

The witch stares at his brethren, bleeding out on my hardwood theater floor. "You really shouldn't have done that."

His eyes are strained with something like devastation. His hand spins in front of him and I hit the floor beside Sammie. The blood in my veins turns to wire. A puppet riddled with agony. Anjelica has homed his talents to what hers once were. If she can't inflict pain, she's taught her coven to how to use her skills. Now, instead of one sadistic witch, there are four. Well, three now. Still, two more than there used to be.

"What do you want with me?" Sammie whimpers.

Fire lances through my core at the sound of pain in her voice.

"You and the shadow witch you have allied yourself with will come and undo the binding spell you cast."

"I didn't cast the spell. And neither of us is going to help you. Or her."

Anjelica.

Sammie and Serena both fought her. Serena bound her magic as punishment for the centuries of cruelty her mother dished out to other species and, no doubt, her own magical folk. Pure evil is an understatement.

If Theo's life didn't depend on hers, Anjelica would be dead right now. What peace that would bring to witches and vampire alike. Who knows who else she's tortured over the past three centuries? I dread the thought.

The door to the lecture theater rattles. The students are here. The witch in charge snaps his attention to the doors. "Who's that?"

"Students. You need to leave. You wouldn't want that magic of yours being exposed, would you?" I snarl.

He frowns at me before meeting Sammie's gaze. "I'll be back, witch. And you will come with us."

Sammie opens her mouth to reply. He waves his arm past his shoulder and over his head and the four of them disappear. The blood that stained the wood floor moments ago vanishes, too. Sammie slumps to the floor. I scramble to where she trembles on all fours. "Sammie?"

She sighs a whimper. "Heavens above, that hurt."

"I know. They're gone now."

"I know, Lewis. What I didn't know is that shadow witches can appear and vanish on command. Remind me to hit Rena up about it." She sits up as the door rattles under many hands. I jump to my feet and pull her up.

"I shouldn't be in here with you. Especially with the door locked." She looks from the spot where we stand to the shadows.

She's going to hide?

"Sunshine?" I say, a pleading call for her to stay.

She gathers her bag and slips into the shadows behind the old theater curtain. I shake my head at her and walk to the door. Turning the lock, the door almost knocks me over, with the gathering of students behind it.

I raise a hand. "Wait up. We may be running a little late, but you can still use manners." I school my face to stone and displeasure. The students take a step back as one.

Smart kids.

I wave a hand toward the seats and they sheepishly file into the room, winding their way up the stairs and settling into seats. Everyone is quiet. Like a bunch of kids caught with their hands in the cookie jar. All that is, except one. The brunette.

She scans the room, as if knowing someone else is here. I stare her down until she eventually thinks better of her attitude and slumps in the chair. I flip the screen on and pull up the slides.

"Let's begin."

⟩·⟩⟩·⟩·◐·⟨·⟨⟨·⟨

I would know that stench anywhere.

Demons.

First four shadow witches, now a pair of demons. What the hell is today? Some sort of test. Supernatural predators 101? My patience for this shit is wearing thin. Sammie walks beside me, unaware the two guys behind us have been tailing us for the past ten minutes. We make our way to the campus library for the last part of the day. Sammie has to study and I need to mark some late papers. We don't sit together; we're not stupid.

Sammie flicks me a smile before heading for the long study tables in front of the stacks. I wind my way up the stairs to the usual study room. The one with the glass wall, so I can still see her, and she can still see me. While at times that is a major distraction, especially in the first few weeks after her bond snapped. Now, we can manage it better.

I set up my space, laptop and textbooks, the printed papers to one side as I lean back in the chair, tapping the red pen on my lips. I read the first line and glance to the tables below. Sammie's head is down, her pen moving fast across the page of her notepad.

Returning to the paper in my hand, I reread the first paragraph. Weak introduction riddled with repetitive prose and vague statements. No strong argument here. I make a note on the side of the text reflecting this. Something tugs in my gut. I swing my focus from the paper to Sammie's table.

It's empty.

I stand and move closer to the glass wall, trying to search between the stacks from my higher position. But the tug in my gut turns to an ache.

Fuck.

Her things are still sitting on the table. Her phone is on her notepad. Did she go to the toilet? I drop the paper and pen on the desk and fly out the door and down the stairs. Trying to restrain my speed to a normal human pace, I hunt through the stacks. The smell of demon hits me like a truck after the third row.

Books are scattered over the floor between the stacks. Like someone was putting up a fight, trying to grab anything they could to slow down their attackers.

Fucking hell.

I stop.

Close my eyes and breathe.

The scent lights up like a trail in my mind. They dragged her toward the back entrance of the library. I glance behind me to make sure nobody is around. A handful of students stand by the reception desk. I stalk toward the back of the library. The second I round the last row of ancient books, I fly out the back door and toward the scent.

The trail tracks toward the forest, backing onto the university. I pick up speed, so fast the human eye would not register the movement. Debris flies from the ground under each footfall. Bark splinters from trees as I speed past. The scent is almost sickly, I must be close. Running water sounds to my right.

"Get your hands off me!" Sammie screams.

Blood thunders through my head, and I spill into a clearing. Releasing her, the two demons circle her like she's prey. Her hands are adorned with balls of fire. Fucking end them, Sunshine.

She notices me staring just short of the clearing but doesn't let it show.

"What do you want?"

"Your relationship status with the vampire for a start," one hisses, running a hand through his dark hair. The chains on his jeans jingle as his arm moves. The leather vest he wears covers a white T-shirt. Motorbike boots that are scuffed and worn finish his look. His comrade is much the same, only a thinner version of him, with amber hair and wide brown eyes. He's a young demon. The council must be running short on trained guys, or these two are outside contractors. So the council can wash their hands of them.

"We should have some fun with her first," the younger demon says.

The older guy tilts his head, as if sizing her up from where she stands.

Animal.

"Why do you need to know my relationship status?" Sammie demands.

"Oh, we personally couldn't care less, sweetheart. But our associates are very interested," the older demon says, stepping closer. Sammie raises both hands. He laughs at her.

She throws a fire ball, singing his hair as it sails past his head. A warning shot.

"You stupid little bitch!"

"I suggest you crawl back into whatever dank hole you slithered out of unless you want to be burned alive," Sammie says.

The younger demon takes a step back. His older comrade shoots him a look of pure annoyance.

"What? This job doesn't pay well enough to end up barbecued, Sal."

Sal moves into Sammie's space in a flash, and his hand lands around her neck. I internalize a growl, letting her defend herself.

The flame snuffs from her hands. She gasps in his grip. Sal pulls a small dagger from his boot and traces a line under her right breast. Copper fills the air. Fire burns the back of my throat. My grasp around the tree beside me tightens, and it cracks all the way to the top branches. The demons still, shifting their focus to where I stand.

"Well, well, if it isn't lover boy," Sal says. He pulls the knife from against Sammie's skin and licks the blood from the blade.

Spots filter into my vision on both sides. The younger demon shuffles on the spot before fleeing back through the trees.

"Ugh, teenagers. Gotta do everything myself these days. Fucking useless pricks," Sal mutters, striding to where I stand, stance wide, hands balled to fists.

Fire dances over Sammie's palms once again, and I side-step the demon. Fire envelops him a second later. He sinks to his knees and rolls on the piney forest floor. Sammie tosses another round of fire at him, keeping the flames alive.

"Stop! Tell her to stop!"

I bend down and level my eyes to his. "I wouldn't dare tell her what to do. That was your mistake."

He flips frantically from side to side, dousing the flames. The scent of scorched flesh fills the space between the tall pines. Sammie appears at my side and brings her hands down, blowing out the last of the flames with wind. "Leave us alone. Or next time, I will toss fuel to the fire."

She stalks into the trees. The demon struggles to his feet. "Whatever, this gig's too cheap anyways."

"Take some advice, Sal." I catch his gaze.

His eyes burn into mine. "From a blood sucker. I'd rather choke on my own—"

"Leave well enough alone. Or next time, I'll rip your head from your fucking shoulders. And if you come within a hundred yards of that witch," I wave a hand toward Sammie's receding back, "I will end you, slowly."

Sal laughs, and his rumble turns to a hideous crackle.

"What's so funny?" I hiss.

"You all but confessed what the council wants to know. Vampires are supposed to hate witches. Separation of the species and all that. You defending her, getting all touch her and die. She's your mate, isn't she?"

Well, Fuck.

If this dipshit demon figured it out, it won't be long until other supernaturals do. In the meantime, I can squash this threat. Sal's eyes widen as I stalk to where he stands. The stench of fear all but drips from his trembling body.

"I mean, I have nothing against it, man. I'd tap that too, if she'd let me." His voice is a shaky half-laugh. His backpedaling is pathetic.

The fire feeding my rage flares with his filthy words. My fangs descend. I wouldn't bite a demon if my life depended on it.

"That's too bad, Sal."

I rip his head from his shoulders. His body collapses at my feet. I toss his bloody head, with stunned wide eyes, onto the limp mass. The fire in my throat ebbs.

"Better luck next time, demon."

CHAPTER 12

SAMMIE

Lewis's hand grips the damp cloth, his knuckles white. I sit on the ensuite vanity, my shirt and bra on the floor, as he cleans the cut from the demon's blade. Who knows what filth it carried? An infection is the last thing I want right now. I have finals in a few weeks. A mate to protect and a best friend to help.

With that thought, my gaze drifts to my phone. I tap the screen. No notifications. Shit. Serena's been gone for two whole days. She has one left before I go asking for help. Maybe Denver . . . He seems to know more than he lets on.

Stinging under the soft flesh of my right breast brings me back to the present. Lewis's brown eyes crinkle with worry. His free hand grips the marble vanity like he's going down with the Titanic. Oh wow, maybe he saw her in real life before she sunk to the bottom of the ocean. I make a mental note to ask later. I touch his jaw with my fingers and turn his face to mine. "Hey."

The rag in his hand falls to the bench, and he pushes my legs apart, moving between them and enveloping me in his warm embrace. "Hey, Sunshine." Gravel ruins his voice.

"I'm okay, Lew. We're okay."

He sinks his head into my shoulder. Maybe he should feed. I want him to feed. I want him, period. There's something about being in constant danger that has my libido through the roof. Or maybe it is the mating bond. If this is how we get to spend the rest of my days, I am not complaining. His thumb brushes my nipple, and the next breath is stuck tight.

"If anything happens to you, Sammie." His heart thunders against my chest. I wish we didn't have clothes between us right now. I slide a hand under his navy sweater and find his hard stomach. He presses his hardness into my thigh. I lose a huffy laugh and track circles over his stomach with my finger, working my way south.

"Nothing is going to happen to me. I'm not going anywhere, lover boy." His smile grows, and I feel it against my neck.

Heavens, I love this man.

His roughness.

His strength.

His vulnerabilities.

His pure need for me. His all-encompassing love. It's deep and nuanced and beautiful. And I will live every day after this one, giving him the same, as long as there is air in my lungs. My breaths have turned ragged.

"Sammie?" He pushes back, searching my face. His hands cup my jaw. "What is it? Is the cut bothering you?"

I shake my head.

"Did I crush you?"

I huff a laugh and smash my mouth to his. He deepens the kiss, pushing his tongue between my lips. I open for him. His hard length rubs against the fire at my core. I never want to lose this. Ever.

I pull back and find his gaze. "Lewis?"

He growls and drops his forehead to mine. "Yes, Sunshine?"

"I don't want to spend another day without you in it."

"Me either."

"Promise me, whatever comes, we will get through it together?" My voice is all but a plea. My throat is so tight I can barely breathe.

"I promise, Sammie."

"Lew?"

"Mhmm?"

"Please take my clothes off."

He rumbles a laugh and kisses my nose. "Your wish is my command, Samantha." His voice is breathy. It starts a fire in me. A raging bonfire. I push my jeans from my hips and jump off the vanity. A second later, they hit the floor. Lewis blurs. The next heartbeat over, he's naked and crowding me against the vanity.

He slips his hand into my blue lace panties, his thumb circling my apex. I groan and he claims my mouth with his. Having to be constantly with him is no burden to me. The tether may be an inconvenience, but it's given us this. Close proximity. It fuels our mating bond. For a moment, part of me wishes we could leave it in place. The practical part of me knows it's not a good idea. There is no life for either of us if we can't choose the things we do and places we go individually.

I grip his hard length, and he leans into me. Lewis gets heavier and heavier as the minutes click over. I push wind between us, enough to keep him an inch from my skin. But all I want is his weight on mine. His skin pressed against my own. For a moment, I wonder what we would have been like if I had met him when he was human. The air steals from my lungs, and I gasp.

Lewis breaks from the kiss and grabs my arms. "Sunshine?"

"I'm sorry—" I straighten and shake my head. "I just— I."

"What is it?"

My chin wobbles. Tears burn and fill my eyes. I am grieving for a version of Lewis I have never known. "I had a thought."

"What thought?" His brows pull down.

"What we—" I shove my head in my hands. "You, before."

"Before?"

I drop my hands and meet his gaze. Tears run down my cheeks. "I was thinking about what you and I would have been like before. When you were human. It's crazy, I know. I wasn't even born then and you—"

His finger presses against my mouth. "Shhhh."

I swallow and try to imagine what he is thinking. I never should have brought it up. Dammit, I'm an idiot.

"When I was human, I wouldn't have known what to do with someone as extraordinary as you, Samantha Williams. I paled in comparison. At least, as I am now, I can hope to meet your expectations. Your love is the greatest honor I have ever had the great fortune to have bestowed on me. Now shut up and let me show you how much I need you. How much I adore every inch of this stunning body of yours. How much I love you." The last three words shake. His shoulders rise and fall in deep, deep cycles.

My Lewis. Eternal and stoic. As always.

He plucks me up from the vanity and places me on his hips. His hardness pokes my butt, and I giggle. He kisses tears from my cheeks as we wander toward the bed. He drops me on the soft mattress. His eyes darken as he studies every curve, every angle on my body. Heat flushes my face, and I fight the urge to cover myself. His gaze lingers on my breast before dropping to my aching, wet center.

"On your knees, Sunshine."

"Um, okay." I kneel in the middle of the bed. He waves a hand, gesturing for me to move backward. I keep walking backward on my knees until his hand stills. My feet touch the headboard.

"Better," he growls. "Now, be a good girl and part those knees further."

My breath turns choppy. My heart thunders, but I spread my legs, and his eyes burn into mine. "Lewis?"

"Turn around and grab the headboard, legs spread." He tilts his head as if thinking something over.

I do as I am told.

The bed dips. His head appears on the pillow below my knees.

Oh, goddess.

I can't talk.

Words lodged, air sticks in my lungs. His hands grip the inside of my thighs.

"Tell me if you want me to stop, Sunshine."

It's all I can do to nod.

His fingers trail circles on the insides of my thighs. Not where I want them at all. The ache blooms and the heat and wetness floods my center. The bundle of nerves only inches from his mouth throbs. I try to force breath into my lungs.

Breathe in.

Breathe out.

Heavens, I could come just watching him underneath me.

His fingers track higher, and I whimper. A hand slides up my stomach and to my breast. I lean into his touch. His fingers flick my nipples, sending me higher with every sharp movement. I swear if he doesn't touch me soon, I will internally combust. Being an elemental, it could totally happen. I huff a laugh at my internal joke.

"Something you want to share with the class, Miss Williams?" he growls.

Holy fuck.

"No, sir," I rasp.

"Are you sure?" His finger brushes my apex, and I whimper, arching my back.

"I—" His finger lightly sweeps over my wetness, and I moan. His fingers pinch my nipple. "Lewis, I—"

"Yes, Miss Williams?"

I drop my gaze to his. His eyes are so dark, almost black. He needs more noise from me to keep from slipping into his instinct. "Lewis, please, I need you."

"I will decide when you are ready, Sunshine." He circles my apex with a finger. All I can think about is his mouth on my folds. His tongue over my apex. Sucking me into oblivion.

"What do you want from me, Sunshine? Anything you want is yours."

I try to steady my breaths to reply. "I want you. Inside me. Stretching me. Filling me up, Lewis. I need you to bite me. To let me come around you. To feel you spill inside me, everywhere."

His eyes dip to black.

No . . . Lew.

"Lewis, please, stay."

He groans.

Shit, too much. I shift above him and his hands clamp around my thighs. With a long groan, he opens his eyes. They're brown, but hooded.

"Fuck me, Sunshine. You are so fucking perfect, my girl. Before I get anywhere near you with my cock, you are going to come on my face."

I huff a strangled laugh and shrug a shoulder. "If that's what you want."

"I want to watch your face when you fall over that edge. Hold on to the headboard."

I slam both hands onto the upholstered headboard and drop my gaze to his.

"Good girl. Now, don't you take those eyes off mine. Or you will be punished."

I yelp. "Huh?"

His mouth pulls into the cheekiest smile. "Every time you take your eyes off me, I am going to stop."

"Okay," I say, nodding.

"Are you ready?"

"Yes."

"Good," he growls, and his tongue sweeps up the center of my folds. I all but buckle with the burst of pleasure. Sparks ignite. I want this to last. I want to give him what he wants.

"Eyes on me, Williams."

I realize they wavered slightly, and I meet his stare with everything I have.

"Remember, I need to hear you, Sammie."

"I know," I rasp.

He flicks his tongue over my apex and my eyes shut automatically. He stills underneath me. "No, please don't stop."

"You closed your eyes."

"Sorry, please don't stop. I won't do it again."

He sends both hands up my stomach, finding both nipples. Tweaking them, he suckles my inner thigh. Heat flushes through my entire body. I want his mouth on me. Now.

"Lewis, please."

"Patience, Sunshine. I want you so wet."

"I am," I pant.

"I decide when you're ready."

He continues to suckle my inner thighs, one after the other. Kissing his way up, he finally sweeps his tongue through my folds again. This time I train my gaze to his. His eyes soften. This is what he wants to see. Me, and pure, utter bliss. It's all yours, Lew.

I stagger through each heavy, deep breath, keeping my eyes on his. His hands work each breast, and he flicks his tongue over my apex. My face contorts with pleasure. He smiles and returns his hands to my thighs, widening them further.

He suckles my apex. My whimper turns to a full-on cry as his fingers sweep through my folds. "Lewis."

"Mhmm."

The rumble from him vibrates through me.

Oh. My. God.

He licks and suckles my apex. Alternating between a finger inside my hot core and dragging his tongue through it. Every fiber in my body is on fire. My breath is so shallow it burns.

"Sunshine?"

"Ah, yeah—"

"You're so fucking wet."

He slides two fingers into me, slowly. His tongue flicks over my apex faster. Heat burst through every inch of me. I'm so close.

"Lew, I'm nearly . . . Ahhh."

He slows his movements. "Not yet, beautiful."

I whimper. "Why not?"

He sweeps through my folds again and his hands grip my hips. "Open your eyes, Sunshine."

I do as I am told. His brown eyes are so dark. He must be fighting the instinct hard. "When you come, do it loudly."

Loudly?

But Denver's home.

Finally, I nod, choppy breaths stealing my words.

"You ready?"

I nod again. He widens my legs further. I grip the headboard to hold myself up. My apex is so close to his mouth now. He smiles before he drags his tongue over me and thrusts three fingers into my center. I fight the wave off, wanting to last a little longer.

"God, Lew."

My eyes slide closed. His fingers move from my heat and his tongue stops.

"Sorry," I rasp.

"Don't be sorry. Come on my face, beautiful."

"Okay."

I hold his gaze. He inches his three fingers inside me, excruciatingly slowly. I whimper and he smiles. I keep eye contact. He pumps his fingers slowly. When I don't break eye contact, he flicks his tongue over my apex.

A moan turns into a cry. I grip the headboard. My legs shake. Lewis growls and the vibration soars through me. He sucks my apex, hard. I writhe over his face. His fingers pick up the pace. I keep eye contact. His eyes burn into mine.

I love this man so many ways. But this is one of my favorites.

He suckles and licks, so fast, I am not sure it's within human sex capabilities. The heat in my center releases with an explosion. I cry out. The first sound echoes and I can't help the strangled cries that spill from my mouth. Lew's eyes are hooded, delight flashing through them with my noisy release.

Wetness fills my center. Lewis laps it away with his tongue. Claiming every wave of my orgasm with his fingers and mouth. Ragged mewls continue as I ride his mouth through the last of the waves. His brown eyes never leave me.

Now I understand why he wanted this. The look of pure adoration as I slipped over the edge was breathtaking. When my body stops convulsing from his ministrations, I shuffle backward. Now, it's his turn. He watches as I crawl backward to his lap and then further back.

"Sammie—"

"Shhhh, your turn."

His hands grip the bed. I grasp his hard length in my hand. It's warm and velvety. Muskiness reaches my mouth, and I take him in.

All of him. A second later, his eyes are closed. His breaths are ragged. His teeth descend. Good man.

And I swear I hear footsteps at our door before they fade down the hallway.

CHAPTER 13

SAMMIE

My hands shake around the pendant that has hung from my neck for years. Serena nods and I try again. Three rotations anticlockwise to travel backward. She says going forward won't work for me. At least, not yet.

We stand in the driveway in the morning sun, trying to beat time at its own game. Last night she returned. And she's too quiet. I insisted she stay with us, and she crashed in my old room. I guess it's the spare room now. She chews her lip, watching as I turn the center gold circle on its axis thrice.

Resting a hand on my shoulder, she gives me an encouraging smile. Everything blurs and stills. The ground beneath my feet slips. Her hand tightens on my shoulder. If we are touching, she should travel with me. Contact is how it works, apparently.

Lewis told me about his experience when I passed out on the snow. How Serena had taken his hand and promised to get me back. I can't imagine how much he hurt in that moment.

The ground jerks.

The gravel crunches against the soles of my boots. The manor stills and returns to historical, detailed clarity.

Ugh. I will never get this!

"It's okay, let's grab come coffee and try again this afternoon." Serena releases my shoulder, offering a comforting smile.

"How long did it take you?"

"A while. And I'd been practicing shadow magic for years before I discovered this little trick."

"Oh."

She wraps an arm around me, and we amble up the stairs and inside. The aroma of coffee hits the minute the door closes behind us.

"Coffee?" Denver calls. He's home again today. Saturdays are his hunting day, so Lewis told me.

"Sure," Serena says, sliding into a seat at the island bench.

I drop beside her. "Where's Lewis?"

"Study, something about overdue papers. Too many distractions." He winks at me.

Heat floods my neck and face. I know exactly what kind of distraction Denver is talking about. And the thought that Denver has let images of Lewis and me into his conscious makes my stomach flip. I swallow down the butterflies that fluttered up from my stomach and accept the mug of coffee he slides into my waiting hands.

He smiles. His brown eyes, slightly lighter than his little brother's, linger on mine. I drop my attention to the mug and wrap my hands around it further. Being outside for time travel practice has frozen me to the bone. Serena's focus alternates between Denver and me. I sip the coffee. It's hot and sweet, the way he always makes it. I love it.

Denver shuffles back to the coffee machine, sliding a mug under the dripper for Lewis. His usual navy mug with a gold emblem is chipped and most definitely seen better days, but he never wavers. Serena's coffee appears a minute later, foamed and dusted with chocolate powder. "Thanks, Den."

"Any time, shadow witch." He winks at her, too. I almost feel better he did.

Almost.

"Something smells divine out here." Lewis wraps himself around me and I lay my head on his shoulder. "How goes the time jumping practice?"

"Good, she almost left the present this time." Serena smiles at him.

"That's great." He pecks my cheek.

His navy mug appears, and he slides onto the seat at my right. Denver meets his gaze and holds it. Something unspoken flicks back and forth between them. What I wouldn't give to know what's in both their minds right now.

"Got any of those bagels from yesterday day, Den?" Serena breaks the silent exchange.

"Ah, yeah, somewhere in here. Wait up." He turns back and rummages through the fridge in a blur. A second later, he is facing us, holding three bagels lathered with cream cheese.

Heavens, yes.

He hands me a plate and pushes two into the waiting hands on either side of me with a chuckle. "Anyone would think you lot never get fed."

He shakes his head and slips another mug under the machine. A large forest green tin mug, with the sawmill's logo on the side in white. So very Denver. Once his is made, he claims the stool by Serena. The four of us inhale our coffee and mid-morning brunch.

"Are you hunting today, Denver?" I ask.

"Yup. You coming, Lew?"

Lewis looks at me.

"You should, I can stay out of your way, but near enough to suit the tether."

"Sure, looks like it's a family trip this time."

"Count me in, I could use some sunshine and fresh Vermont forest air," Serena adds before she bites into her bagel.

"See if you can keep up with us, magicos." Denver rips the side out of his bagel.

I huff a laugh at his new word. He's been testing out new magical nicknames for Serena and me for days. So far, we have heard and appropriately rejected, summons sisters, magical martyrs, Wiccan wenches, shadow and light girls. The last one wasn't too bad, but a mouthful apparently. So, the hunt to nickname the magical duo of elemental light magic and shadow magic continues. It's entertaining and I would do anything to keep a smile on his face after the last few weeks he and Lewis had to live through.

We don our coats after washing our mugs and plates. Letting the boys lead the way to the forest that backs onto the manor grounds.

"Try to keep up, pagan peasants." Denver's face splits into a cheeky smile.

Lewis punches his arm, hard.

"Stay in view so we know which direction to aim for," Serena says.

"You're on!" Denver calls behind as he takes off. Lewis follows.

Serena grabs my hand. "Ready?"

I close my grip around hers. The ground blurs and we appear a few feet behind the blur of the boys. Serena squeezes my hand, her other clutching the pendant. A heartbeat later, the boys are lost between the trees and the tether tugs in my core. Serena flips the pendant, and we sweep past tens of trees in a blur, catching up to them again. We stop behind a thrush of bushes and still, as the boys slow and circle a deer. A buck.

The animal trembles, its instincts are on the money, it understands these are its last moments. Lewis closes in at its head, Denver at its side. The buck lowers its head and paws the ground, not going down without a fight or at least some show. Denver is quick. A second barely clicks over and the beast's head is at an unnatural angle, its body quivers against the ground. Both brothers sink fangs into its neck.

Serena turns away. "Shit, Sammie."

I hold her hand tight. It's not like I haven't seen Lewis hunt before. But never the two of them. I can't take my eyes off the animal.

Thank god it was quick. The brothers may be supernatural predators, but they are not cruel.

Serena tugs on my hand. "Let's go, babe. The smell is making my stomach heave."

I stagger backward, following her back into the thick of the piney trees. I wonder if the way vampires hunt is some of the reason witches and demons dislike them. Gauging by Serena's reaction, I think it may have played a part. Nature is not always pleasant.

Goosebumps flood my skin as the wind changes.

I stop in my tracks, dropping Serena's hand.

She turns back. "You okay?"

I rub my hands over my arms, trying to warm the chill that crept into my bones. I don't know if it's from the icy breeze or the hunt. "Yeah, I'm good. Don't you think we should wait for the boys? Tether and all?"

She studies the forest around her for a moment and turns back to me. "Fine. When those bloodsuckers are done. We are out of here."

"Rena," I growl.

"Sorry, old habits die hard. Especially when you witness that." She waves in their direction.

"We are not exactly innocent beings either," I mutter and meet her gaze.

She steps into my space. "None of us get a choice in this life."

"I am beginning to understand that."

"So, I had an idea about the tether," she says, bumping my shoulder with hers.

"Oh, yeah?"

"We need to make a trip."

"Where to?"

"When to."

"Oh."

She laughs and grabs my hand. "We can put Lewis in stasis, so the tether doesn't leave him vulnerable again."

"You can do that?"

"I can, I don't know if he will agree to it though. It's basically a sleeping spell."

"We need to break the tether, or he is going to be at risk for the rest of my life."

"I know. That's why I was thinking maybe we don't tell him."

"Rena," I growl her name for the second time in ten minutes.

"It is a small sacrifice to free him from a problem that could be the death of him, literally."

"I guess." I chew my bottom lip. He's going to be angry when he wakes up. But if we can break this tether, I will take his anger at me over him being hurt or worse any day.

"Let's do it." I squeeze her hand.

"Right, back to the future we go." She laughs and grabs her pendant.

"First, though, we have to wait for the boys. When Denver settles into his weekend ritual of research and relaxation, we do the spell together, then time hop for like a couple hours. It shouldn't take too much longer."

"Solid plan, girl."

The brothers rush past us in a gust of a blur.

"Take us home?" she asks, nodding to my pendant.

"I thought forward was too hard?"

"Well, backward seems to be improbable for you. Try forward. Imagine us arriving home and walking over the threshold. That would possibly occur in around two minutes. Making our arrival 11:57."

"Okay, hold on."

I grab her hand again and shut my eyes, fingers firmly around the center gold loop in my pendant. I envision arriving over the threshold at exactly 11.57 and turn the loop clockwise this time. The ground slips. Serena's hand tightens around mine. Air leaves my lungs.

For a moment, all I can hear is white noise and the beating of our two hearts. I replay the image of the threshold, our boots scuffing over it, the minute hand on the clock in the manor foyer ticking up to the fifty-seventh minute.

Something hard meets the underside of my boots, and I open my eyes. Serena drops my hand.

I take a moment, blinking. The wooden front door of the manor is inches from my face. I huff an astonished laugh and turn to Serena. "Oh my god, I did it!"

She opens the door, and we lean in to find the clock. The minute hand flicks to the fifty-seventh minute on the round heirloom wood and gold clock over its shimmering pearl face.

Serena crosses the threshold and pulls her coat from her shoulders. "I knew you could, Sammie." I follow her in and shut the front door. I hang my coat on the brass hook beside hers. I like them together. Every day, this massive house feels more like home. Having Serena here makes it even more homely.

We settle into the sofas, soaking up the warmth of the fireplace. I toss a handful of fireballs into it, to help it along, and Serena picks up the novel Lewis had been reading from the side table. Pride and Prejudice. Seriously, these two. It's not like they lived through it or anything. I chuckle to myself and lie on the sofa.

"Sammie."

I crack an eye and find Serena's face crumpled. I bolt up and swing my legs, feet hitting the floor, and am beside her instantly. "What is it? Theo?"

She forces a sad smile. "I miss him, is all."

I hug her shoulders and lay my head on it. "I bet you do. I can't imagine . . ."

She tosses the book back to the side table. "These stupid regency novels always make me upset."

"Once we break this tether, we can force your moth—Anjelica, to undo the spell on Theo. Then you won't ever have to toss another regency book."

She laughs and lowers her head to mine. We sit hugging for a moment, the only sound the crackling fire. The front door opens, and the boys burst into the foyer, pulling their snow dusted coats from their backs.

Serena gives me a small look.

Are you ready?

That's what she's asking.

Absolutely. I smile back and nod.

We rise from the sofa as one and make our way to the boys. I snuggle into Lewis. "How was the hunt?"

"How did you get back here before us without triggering the tether?" Denver raises an eyebrow.

"Sammie time jumped us here. So, when we arrived, you weren't too far behind us, with your super speed and all." Serena meets Den's gaze.

"Tricky witches." He chuckles and heads for his library.

Research time. So predictable.

"On that note, I have more papers to mark. Sometimes I wonder why I do this to myself," Lewis mutters, wandering to his study.

I turn to Serena. "What do we need for the stasis spell?"

"Nothing, just an enchantment."

"Okay, what is it?"

She takes both my hands and leads me to the closed door of Lewis's study. "Close your eyes and repeat after me."

My eyes flutter shut, my grip around her hands tightens.

"Inside the minute, part of the hour. Lewis will stay as he is now. Til the words are spoken true. He will not wake until we are through."

I repeat the words. We chant them on breathy words until we hear a thud inside his study.

"It worked," Serena whispers.

I crack the door and poke my head in. Lewis is asleep on a pile of papers. Red pen in his hand. His back rises and falls peacefully. I smile, looking at how gorgeous he is. My stomach twists as I remember this isn't his choice, and I am going behind his back. I am doing this for him. I only hope he doesn't wake before we return.

What if Denver wakes him up? Shit.

I turn the lock on the inside of the door and pull it closed. Denver won't be able to get in.

Hopefully, both men stay in their spaces until we return in a few hours.

"Let's go. We need to make this quick."

Serena nods and grabs my hand. She spins the pendant loop, and the ground vanishes for the umpteenth time today.

I open my eyes, and I almost don't recognize the city around me. One feature on its shortened skyline grounds me to place.

The Empire State Building.

"What?" I breathe.

"You mean when. They finished building it a couple of months ago. It's 1932." An elegant smile blooms over her face.

"It's magnificent!" I gasp a laugh.

"It is, but we are not here to sightsee, babes. There's a thrift shop we need to get to before they sell an item I've been tracking for weeks."

"How—"

"Probably best you don't know everything Denver and I dig into."

"Okay?"

"Come on, it's a few blocks from here." We step out of the side alley and into the bustling streets of Manhattan, 1932. I can't peel my attention from the buildings, the people, the cars and cabs. The attire. The wardrobe in the old movies hasn't done this time period justice. People took so much pride in their wardrobe. It's simply amazing.

Commuters give Serena and me odd looks. I guess the jeans and sweaters we are wearing are not exactly status quo. I follow the back of Serena through the crowd. She disappears through the front door to an elegantly decorated thrift shop, and I follow. The doorbell dingles and I close the door behind me. Cigarette smoke wafts around the small shop in clouds. I cough into my elbow, my eyes watering.

"What can I do for ya, doll?" a middle-aged man in a double-breasted crumpled suit says to Serena. I wander around the shop, taking in the treasures the folks of the thirties have deemed unwanted. A pearl necklace and a fob watch sit side by side in a glass case. Rows of green velvet display cabinets, their frames made of dark hardwood, flank the perimeter of the shop. On the center floor, twin art deco sets of drawers sit back-to-back, their draws hanging out in various depths. Treasures of days gone by drape the walls of their confines, as if teaming to escape.

"I am looking for a trinket of sorts. It's a small silver pentagram with five gems, one at each point. The chain it's on is byzantine, around a foot long," Serena says.

The man looks at her for a moment, then moves to his left, pulling out a shallow draw. "Something like this?" He plucks the very pendant and chain and lets it swing in his hand at Serena's eye level.

She huffs a laugh. "That's it!"

He drops the chain back into the drawer. "It's not for sale."

"What do you mean, it's not for sale?" I ask, stepping beside Serena.

"I mean, I am not selling it."

"I will pay double what it is worth." Serena shoves fifty dollars onto the counter between him and us.

He slides it back. "I said, I'm not selling it, girly." Pulling a pack of cigarettes from inside his jacket, he strikes a match. With quick inhales, he lights his cigarette and tosses the match into the ashtray beside an ancient brass register.

Serena leans forward, and he matches her stare. "I will be taking the pentagram with the silver byzantine chain."

His eyes dull for a heartbeat, then clear. His hand moves to the drawer and pulls out the pentagram and chain. He places it in Serena's waiting hand.

"Thank you. Now, was that so hard?" She rolls her eyes and ushers me from the shop.

"We stole it?" I cringe.

"Babes, the man rips people off daily. One pendant he obviously knows nothing about will not break him."

We mix in with the crowd, working our way back to the alley. The city smells different. The skyline is much shorter than it is back in 2024. The way the men and women speak is almost amusing, like something out of the Godfather films. Or Grease. We slip into the alley. Serena checks over the pentagram in her hand.

"What is it? I mean, besides a Wiccan symbol?" I ask.

"It belonged to Theo's father. My mother stole it from him. Which makes it the perfect talisman to undo both the tether and Theo's spell."

"Oh Rena, that's epic!"

"It is. Only a talisman housing dark energy from a shadow witch can be used against them. Bart was her original enemy. She hated him. So, she made it her business to bring him and his family down . . . Theo lost everything because of her." Her eyes shine with unshed tears as she adds, "This, right here, is poetic justice, Sammie."

I shake my head, focus fixed on the silver pentagram in

her hand. Something so small, holds that much dark energy? That much power? Magic will never cease to amaze me.

Serena breaks the moment. "Let's get out of here, babes. Take us home."

"You think I can do it?"

"Only one way to find out." She smiles as I take her hand. I focus on the time, an hour from when we left. The space in the foyer, the clock on the wall. Our feet on the marble floor. I spin the pendant. Instantly, the sickening feeling of falling swells around me.

I cry out.

Serena's hand tightens on mine.

The white noise fills the void.

It's deafening.

CHAPTER 14
SERENA

We slam into the marble of the manor floor inches from Lewis's study door. Shit. Sammie moans but pushes to a stand. Her body shakes. Maybe that far forward in time is too much for her?

"What happened?" she asks, hands trembling in front of her as she looks them over.

"Rough landing." I laugh, but it dies out. I shouldn't have pushed her so far.

"Lewis," Sammie breathes.

"Take my hands again."

She does and we inch closer to the door.

"Inside the minute, part of the hour. With these words spoken true, we see. Lewis, we set you free."

A groan slips under the study door and Sammie releases me instantly and knocks on it. Shuffling echoes with a curse before Lewis unlocks and opens the door. His hand sweeps over his face and then slides through his hair. Sammie slams into his chest and his brows drop.

"What did you do, witch?" His voice is a low rumble as his eyes fall shut.

I know he is talking to me. "Nothing much. How was your sleep?"

His head tilts, and his mouth flattens to a thin line. "This was your doing?"

"We needed the tether to not kill you for a little while, that's all. Everything's fine. Go back to your papers, Professor."

Sammie steps out of his arms and throws me a warning glance. I raise my hands in surrender.

"Fine, I have places to be anyhow. See you two later." I make my way to the spare room to gather my bag and slip on my regency dress. I want to try breaking this spell using the talisman. If I can, I won't need any part of my mother to wake him. I don't want Anjelica anywhere near Theo if I can help it.

Raised voices float down the hall from the living room.

Oh crap.

Lewis is one overprotective male sometimes. Not that I blame him. I know exactly what it's like to be without your mate.

"You had no right to do that, Sunshine." His voice is no more than a feral growl.

I guess not telling him was a bad idea.

"We did it for you. To break the tether so you can get your life back!" Sammie meets his tone.

Give it to him, girl.

I chuckle to myself, those two are like the storm and the fury all rolled into one. Sunshine, fierce and hot. Lewis, the storm, an all-encompassing thunder clap.

"If anything had hap—" His voice breaks and something thuds to the floor. I pluck my bag from the bed and wander toward the living room. Sammie stands, cradling Lewis's head against her stomach. Her face is wrecked. His is buried in her stomach as his shoulders shake.

I can feel his devastation from here.

Fuck.

My cue to make myself scarce.

"I'm sorry, Lew. You can be angry and upset with me for as long as you need to. But I am going to do whatever it takes to free you, you hear?" Sammie's words are soft, coaxing.

He stands and smothers her, folding her into his chest. "Don't you ever do that to me again, Sunshine."

"I promise. I won't leave you again."

He growls into her hair. "Ever, Sammie."

Her hands move into his.

I slip out the front door.

Maybe it's the warmer London air, maybe it's not. The coven is restless tonight. Rumors have made the rounds. Every family has all but picked a side. I grip my skirts, not making eye contact with any member of our small band of witches. Not wanting Mother's wrath. Not with the constant churning stone revolving in my gut since we made those herb elixirs.

Theo sits across the hall from me. Eyes fixed on mine. His family beside him, bar his father. Every second of the last moment we shared replays over and over in my mind. Right until the point where he dropped to one knee and Mother tore me away from him.

She sits tense and upright on my right. Her hands crushing the bundle of sage she has been carrying for the entire night. Wax moats surround the candles, now almost burned to stumps. Lining the floor, some on the rafters overhead, they flicker and sway as the doors to the hall open once more.

Bartholomeus strides to the center of the hall, his robe drifting across the wood floor behind him. Hood down, he stops and takes in the faces of every single member of our coven. "It has been brought to my attention that my leadership of this coven is being scrutinized and undermined."

He paces a short space between the candles. Other witches shift in their seats, not daring to take their eyes from the leader. Mother's face is placid, as if he just announced pleasant weather. I glance at Theo, his head hangs, his hands twist around the ends of his robe.

I miss his warmth, his laugh, his conversation. Mother has ensured my days are filled with Wiccan work, rituals, and study. Spouting that a girl of my class and upbringing needs all three to make an impression to suitors at court.

I dread the thought.

Tonight, Theo is wearing his usual navy coat and tails. Underneath the robe, I see his riding boots, his dark trousers.

"My influence over this coven has been the makings of our small cohort, to that of what it is now. Every effort I have put forward for our betterment. Should you disagree with this statement and my leadership as a whole, please rise." He raises his hands, as if encouraging members to show their displeasure.

Mother stands instantly.

Her hands drop to her side. Her gaze burns into Bartholomeus's.

Slowly, other members stand. Our leader's face falls. Theo's brows lower and he scans the hall as more of our brethren stand. After a moment, almost half of the coven is standing. Some have their gazes on the floor, as if this act of rebellion is not their own choice.

Did someone influence them, or blackmail them? Is this simple gesture, this show of unfaith, the result of a sour bargain?

Mother steps forward. "As the second in line for leadership, I invoke succession of this coven. You may step down, Bartholomeus." Her stance is tense, a mere foot from the leader, she stares him down.

"I appreciate your enthusiasm for leadership, Anjelica. However, this is neither unanimous nor is it a majority vote. You have less than half convinced."

Ah, so he is not naive to her influence.

She would do whatever she deems necessary to overrule Theo's father and oust their family.

"I expected that response, Bart." She sneers before returning her face to a more pleasant facade and studying the faces of those still standing. "So, in lieu of your concession, I challenge you to a duel. Elemental versus shadow."

The gasps that follow echo around the room long after the sound passes. My heart flings in my chest and I wring my skirts through trembling fingers.

A duel?

Elementals are a fair match for a shadow witch. In fact, they are the only two types that can directly cause death with very little effort to each other.

Heavens above . . .

She intends to kill him.

Theo stands and moves to his father's side.

"No," I utter.

Bartholomeus turns to his son and rests his hand on his shoulder. "It's alright, Theo. Sit with your mother and sisters, lad."

He hesitates, but does as instructed.

I rock back and forth in my seat, desperate to be at Theo's side. Mother throws me a bitter glance. I drop my eyes to the floor. She may be my blood, but I want no part in her sadistic games. Our leader raises his hands and lowers them, indicating to those standing to sit.

"Have it your way, Anjelica. However, should this end badly for you, please know Serena is always welcome in our family."

Theo offers a sad smile.

My chin wobbles.

I swallow past the lump in my throat, threatening to cut off my air and breathe deeply, trying to stifle the tears now burning behind my eyes. Heat flushes my neck. Embarrassment, devastation, terror. The members of the coven stare at me, some with sympathy, some with outright distaste at my lack of support for my own.

"Three blows or to the death, Bart?" Mother coos.

"Three blows will suffice, Anjelica. Let's not get dramatic."

"Have it your way, oh benevolent leader." The sarcasm in her voice drips from each word. Part of me hopes he will hurt her enough to push this ludicrous idea of being coven leader from her head. She claims everything she does is for my benefit. But I fail to see how becoming coven leader at the expense to Theo's family is for my benefit.

Bartholomeus sheds his robe and tosses it to his wife. Members move back, pressing up against the wall of the old hall. Too stunned to leave. Too eager for a show of power from the two top witches in our coven to hide their eagerness.

Mother circles him, her robe still around her shoulders. Her hands by her sides.

Gaze locked on the stoic face of the man who has led us for the past decade. Right now, I wish the dusty old boards of this hall would splinter and give away underfoot. I wish I was anywhere else but here.

Mother throws a hand up and slithers of silver streak toward Bartholomeus. He dodges the deadly blows, and they disintegrate behind him onto the floor. People shuffle back further, fear flashing across their faces. Bart curls his hands by his sides, a cluster of sparks in each hand burst into fireballs.

Mother huffs a laugh and breaks eye contact.

He throws them at her in unison.

She turns her back, flinging a hand over her shoulder,

returning them to sender. The movement is so quick; he doesn't move in time. One slams into his shoulder. Instantly, the acrid tang of burning flesh fills the hall.

Gasps spill from every agape mouth.

Mother turns to face him, ever so slowly. "One down."

Raising her arms over her head, she releases dark trails that spiral and flood the room. Every inch of the space is shrouded in darkness. Her shadows are deadly when she wants them to be.

I hold my breath.

Murmurs weave through the darkness.

A small child cries.

A low growl rumbles through the dim fog and the force of a hurricane clears the shadows a moment later. Theo's father stands, eyes closed, hand swirling around an invisible sphere before him. Mother stalks toward him and plucks an athame of pure silver from under her robe at her hip.

A second later, she is suspended in the air above Bartholomeus. Her face twists with hate. She screams and he lets her fall to the floor. The thud of her weight on the wooden boards is sickening.

"One, Anjelica," he bites out.

She pushes from the floor and inhales, long and slow. I know that face. Pure rage. I have seen it many times. I grip my skirts harder, my knuckles turning white. I watch as our leader summons a ball of water. It swirls in a perfect orb between them. He raises a hand, and it rises above Mother.

His hand snaps into a fist, and it drenches her.

She gasps, saturated and dripping, hand tight around the dagger.

Members chuckle.

Something raw and feral purges her throat. She flings the dagger into Bartholomeus's chest and closes the distance between them. "You will pay for that, Bart."

He pulls the dagger from his flesh. Blood runs down his shirt. He looks at the wound before returning his focus to Mother.

"Two all, Anjelica. And this is far from over."

She snarls at him. All semblance of manner and lady-like behavior squashed by her current need for revenge. Or power.

"Last round, then you leave," she hisses.

"We will see about that."

Theo is studying the wound on his father. He would be itching to get to him to heal him. His magic, while it drains him, is so rare it is all but miraculous.

Mother backs up a step and summons her shadows, this time, she sends silver spears of lightning into the darkness.

What is she doing?

She can't possibly home in on a target in the darkness. Deadly silver spears fly toward the center of the hall. Some find their mark, others sail past. Terrified cries of members split the hazy air around us.

A warm hand slips around mine.

"Time to leave, Seri," Theo says, tugging me from my seat.

I fumble my way through the smoky space behind him. Something thuds in front of us and the amber lights of east London widen as the door cracks open. He pulls me through, and we run for the forest.

Once in the deepest park of the park, Theo stops and pulls me into his embrace. Whimpers flood from my throat. He rubs my back in circular motions, speaking softly. What on earth possessed our parents? They are both insane. They will be lucky if no other witches are hurt. How can they possibly think this is a good idea?

I push out of Theo's hold. His face is soft. His green eyes search my face.

"What is it?" I ask.

He huffs a laugh as his thumb brushes my cheek. "Are you alright?"

"I'm fine."

"Whatever happens, you have a place with us. My family is your family."

Heat flushes my neck and face. The only thing I want in my life is to be Theo's family. His everyday companion. His confidant.

His wife.

"Theo, can I do something?"

He closes the gap between us and rests his forehead on mine. "Anything."

I steady my breaths and lay a tentative hand on his chest. My heart thunders against my ribs. I swallow, and my fingers tremble on his jacket. His hand presses onto my hip. I lift my head and touch my lips to his.

He smiles. His shoulders heave and his other hand comes to rest on my hip.

"Seri." My name is a low rasp.

Our breath mingles. I press my lips to his again. This time, he claims my mouth. Every thought flies from my mind.

Breath leaves my lungs.

Time stops.

I have found heaven. This, he, is my heaven.

His hands leave my hips, and I pull back a little. Opening my eyes, I search his. Absolute adoration lines the gorgeous green eyes I have loved since I was a little girl.

His warm hands cup my face. "Seri, I want to—"

I slam my mouth to his. He chuckles against it. I kiss him with every fiber of my soul. I, we, have waited so long for this moment. He deepens the kiss, and I lean into him, not trusting my legs to keep me standing. His hand slides behind my neck and into my hair.

Heavens above, Theo.

Breathless, he breaks away and studies my face for a moment as a simper grows on his.

"What?" I whisper.

"I love you, Seri. I always have."

I trace the angles of his jaw, and his face turns to pure bliss under my touch. I reach his chin, and he turns his head, kissing my palm.

If I could spend every day reliving this moment . . . I would.

A boom crackles through the trees from the direction of the hall. We turn as one. The orange hue of enormous flames engulfs the hall.

Oh no.

Theo takes off toward the hall. I lift my skirts and follow him as fast as the wretched layers allow. We reach the hall and find members huddling around in groups. Some cling to each other, others stalking around the front yard. I don't see Mother or Theo's family.

"Stay here, they must be inside," Theo says, rushing into the burning building.

I slap a hand over my mouth. A woman comes to stand beside me. She offers a sympathetic smile.

What's that supposed to mean?

"What happened?" I ask.

"Fire balls. Lightening. Chaos and madness. Both of them."

"Are they still in there?"

"What? No, they were so consumed by their duel, they didn't even notice when the hall went up in flames. We were all outside by then."

Oh heavens, Theo.

I take off toward the door.

"Get back here, lass, you will be burned to death!"

I cross the threshold. Smoke stings my eyes and fills my lungs.

It burns.

I hold a hand up to my mouth and nose and stagger inside further. "Theo!"

Timber cracks above me.

"Theo!"

"Seri, get out of here!"

"Where are you?!"

"I-I'm stuck."

I whimper and hold an arm out in front of me, moving further into the fire. The smoke all but steals my breath. Eyes watering, I spin, scanning every side of the blazing hall.

Then I see him.

He's pinned under a beam. It must have fallen moments after he made it inside. He tries to move it. But he's a healer, not a fighter.

I rush to him, dropping beside him. I tug on the beam. It burns my hands. Charred flesh stings my nose. I lift hard. It budges a little but doesn't lift.

"Go, Seri."

I shake my head violently. Tears fly from my cheeks, burning up in the air, not even hitting the floor. "No."

I'm a shadow witch, not an elemental. I can't use wind or water. Maybe the silver lightening Mother uses? I close my eyes and dig deep into my core, pulling at the energy writhing inside me daily. I moan as it singes through my veins and crackles its way to the skin's surface of my palm. "Ahhhh."

"Ser—"

I fling both hands, splayed open, toward the beam. A shard of silver crackles around it and disintegrates.

Again.

I drive more force behind it this time. The burning is excruciating. I growl, tossing multiple shards into the wood. It splinters, snapping in two. I huff a feeble laugh of astonishment and pull the parts of the beam from Theo.

He is drowsy. The smoke having claimed his lungs.

"Get up, Thee!"

He moans as I tug both of his hands.

"Come on!"

He moves onto all fours, and I help him stand. Putting myself under one of his shoulders, I guide him to the doors. His right leg drags limp behind him.

A handful of heartbeats later, we are lying on the damp ground. His eyes are open, and his face is covered in ash. Women rush to help us. I sit up. Theo smiles at me, his hand finding my face.

"Seri," he chokes.

"Theo?"

"Let me heal you."

I look down at my hands, my arms. Gray raised lines cover my skin. I press a finger to one line and blinding pain shoots up my arm. "Ohhh."

Theo presses a palm to mine. Instantly the pain ebbs, the heat replaced by coolness. His body jerks and his eyes roll back in his head.

"Theo!"

"Theo!"

CHAPTER 16

LEWIS

Serena looks terrible. Trying to help multiple people across alternate timelines must be exhausting. Sammie leans into her on the sofa. They study the spell one last time. Apparently, the talisman they ran off to acquire after knocking me unconscious for three hours will do the trick.

Denver is skeptical, but it wouldn't be the first time a shadow witch has shown him up. He stands, arms crossed by the fireplace. His eyes fixed on the two witches. They mutter under their breath, practicing the enchantment without the rest of the spell requirements.

"It must be said in unison. Not broken by either of us forgetting the words. It has to match. Syllable for syllable," Serena reminds Sammie.

"Yep, let's do this," Sammie says.

"You're absolutely sure you remember it word for word?" Serena asks.

"Yes. Can we start?"

The shadow witch sighs. "Fine, this should work. If you touch, before the waiting period elapses, you will stay bound. So that means no contact at all until," Serena glances at the time on her phone, "midday tomorrow, exactly. Otherwise, you'll remain bound. Which would be evident after the tether is broken. You all onboard with this?" She looks at me.

I must be 'all'.

I nod. "Go ahead."

Denver's arms fall to his sides, and he steps closer. Sammie makes a circle of salt, inside it a pentagram of the same earthy substance. Serena places a tall pillar candle at all five points and steps inside the circle with Sammie. I stand, not sure what to do with myself while the girls work. They join hands and close their eyes, hanging their hands. Serena counts in and the chanting starts.

The flames of the candles shoot up instantly, burning high and fierce.

Denver appears at my side, glancing a worried look my way.

"Think this hocus pocus will work?" he whispers.

Serena rolls her head on her shoulders, but doesn't open her eyes, nor does she stop the chant.

I nod but dip my brows in warning. I don't want something happening to Sammie because people lose their focus.

The chanting grows louder, and the flames reach higher. An itch starts in my veins. I shuffle on my feet, still restless. The itch turns to a burn. The girls call the words loud and fervent.

Sammie winces, and her grip tightens around Serena's hands. She must be feeling the same fire I am. The pentagram swings from Serena's hand. The air around us turns stifling.

Denver clears his throat, his gaze alternating between me and Sammie. If I didn't know better, I would say he's as worried for her as I am.

Good.

A force tugs in my gut, and I stagger backward and fall onto the couch. Sammie cries out and slumps to the floor. Denver rushes to the circle. Serena holds up a hand.

He stops short of breaching the salt border.

"Don't. Nobody can touch her until she comes too. Lewis, you, okay?" Serena says.

"I'm fine. What's happening?"

"The tether is broken. You cannot touch her for at least twenty-four hours. Nor she you." She shoots a warning between Den and me.

I drop my attention to Sammie. Her chest rises and falls in a steady rhythm.

"Why is she out to begin with?" Denver asks.

"She's not immortal like you two. It is a greater toll on her body."

I feel the blood drain from my face. Neither my brother nor the shadow witch mentioned this part.

"Why didn't you tell me about this?" I snap.

"Sammie knew. She was the one with the greatest risk. It was her choice," Serena says, but her gaze is locked on my brother's.

He knew.

I am going to kill him.

How could he let her do this without telling me everything?

I turn and fly out the front door. A heartbeat later, Denver is by my side. I push faster. A blur between ancient forest pines. Clearing the tree line, I slide to a halt short of tipping over the cliff hanging above the ravine. Water cascades over worn stones below.

I scream into the open air and drop to my knees.

Footsteps behind me signal Denver's caught up.

"How could you let her do this? Without telling me?"

"It was her choice, brother. Not yours."

I stand and spin to face him.

He's calm. Hands by his side. Face soft, eyes empathetic.

"If anything happens to her, Den."

"I know, you'll kill me." He smiles.

I growl and stalk so close my breath lands on his face.

"She did it for you, Lewis. Just let somebody help you, for once in your stubborn life."

I can't speak. Every breath cycles through too fast.

Denver tilts his head and frowns. "You had more to lose Lew, she knew that. She wouldn't accept a life with you being vulnerable. Your Sammie is one brave girl."

"I know," I choke out. I replay Denver's face the moment Sammie crumpled to the floor. My gut flips. The combination of fear and surprise is too much. Afraid for Sammie. Surprise at my big brother's reaction to her falling. "You need her too?"

Denver jerks backward. Brows lowering his mouth gapes before closing. "No, I—"

"It's okay, Den. Sammie likes you. If anything happens to me—"

His hand shoots up between us, and he closes his eyes. "Don't even go there, Lewis. She is your mate. I've had mine."

"It wouldn't be the first time we have shared. And I love you both."

He huffs a tentative laugh and scuffs his boot over the edge of the cliff. Rocks fall into the rushing stream below and disappear.

"It's not because I don't like her, brother. That's not it at all. But I can't imagine what it would have been like to share Zahli. How I would have even coped with that?"

"You don't have to think about it right now. It's just an idea for a possibility in the future."

"You're going to turn Sammie, then?"

"No! Absolutely not."

"Lewis, how could that work if the two of us are immortal and she isn't?"

"Like a family. Quality over quantity."

He shakes his head but thumps my arm. Conversation over.

I lean against the nearest tree and run my hands through my hair. I don't want to spend the rest of my days without Sammie and Denver. But I don't want my brother to be alone if something happens to me. Be the third wheel. That was me when he had Zahli.

Sure, I had flings. Loneliness is a sneaky bitch, always sliding into your bed when the other half is cold. I want better for my brother. I want Sammie to have as much love and adoration as possible. And for that, I am willing to share.

Denver is first through the door. He makes a beeline for the living room floor. I am right behind him. Sammie is sitting on the sofa; Serena is by her side. It's only been an hour since the spell. I can't touch Sammie until tomorrow. I don't dare get any closer, not trusting myself to stay away.

"Lew?" Sammie's eyes find me. The word slurs, as if she is groggy.

"I'm okay. How do you feel?"

"Like a truck hit me. I'll be fine." She smiles and leans her head onto Serena's shoulder and her eyes fall closed. My gut clenches and I force breath from my lungs. Breaking the tether has taken a very real toll on her.

"You must be hungry. Can I get you something?" I ask.

"Maybe a sandwich. Or just half a one."

"Be right back." I linger on the spot. Wanting more than anything to cradle her against me. To make sure she's alright. To breathe her in. But there is no way in hell she went through all that for it to come to nothing. So, I turn on my heel and head for the kitchen.

I pull a loaf of bread from the bread bin and have two slices with chicken and salad, no mayo, done in less than a handful of heartbeats. I pluck a tumbler glass from the top cabinet and pour her a glass of OJ. Our well-stocked kitchen accommodates everything you could possibly want for meals and entertaining. I open a large drawer in the center of the island bench and grab up a wooden tray.

Denver appears at my side, hands waiting, his face pulled with concern. "I can take it to her. It will be easier if you don't get too close."

I nod, sliding the tray toward him. He lowers his hands before picking up the tray and disappearing into the living room. I grip the side of the island bench and drop my head to the marble top. A moan rumbles out on its own accord.

I hate this.

I hate Sammie was placed in this position. I hate Anjelica for putting us through this. So many things are her fault. I tried to prevent this and failed epically. So mostly, this is my fault.

"She'll be fine, Lewis. Denver can stay with her until this time tomorrow. Tomorrow night at the latest. She can't be close to you. Sorry." Serena leans against the counter, her arms folded across her chest.

"I hate this," I mutter.

"I know it's not ideal. My mother's plans never are for others. There is always another twist coming. Usually, it's not a pleasant one. In the grand scheme of things, the two of you got off lightly. She's done far worse for less, to so many others."

Her face is contorted, as if speaking the words drags up too many horrible memories. I can't imagine living with someone as vile as Anjelica as family, let alone a parent.

"Did you want to stay with her instead? Denver might not be comfortable with the current arrangement," I say.

She turns as if checking back on the living room and its occupants. "He seemed fine a moment ago."

"Sure. How close is too close? For me, I mean."

"Well, considering you had an entire cabin and couldn't stay apart. So you know . . . I'm going to head back to my house. It's been a while. I should at least check in on things." She looks toward the front door. "If I were you, I'd say stay on your side of the house, Lewis. To be safe."

That's what I thought, but I needed to know for sure.

"Thanks, you want me to walk you out?"

"It's fine. I'll see you tomorrow. Call me if anything develops. I mean anything." She wanders toward the foyer, glancing at the two figures on the couch as she passes. I trail behind, trying not to look at Sammie.

She turns back when she reaches the front door. "I mean

it, Sullivan. Stay away from her until the twenty-four hours are up. Or I'll break you myself."

I chuckle, knowing she's entirely serious. I'm glad Sammie has her for a friend. She is protective and loyal. And despite her connection to Anjelica, after all she's done for us, I trust her.

"You have my word, Serena."

She nods, crossing the threshold, and I close the door behind her. I wander from the foyer to head to the hall to my side of the manor. On my way past the living room, I glance at Sammie and my brother for the first time.

They sit on the sofa. Denver on one end. Sammie's head in his lap. Her eyes are closed. The sandwich is half eaten. The juice is all gone. Her breathing is steady. Her heartbeat, strong. Denver notices me lingering and presses a finger to his lips. She's asleep.

I force my feet to move, my gaze to track to the hallway. The house is a blur around me as I make my way to my bedroom. The sight of her head in Den's lap is overwhelming. Heat rises in my core. Flooding my veins. I can't tell whether it is jealousy over my mate touching another male. Or something akin to adoration for the both of them. It is hard to dissect the two emotions.

Almost impossible to figure out which one I should be feeling right now. Because she's my mate. The instinct to protect her and covet her is impossibly strong. But the fact Denver and I have talked about sharing Sammie. That

Sammie and I have spoken about what could be between the three of us flares another cluster of emotions.

A tangle of adoration and . . .

Lust.

Want.

Longing.

I tug the clothes from my body. It's only past noon, but I need to shower after the forest run. I step onto the cool tiles of the ensuite and flick the mixer on. A moment later, the space fills with curling steam and I step under the water. Hot spray envelops me. I tilt my head back, opening my mouth. Water cascades over my shoulders and down my back. I try to ignore the thoughts of the many times Sammie and I have shared this shower.

Her body, warm and soft under my touch, takes over my mind. Her sweet moans and wet heat invade my memories. And I'm hard. Painfully so. Not touching her. Not being near her for the next twenty-four hours will be a challenge.

Serena's right. I can't stay away from Sammie.

I couldn't if I tried.

)))·)·)·◐·(·(((

The glass door to the Mountain Top Inn swishes open under my hand. The snow covering everything outside tracks in with my boots. Chittenden seemed far enough away from Sammie. I couldn't stay in the house with her so close. The woman at the front desk perks up when move toward it. Her white teeth match the fresh snow outside. Her short dark hair and round face, home to kind blue eyes and a wide smile.

"Welcome!"

"Hi. I have a reservation for Sullivan."

"Sure, thing."

She turns slightly to her right and taps on the keyboard. "Yes, here it is. We have you down for a private guest house. Your card details are on file. Just the one night, is it?"

"Yes, thank you."

"Wonderful, Jerome will be here with the caddy to take you across to your house shortly." She pushes a button on the counter. "You're welcome to have a seat here or wander the gift shop for a minute." She waves to my right at the entrance to a small shop. I imagine it's lined with overpriced souvenirs and knickknacks.

Instead, I walk to the window and stare out as more guests drive up. Staff go about their tasks and far in the distance, on one of the slopes, where people are skiing and snowboarding. The door opens and a young man, rugged up in a parker and beanie, strides in.

"Jerome, this gentleman is off to the guest house at the end of the grounds."

"No worries." He holds a hand, presumably for my bag, and I pass it to him. "Follow me. I'll have you settled in in no time."

I push past the glass door and climb into the caddy.

Jerome puts the luggage in the tray of the vehicle, dropping into the driver's seat. "Here for a break then, hey?"

"You could say that."

"The slopes are good this time of year. Or if you're not into that kind of thing, the hiking trails are pretty quiet. All the snow." He smiles and I return the gesture.

"Thanks."

We ride in silence until we reach the last guest house on the estate. It's a two-story cabin with glass windows on every side. A deck skirts the entire structure on the second level. Its peaked roof, now covered in glittering white sports two chimneys. It looks magnificent.

Remembering why I am here, I school my face and jump from the caddy, now pulled up beside the front door. I pluck my luggage from the tray and wave to Jerome. He nods and drives away. Leaving fresh tracks in the snow.

Inside, the house is even more impressive than the outside. With high ceilings, a stone fireplace, a bar, wine storage, a games room and two master bedrooms. Sammie would love this place. I make a promise to myself to bring her here when things settle down. After the brief exploration tour, I drop onto a bench seat at the dining table off the main kitchen and tug my laptop from my bag.

Twenty-seven emails have flooded my inbox since yesterday. I close the program and pull up Google. I tap out search terms for anything related to being bound to a mate. With the tether severed, the risk of us becoming bound is something Serena warned us both about.

Bound to another means what I feel she will feel, and vice versa. If I bleed, so does Sammie. It would be a cruel card to play on Anjelica's part. But it would align with her current methods, and I am worried things are not as fixed as the girls would like to think they are.

After two hours of internet surfing, all conclusions are the same. Being bound to another is a direct result of a broken tether. It's like nature's backup plan should you outsmart a tether. My gut sinks.

That's what I thought. I shove my head in my hands and growl. It rattles my chest. How did our life get so complicated?

My phone vibrates on the bench beside me.

Sammie.

I swipe the screen to answer and tap the speaker icon.

"Lewis?"

"Yeah, Sunshine."

"Are you okay?"

"I'm fine. I just need to give you some space. I didn't want to mess things up after everything you went through."

"I know. You wouldn't though. You always put me first. That's why—"

Her voice breaks, and I hear Denver in the background. His words are soft, encouraging.

"It's alright, Sammie. I understand."

She sucks in a breath. "I miss you."

"I miss you too, Sunshine. You have no idea."

"Oh, hold on, Serena is trying to call. Can I ring you

back?" Her voice is sweet and happy, despite the fatigue I hear in her words.

"Sure."

The call disconnects and I stare at my screen. Not even thirty seconds later, my phone lights up again. "That was quick, Sunshine."

"Lew!"

The second my name leaves her lips, I know something is wrong. My stomach plummets, knots tying themselves around one another.

"What is it?"

"She took him." She's sobbing, her words ride on choppy, shallow breaths.

"Who took who?"

"Jackson, he's gone. Serena rang. My mum rang her because my phone went to busy signal."

"Jackson's gone? Why do you think he's taken?"

"He went to school today but didn't come home. He always goes straight home."

"Who would have taken him?"

But I already know.

"Serena said my mom found a note. She wants both of us in exchange for Jackie. Lewis! What do we do?"

"I'll be there soon. Stay with Denver. Whatever you do, do not give her what she wants, Sammie."

I slam the phone on the bench, losing a string of curses.

It never fucking ends!

Fuck.

I toss my belongings in the bag I brought and throw it over my shoulder with my satchel. No Uber home this time.

I walk into the snow. A crowd of skiers are making their way back to their accommodation. I walk as fast as humanly possible until I reach the end of the drive of the resort. Checking for cars and hikers, I make sure the coast is clear. The incoming show fall has chased everyone inside.

I take off in a blur.

I will be home in under an hour.

I need the Mustang for this one.

Lewis paces the floor beside me. Denver and I stand between him and Sammie, keeping them apart. It's beyond cruel, but we can't go backward now.

Sammie's phone lights up.

A text. She taps the screen and reads the message. By the way her face crumples, I can tell it's her mom.

"Just breathe, babes," I offer.

Sammie clicks the phone shut and rocks back and forth on the sofa. What a fucking mess. How the hell did my mother know the tether was broken? It's no coincidence the day the tether is undone, Jackson is taken. Sammie sways on her feet, rubbing her hands on her thighs, she is anxious, upset and not coping. And Lewis can't help her.

Ugh, this is utter shit.

Denver steps over to her. She looks up, her face breaks with a sob. He guides her to her feet and folds her in his arms, holding her. She chugs through sobs. I glance at the stunned, pained face of Lewis. Having his brother wrapped around his mate must be messing with his head big time.

Lewis shakes his head, as if dislodging a thought, and drags his focus from his brother and his mate and looks to the flames, now burning high in the heath. I should get him out of here before his willpower vanishes.

"Sullivan, you're with me." I walk to the fireplace and grab his hand, leading him down the hallway and through the double glass doors. The last time we headed through these doors, Sammie almost lost her life. Now she is at risk of losing her brother. I know Lewis is tallying up all the ways his being in her life has been to her detriment.

"Where are we going, Serena?"

"Not far, I need to get you away from Sammie and Denver before you do something stupid."

He stops and I drop his hand. I turn back to him. He runs a hand through his messy blond hair and turns his gaze to the back of the house. "She'll be okay with Den."

"You are taking this very well, Lewis."

"How else could I take it? Everything turns to shit. Everything is my fault. I should never have spoken to Sammie. She's better off without me."

I knew that was coming. With a sigh, I wander to the lake behind their house. In the sunshine, the snow glistens and the water moves sluggishly around the wooden dock the brothers built. I sink onto the end of it and stare into the ripples of icy water. Lewis drops beside me a moment later.

"You can't beat yourself up for everything that happens to her, you know."

"You wouldn't understand."

Of course I do. I have my mate literally frozen in time. Hiding from the world's most sinister witch ever to live.

My own mother.

I've tried for centuries to keep harm from Theo. To keep her from Theo. I know that no matter how hard you try, sometimes evil wins. Some things are beyond our control.

"You're wrong, Sullivan. I know all too well about trying to protect your mate. I have been doing just that for centuries. Not everything can be prevented."

"You have a mate, shadow witch?"

"I do. He's also a witch. A healer."

"Where is he?"

"In France."

"And you're here, why?"

"It's complicated. I can't be around him like you can with Sammie. That's not an option for me until—"

"Until?"

"My mother is out of the picture. Which is also complicated, because I am bound to her."

"What? How?"

"She bound me to her and our coven leader when I was young. I had no idea what it meant. Not until the day she killed him. The bond broke. The only thing that kept me alive in those following hours was the one I shared with her. Theo, my mate, is the son of the coven leader she killed. If she found out he's still alive, she wouldn't hesitate to kill him too. World's longest grudge holder, my mother."

"Fuck. I'm sorry."

"Yeah, me too." I trace the grain in the weathered boards underneath us.

"When Anjelica dies, what happens to you?"

"I was hoping to have the bond broken before I had to find out. The talisman we got to help you and Sammie it should do the trick, but I would need her to do it for me. Only an elemental can break a shadow witch bond. I don't have the heart to ask. She's gone through so much already."

"She would do for you in a heartbeat, Serena. You two are practically sisters."

I huff a laugh. I guess we are.

"Do you know the spell to break it?" Lewis asks.

"Yes, it's in my grimoire."

He goes silent and stares across the water. I hug my coat around my body tighter.

"How about this? You and Sammie break your last connection to her. Den and me get Jackson back."

"How are you going to do that?"

"Stealth and speed."

"I suppose we could do a tracking spell. But if she catches you, Lewis, it will not end well for either of you."

"I'm aware of your mother's motivation, Serena. I have been running from them for centuries, as you know."

I laugh and bump his shoulder with my own. "Oh, I know. You are the reason I met Sammie. I was supposed to be keeping tabs on her and her family, so they didn't help you out of your curse."

His eyes widen. "I didn't know that."

I stand and drop my hand. He takes it and pulls up to his feet.

"I can get something of Jackson's and be back in an hour," Lewis offers.

"Okay, I'll get my grimoire and everything we need for the locator spell and the bond breaking spell."

He turns to head inside.

"Lewis?"

He stops and turns back.

"For the record. I'm glad you and Sammie found each other."

A smile blooms over his face, filling his brown eyes. "Me too."

)))·◉·(((

The locator spell takes three minutes and Lewis and Denver are gone in less time. I pray to the goddesses they get in and out without being detected. Last I heard, my mother's held up in some abandoned mansion in the burbs of Portland. If the brothers are not back in a couple of days, I'll pay her a visit.

"What does the spell involve?" Sammie asks.

I slide the grimoire sideways on the kitchen island bench so she can read it. The ingredients we need are on the marble top, ready to use. I check them off in my head again, double checking we have every one. Athame, sage, salt, cinnamon, my blood, Mother's blood, chalice, matches. I think we're good to go.

"Will your mother realize the bond is broken?" Sammie asks.

"Maybe, maybe not. I felt it break when the coven leader bound to me died. However, the bond was very new. This is literally hundreds of years later. She may feel something or nothing."

"So, we are kind of doing this blind?"

"Unfortunately, yes."

"Ugh, the last person I want to see right now is your mother, Rena."

I have to laugh, what else is there to do? "Just hold off incinerating her until we get Theo back, please, girl."

"Cross my heart and hope to die." She smiles, and it lights up her entire face.

"God, don't say that, Sammie. She will hear you."

This time she bursts out laughing and I shrill out the chorus of "What Is This Feeling?" From Wicked. Which elicits hysterics from her. We clutch our stomachs and let the giddiness take over. After a moment, the giggles subside, and we refocus on the task in front of us.

It's not really funny. The reality of dying around my mother is higher than most other people's parents. Substantially so.

My phone pings.

Lewis.

"We found the house. Going in. Update soon."

"Okay. Stay safe, Sullivan."

"10-4."

I roll my eyes at his old man slang and update Sammie. She forces a smile. I know the waiting and worrying is killing her.

"They'll be okay. They have the advantage. Plus, being vampires, they're mostly immortal and super speedy, you know." Like it's her first day in the world of supernaturals.

"How are they supposed to get into your mother's house if they are not invited?" she says, stilling, her eyes widening.

"I lived there for a couple of decades. Before it was run down. I invited them in before they left."

"Oh, it works like that?"

"Should do."

"Should do?!" Her eyes widen. "What if it doesn't?"

"Then the boys will have to get creative."

She goes about rereading the page, her finger running across the handwriting letters with old ink. Being able to divide and conquer, with Sammie and Lewis no longer tethered, feels right. I have missed her.

"Hey, you wanna come with me to see Theo?"

"Oh, I thought I couldn't."

"It should be okay if we're quick. Plus, it's been longer than usual since my last visit. I am dying to see his handsome face again."

"Sure, but you should do the time travel stuff. I don't think I'm that great at it."

"Okay, I'll drive."

Sammie throws her head back and laughs. It is so good to have her back.

)))•◗◖•(((

It took all of five minutes for Sammie to break the bond. Since hell didn't rain down on us, I suspect Mother doesn't realize it's broken. I felt a twang of an ache as if something snapped in my chest and then nothing.

I wait in the living room dressed in my regency clothes, stuffing items into the pockets I sewed into the skirt decades ago to hide my modern-day things. They're deep and I make sure I have my phone silenced, plus my small dagger I never leave this century without.

With the bond between my mother and I broke, I plan to wake Theo up. Now we are no longer connected, it's safer to include him, than to have him suspended in time, helpless. Sammie appears from the hall, her dress glides on the floor behind her. Her hands wander the lace and layers of her blue dress.

She's stunning. I pull my phone out and snap a picture for Lewis. I'll send it to him later. It's going to do his head in.

"This is so cumbersome, but it is so pretty," she says. "All I need is one of those fans, then I can bat my eyes and pull a handsome suitor." She grins as if that's the funniest thing ever spoken.

"Trust me, girl. The one you have is much better than the types from the time we are going to."

"Oh, I know. Can't I live like Elizabeth Bennet, just for one day?"

I roll my eyes at her, and she snorts a laugh. She grabs my hand.

"Not where we're going. Now, let's get out of here."

Sammie composes herself, straightening her skirts with her free hand. I spin the inner circle of my pendant. The world blurs and we hit the hard mud floor in a heartbeat. Sammie releases her hold on my hand and turns, taking in the dim cellar.

The stretcher holding Theo is all I can focus on. The sounds of the family above us in the small farm French farmhouse. The scent of sage and cooking drifts through the wide cracks in the floorboards. Two lanterns light the space, one by the stretcher. The other by the small trapdoor that leads to the house upstairs.

"Will they know it is you?" Sammie asks.

"I knock, a pattern we established ages back, so they know I am visiting. They tend to Theo daily, but otherwise, he's undisturbed. Last time I was here, a witch hunt consumed the place. Pyre-wielding maniacs and all. It was a close call."

"What happened?" Her brows drop. I take my eyes off Theo for a second.

"I moved him temporarily. A few hours later, the drama subsided. And things went back to the status quo. But there will be more. Many more."

"Heavens." She wanders to where Theo rests peacefully suspended in time, who looks like he is simply asleep. His arms rest over his chest in an X pattern. His legs are straight. His bed-clothes are the ones he fled in the day we ran.

French chatter seeps through the floorboards. My French is good enough to understand what they are saying. Crops, something about a fattened beast being ready. Will the scout be coming back?

What scout? I make my way to the door and knock, three times, then two, then pause, then three.

The trap door lifts. The surprised face of the woman of the house finds mine. "Oh, mademoiselle Serena, *vous m'avez surpris!*"

"Sorry to startle you, Marguerite," I say in her tongue.

She eyes Sammie behind me. "*Qui est-ce?*"

"This is Sammie. She is elemental. Ah, *élémentaire.*"

"Ah, *oui.*" She gestures for us to come upstairs. We follow up the stairs and into the bright kitchen of her home. Two stunned faces meet me, their gazes flickering between Sammie and me. Jacques, her husband, and Henri, her son, almost of age now, sit with widened eyes and spoons suspended halfway to their mouths.

"*Mes amours, voici l'amie de* mademoiselle Serena, mademoiselle Sammie."

The older man nods. The son swallows, his eyes fixed on Sammie's face.

"Hello. I mean—*bonjour?*" Sammie offers.

Heat flushes the boy's face, and he returns his focus to his bowl.

"You said something about a scout?" I ask Marguerite.

"*Oui, il est venu il y a deux jours.*" She nods as her brows lower, and moves to the bench, taking up a large knife and chops potatoes.

"He came two days ago? What did he want?"

She holds both hands up, as in I have no idea. Mother would have sent him. No witch wanders aimlessly in these parts, with regular witch hunts and all. How the hell did she find out where Theo is—when Theo is? I chose this time period specifically because the English are not welcome here. The ongoing war makes sure of that.

So, he must have come from our current time. That means she is far too close. I can't wait for her to find her way here and kill Theo.

"*Merci,*" I say and guide Sammie back down the steps. We stop short of the sleeping Theo.

Sammie glances back to the trapdoor. "What happens now?"

"We wake him up."

"I thought you couldn't?"

"I'm not bound to her anymore, which means any spells I cast while I was shouldn't be affected. Hopefully."

"It sounds risky, Rena. What if he wakes up, only to die?"

I meet her gaze. Her face is as pained as the ache in my heart. I cannot lose Theo. I refuse to let her win.

Not now. Not ever.

"He is a sitting duck here. I have no other choice."

Sammie chews her lip but nods. "Sure, what do you need me to do?"

"Here," I pluck a piece of paper from my deep right pocket. "Chant this with me."

She takes the paper and studies it. "Right, where do you need me?"

"Take his hand. And mine. It has to be a continuous loop."

We join hands and hold Theo's.

For a moment, I hesitate. I haven't seen Theo for over two hundred and fifty years. Awake at least. Haven't felt his warm hands, his wide smile, his gorgeous green eyes lit up.

"It's okay, Rena."

I suck in a breath. "I-I. It's been such a long time."

"Then we shouldn't wait another second."

I nod.

We close our eyes. Sammie squeezes my hand, and I start the chant.

Low vibrations tunnel through me with every word in the right order. Sammie's grip on my hand tightens.

Mater terra hic precatio nostra,
Hoc corpus e somno laqueis solve,
Evigila nunc,
Surgite fortis et stabilis,
Evigila nunc

Theo's hand vibrates against mine. Sammie slams her eyes shut. Her mouth forms a thin line. Her face scrunches. For this spell, she carries the burden. Not me.

"Again," she whispers.

Mater terra hic precatio nostra,
Hoc corpus e somno laqueis solve,
Evigila nunc,
Surgite fortis et stabilis,
Evigila nunc

Again.

Louder.

Our chanting grows until the small space around us hums with each word. Wind sweeps around our ankles. Sammie's face hardens, and her grip tightens.

Theo jerks, his head flips from side to side as if he is having a wild dream. My heart thunders in my chest. I can't let either of them go. I won't. Sammie raises both of her hands, taking mine and Theo's with hers. He trembles where he lies, eyes fluttering. Breath leaves my lungs and doesn't return. The wind whips around the three of us like a heat-crazed storm.

Sammie stills.

She releases my hands, and her eyes have whitened completely.

"Oh my god," I gasp.

A low growl seeps from her lips.

Theo sits up, eyes blinking rapidly, dazed.

Sammie collapses to the floor.

Theo crumples back down to the stretcher. Out cold. Again.

"No!" I scream.

I sink to her side and take her hands.

"Sammie, no. Wake up!"

Her breath is gone.

No. No. No. No!

Fuck, Sammie, no.

CHAPTER 18

LEWIS

Beneath the rays of the full moon, the crumbling mess of a mansion sits. It's laced with oak vine, critters, and the distinct stench of witch. The old home would have been impressive in its day, with sweeping steps to double doors. A rotund two-story tower on the left, a robust two-story section to the right. A hip roof with three peaks and two chimneys, the bricked home is trimmed with cream hand-painted fretwork under each peak.

Through the vines and pasty old stone, I can hear the heartbeat of two humans. They know each other going by the conversation tossed back and forth between them. The older one is a woman, the younger is Jackson. I remember his tone and mannerism from the visit to Sammie's house.

"What's the plan?" Denver says.

He leans against his truck now, and I sit on the hood of the Mustang.

"Get in, get the boy, get out."

"Simple," he mocks.

"You got a better one, brother?"

"Yep, set the house alight, they all rush out. We nab the boy."

"How do you plan on igniting that many tons of chalky stone?"

He chuckles. "Fuel."

He holds two jerry cans in his grip, and I scoff.

"It doesn't have to burn it down, just enough smoke they have to get out."

"What if they leave and don't bother taking the two humans with them?"

"Then we will have to risk entering, I guess. Plan A first."

"Fine, give me a can. Meet you back here in two minutes."

Denver disappears without responding. I take off in a blur, splashing fuel over anything around the mansion that'll burn. I sense no wards. Or barrier spells. That's unlike Anjelica. Maybe her plebs haven't learned those yet.

I slide to a halt by Denver's truck, and he meets me a second later. He flicks the lighter lid closed and slides it into his back pocket. "Now we wait."

"Now we wait."

We lean against the truck. The moon overhead reflects off the chrome bummers of the truck. The shadows cast on the ground fade as flames burst to life and grow higher and higher. The cover of darkness was a good idea. I hope we haven't blown it by adding more light.

Smoke billows around the old house. Critters scamper from the vines, racing across the lawn and the pavement to the street. Yelling starts.

Our cue to move closer.

We take cover behind the closest row of bushes and squat. The witches are moving about. All male voices. Anjelica isn't here. That's one blessing, at least. The scouts assemble on the pavement outside the house. No humans with them.

Fuck.

"Looks like it's Plan B, Lew." Denver moves from the bush to the back of the house in a blur. I follow. I bunt the door open with one hand and step across the threshold.

Three heartbeats.

Not two.

Someone else is here.

I step inside. Neither of us feel a thing. Serena's invitation must have worked.

The inside of the house is much the same as the outside. The plaster crumbling from the walls only rises halfway up the high ceilings. A heritage-looking chandelier hangs precariously from the ceiling in the center of the great room. The foyer is visible from the back of the first floor now, with the internal walls sporting so many holes, its innards resemble Swiss cheese.

A broken kitchen sits to our right. To our left, a sitting room. The old dark green carpet is worn, laid under broken occasional chairs and a side table with a crooked top. Old family oil painted portraits line the walls of the great room. Cobwebs hang from absolutely every surface. So much for housekeeping.

"They must be in the basement," I whisper.

Den nods and tracks the stairs that descend. I follow at his back. The pit of my stomach plummets as we descend further into the confined basement space. Denver reaches the bottom and pulls his phone from his back pocket, a second later, the light from it illuminates the cramped space. Two cages sit to the left of the square boiler room. An ancient, rusted boiler sits in a puddle of dank water. Mildew and moss cover half of the stone lower wall. Jackson and a woman I don't recognize are trapped in a cage each.

"Lewis!" Jackson shuffles to the front of his enclosure.

"Hey, buddy. We're gonna get you out of here."

He nods. His hands grip the bars. "Help Mrs. Stewart. She got hit on the head. She was bleeding."

"Denver will get you out. I'll help her."

Den moves to Jackson's cage and motions for him to back up. In one swift tug, the door rips from the hinges and Sammie's little brother crawls out on his hands and knees. He stands beside Den, watching. I pull the second cage door from its pins. The middle-aged woman lies curled up on her side. Her breathing is fast.

As gently as I can, I lift her up and cradle her against my chest. I shuffle backward on my knees until we are clear of the cage and lay her on the cold floor. She moans. Blood seeps from a gash on her head. My throat burns.

Denver drops by her other side and bites his wrist. He holds it over her parted mouth, letting three drops hit her tongue. A moment later, the wound stitches over and she opens her eyes. They widen as she looks between Denver and me.

"It's okay, Mrs. Stewart. They are here to help," Jackson says softly.

She pushes to sit up, focusing on Jackson. He squats to meet her gaze. "Are you alright?"

She nods and clutches her cardigan around her shoulders. Her cream pants are filthy, her shoes are covered in snowy sludge. Her face is dirty and streaked by tears. How long has she been here?

"We need to move," Denver prompts.

On either side of her, Den and I help her to her feet.

"Thank you," she rasps.

We make it up the stairs and back into the smoke shrouded great room. The smoke drifts through the area, thicker than before. I lead Jackson toward the back door we entered through. Denver helps the woman along as we cover our faces with our sleeves. I grab the doorknob of the back door and turn it.

Nothing happens.

Instantly, the smoke vanishes as if washed away. The temperature plummets.

Fuck me.

I spin back and fall in beside Den, shoving the humans behind us.

Two scouts flank Anjelica. "Huh, you really are dumber than I ever imagined, Lewis. And you, Denver, you should know better than to interfere with my plans."

Denver growls and takes a step toward the shadow witch.

I tense but follow.

"What do you want with these two, Anjelica?" I snarl.

"Ah. Well, that depends really. I am a woman of my word, and I don't give up easily. You think you have won, Lewis, but this game is far from over."

"Let the humans go. You want to take your revenge. Take it out on us."

"Sounds fair, AJ, two against three. The odds are in your favor."

I groan internally at my brother's effort to nickname this sadistic wench. Why he bothers, I will never know.

She laughs, throwing her head back. Before homing her sights on Denver. "Boy, the odds are always in my favor."

She throws her hands up and black tendrils fly toward the four of us. I spin and slam Jackson to the ground. Denver pins Mrs. Stewart underneath him. The dark magic passes over us, burning across my back. Someone has their magic back.

Fucking hell.

Who in their right mind would volunteer to unbind this bitch?

Serena is going to be pissed.

We divide and circle the three witches. I highly doubt her subordinates are as skilled as she is. As if reading my mind, Denver lunges and rips out the throat of the one to her right. Anjelica turns on him and slams Den up the wall. An invisible force holding him by the throat. He gasps. I snap the neck of the last scout and go for her back. I smash into something hard. A ward. She has a personal fucking ward.

How the hell are we supposed to kill her if we can't touch her? If nothing can touch her. Sammie wouldn't even be able to incinerate the witch. The ward is impenetrable. Denver thrashes against the stone wall. It crumbles, white dust rains from the cracks he is making with every movement. His strength against the dilapidated old mansion's structure.

"Enough!" I roar.

My canines descend.

Blood red creeps into my vision from the sides. Anjelica releases Denver and stalks across the floor to Jackson. Tugging him to his feet, she drags him toward the foyer. He is practically up against her chest.

Apparently, humans can penetrate the ward. Denver's

gaze meets mine. He must have had the same thought. If we can get a weapon to Jackson, he can at least try to wound her. In the kitchen to my right, dust-covered equipment sits on benches. I scan the surface for something sharp. Toward one end, by a refrigerator that looks like it last run in the 1970s, sits a knife block. Denver rips an iron baluster from the internal stairs and closes in on Anjelica.

"You think you can hurt me with that? You blood suckers really are basic." She laughs.

Jackson twists in her grip, watching me as I inch toward the kitchen. Denver steps closer, drawing her attention. "I have no intention of hitting you with this, Anjelica."

She shakes her head and draws a dagger from her flowing crimson skirts, pressing the tip into Jackson's neck. Blood trickles over his Adam's apple, soaking into his collar. His eyes widen and he tries to make space between them.

I leap over the island bench and pluck two knives from the block. Before the next beat, the iron bar flies through the air, snapping the chain holding the chandelier above their heads. It crashes toward the floor.

Anjelica screeches and jerks sideways, taking Jackson with her.

"Jackie!" His eyes snap to me with the use of his sister's nickname for him. I toss the knife. He catches it in his right hand and slams it into the witch behind him.

Anjelica screams.

Shoving the boy to the ground, she plucks the knife from

her abdomen. I look to Denver. He nods. In a blur, I collect Jackson. He sweeps the woman from the floor where she's been sitting, stunned for the last few moments. We are in our vehicles and flying down the street three heartbeats later.

Jackson sits, pressed against the passenger's side door. His mouth is agape and his face is white. "You're—" He snaps his head back. "You're a vampire." His face twists with disgust.

Oh great.

"One who just saved your ass, I might add."

He straightens and tries to relax. He closes his mouth and slides the seat belt over his chest, clicking it into the receptacle. "Yeah, thanks, I guess."

"You guess?"

"I mean, thanks Lewis."

His face turns sheepish, and he fixes his focus on the road. I swerve the corner and head toward the highway. The further we are from Angelica, the better. In my review mirror, Den's truck sits on my tail.

Good.

"Is Sammie okay? That witch didn't get to her too, did she?" he asks after a while.

"She's fine. She's with Serena."

"Oh," he says, as his heartbeat kicks up.

I suppress a smile. "Sammie will be relieved you're okay."

"Yeah."

He stares out the window for a moment, then turns back to face me. "So, you are like her boyfriend?"

"Something like that."

"What's that supposed to mean?"

"You should ask your sister about it."

His brows furrow, and he clasps his shaking hands behind his neck with a sigh. All's well that ends well.

For now.

The second we collapse into the foyer of the manor, Sammie falls from my arms to the hard floor, head lolling to the side. She's motionless.

No, Sammie.

A familiar hand rests on my shoulder.

Denver.

"Where's Lewis?" I choke out as I look up at the older brother.

He is going to kill me, but he should be here.

"He took Jackson home." Denver drops to Sammie's shoulder on the floor. "Fuck Serena, what the hell happened?"

"We tried to wake Theo. She was doing fine and then her eyes, they . . . They turned white like a possession, and she collapsed. Please, she needs your blood. Before it is too late."

Instantly, Denver bites his wrist and holds the wound over Sammie's lips. Blood swells at the puncture and drips into her mouth. Three, seven, ten drops.

Sammie flinches.

Her heart hammers to life. Dammit, that was way too close. She gasps for breath. Hands under her shoulders, I pull her up. Denver hangs his head, letting out a low, breathy groan.

"Thank you," I utter.

He nods and scoops Sammie up and walks her to Lewis's bedroom, laying her on the bed. I stand in the doorway. Guilt crawls its way through my core. Its ugly, vicious pang twists in my chest. That was too much. I almost lost her. Selfishness and spontaneity could have cost me and Lewis Sammie's life. Tears prickle behind my eyes.

A second later, Denver stands almost on top of me, his face contorted by anger. "What the hell were you thinking, Serena?"

"I-I wanted—"

"You could have killed her! You find another way to wake up your mate. I will not allow you to endanger Sammie when you have other alternatives." He shoves past me. I stand numb, staring at my best friend's sleeping face.

He's right.

It was stupid.

Reckless.

I just. I wanted to have Theo back so damn much. Centuries, I have had to live without him. Enough is enough. I grab the turner in my hands and flick the outer ring. Time to get the hell out of here.

SAMMIE

My head pounding, I pace the short stretch inside the foyer, Denver never more than a few feet from me. This house is too small. Lewis should have been back by now. I open the door and stalk across the porch. I sit in the love seat and try to think of something else. Anything else than my brother and Lewis in the same space as that horrendous witch. They will be fine. Lewis is capable. He's a vampire, for god's sake.

Ugh. I hate this.

I jump from the seat and stalk along the porch. I consider jumping forward ten minutes to see if they arrive home. But I don't want to miss him if he comes a second earlier.

I reach the end of the porch and turn back. Like a swimmer taking a tumble turn before lapping down the watery stretch for another go. I grab my pendant and twist it between my fingers. I know Serena told me not to, but it's my only comfort, especially when Lewis and I are apart.

Movement at the top step catches my eye.

Denver.

My stomach flips at the thought of him around Anjelica. His breathy curse, as I pace past where he sits on the top step, reminds me he made it home.

He is here.

It's Lewis who hasn't returned.

My heart races faster with every menacing thought. The front door cracks open. My hand around the pendant stills. Serena shuts the door and walks to where I pace. Her hands stop me in my tracks, firmly around my arms. "Hey, they will be okay. Please come and sit down."

"You don't know that."

"Lewis has survived my mother for centuries," Serena offers weakly.

Denver shoots her a glance that could melt glaciers.

My chin wobbles as I think about the two of them. "Sammie, hey. He will get Jackson back." I nod, but tears slip down my cheeks.

"I could feel you through the pendant, babes."

"Sorry," I rasp.

She shakes her head and pulls me into a hug. After everything we have been through. I can't lose him now. I can't lose Jackie. If that bitch hurts any of my family. Lewis. Jackson . . .

I will kill her myself.

Tires on gravel split the otherwise quiet. Serena releases me instantly, and I fly down the porch steps as the Mustang comes to a halt at the foot of them. Jackson spills from the car and flies to where I stand. His arms are around me in a heartbeat. He's shaking.

I hold him tighter.

"Sammie," he chokes.

"You're okay. You're here now. But I thought you were going home?"

I run a hand over his head and rub his back. His bigger frame is almost wrapped around me. At only sixteen, I remember he's still a kid. He would have been scared. Breath leaves my lungs. I swallow back the sobs threatening to pour into his coat. He groans and releases me. I wipe my eyes and force a smile.

"I had some questions, so I asked Lewis to detour. You never told me he's a vampire, sis."

My mouth gapes.

Huh, yeah, I guess I didn't.

"Lewis and Denver are vampires," Lewis offers, coming to stand by my side. His hand slips into mine. God, I have missed that.

Jackson glances between us. "Witches and vampires don't—"

"They do sometimes," I say, smiling at him. I can't keep the grin from growing over my face.

"Oh . . . Do Mom and Dad know?"

"Kind of. They know he is my boyfriend."

Jackson looks at Lewis, who nods, before returning his gaze to me. "We're supposed to hate each other."

Lewis pecks my cheek and walks inside with Denver and Serena.

"Obviously, we don't. Let's go inside, Jackie. There's more to this you should know."

Where do I start? How do I tell him about Lewis's curse? About Grandma trying to help and dying for it. That Lewis is my mate. That we were tethered.

The tether.

Oh crap, what time is it?

I pull my phone from my back pocket. 11.58.

Oh no.

I freeze, staring at the digits on the screen.

We were supposed to wait until midday. Lewis wasn't supposed to touch me until after midday. My breaths shorten. My head lightens.

Two minutes shy . . .

A hand lands on my shoulders. I turn back to find Jackson's worried eyes. "What is it?"

I raise my gaze to meet his.

"It wasn't time," I utter.

Serena appears in the doorway. Her shocked face finds mine as she bolts down the stairs and pinches my arm.

"Ouch, what was that for?"

Denver appears by her side a second later. "He felt it."

"What. Who felt what?" Jackson asks, his confused stare swinging between me and Denver.

"Lewis. He felt that." Den forces a sad smile, his stare not leaving me.

Serena hangs hers, her mouth a thin line. "Two more minutes, babes, that's all it would have taken."

I tap the phone again. 12.00.

Lewis walks through the front door and onto the porch. His gaze burns into mine. I race up the stairs and into his arms. He folds himself around me.

"We're bound, Sunshine."

"I know. I'm sorry."

"Don't be. This changes nothing."

I push out of his hold, chest heaving.

"It changes everything, Lewis. If I die, so do you."

"Sammie." My name is a grave plea.

No. He doesn't get it.

We are back where we started, back to him being vulnerable because of me. I scream into my hands.

Warm hands curl around my fingers, coaxing them from my face.

"I do not care. Whatever time we have, I am grateful for."

"No . . ."

"Sunshine," he growls.

"You're not immortal anymore, Lewis. It's all my fault, again."

The pained faces of Denver, Serena, and Jackson stare back at us from the top of the porch steps.

My world seems like it is constantly falling apart. But

somehow, having these people who are my family around me shifts the heaviness of despair and replaces it with a glimmer of hope.

Serena ushers everyone inside and into the living room. I toss a ball of fire into the hearth to help it along. Before long, we are all sitting on the two long sofas. Me flanked by Lewis and Jackson. Serena is next to Denver.

I take a selfie of Jackie and me and flick it to Mom. With a text letting her know he is safe and with us. She sends back a long text, saying how proud she is of us both.

"So, I guess we all have some catching up to do." Denver breaks the silence between the five of us. Jackson looks around the house as he listens to the explanations Lewis and Denver give. Telling him a brief version of their live story, including who Angelica is.

"Why did she take me and Mrs. Stewart?"

"She's trying to hurt Sammie and Serena. They recently broke a curse she had held over Lewis for centuries."

"Oh. Way to go, sis." His face lights up in a smile. "Are you like a super witch now?"

I huff a laugh and tuck a curl of hair behind my ear. "Ah, no. It took two of us, little bro."

He glances at Serena and blushes.

Jackson recovers and turns to me. "So, you two are dating?"

I look at Lewis, and he smiles at me, running a hand through my hair. My heart beats a little faster and warmth grows in my core. His fingers trace my cheek before he looks back to my little brother. "We are dating."

I nod, confirming.

"So that's it? There's nothing else? What was all that on the porch about then?"

"Oh, we, um—" I start.

"They're mated," Serena says.

Jackson glances at her before studying my face, brows lowered. "What do you mean, your mates? Witches bond with other witches. Not vampires."

"Not usually, no. But, while it's rare, it isn't impossible," Lewis says.

"Oh. So, you are like stuck with each other, like forever?" His face screws up.

Denver chuckles.

Lewis flattens his growing smile. "It is no hardship to be paired with your sister. It's my privilege."

Jackson alternates his focus between Lewis and me.

"And we are bound. We were tethered after I broke his curse. We got through that but now . . ." The words lodge in my throat. "Now, we are bound. What he feels, I feel and vice versa."

The words are heavy. I hate them. I hate that my mortality once again endangers Lewis's life.

"Okay, so if I do this," Jackson punches my arm, "Lewis felt that?"

Lewis rubs his arm, then mine and drawls, "Yes, he did."

Lew talking about himself in the third person is hilarious and I chuckle.

"Cool!" Jackson wriggles his eyebrows.

"Yeah, not really Jackie, his life is effectively tied to my own. I'm mortal, he shouldn't be."

"Oh yeah, that part sucks. I guess."

"Alright, well, if show and tell is over. How about we divide and conquer? I have research to attend to. Maybe something in my library about being bound. Or Google, you never know."

Serena stands. "Let me show you to a room, Jackson. I think your sister and Lewis could use some downtime."

My little brother simply nods and follows her to the guest wing of the house. Denver crowds my space as I stand. He pulls me in for a hug. "I'm glad you're okay, Sammie."

"Oh, I'm okay."

He releases me. "Serena told me what happened." His jaw feathers, but he winks at me. My heart leaps. He hasn't told Lewis I almost died trying to help Theo. He won't, I'm guessing.

A hand slips into mine from behind.

Denver smiles softly before heading toward his library.

I turn back to find the happy, loving face of Lewis. "You two are getting along well."

I smile and bury my head in his neck. I moan and press my body to his. His hands run behind my neck and into my hair. "Shall we test out this new bond, Sunshine?"

God. Heat pools fast. I swear now the tether is gone, the bond between us from being bound is a thousand times more sensitive.

"Lew, yes, please." Twenty-four hours is far too long to go without touching this gorgeous man.

He sweeps me off my feet and into his arms. A blur and a moment later, we are inside his bedroom and the door shuts softly behind us. "Where do you want to start?" Lewis whispers, dotting kisses down my neck.

"Anywhere you want."

He drops me to my feet, eyes wide with surprise. "I felt every kiss I gave you."

This is going to be a new level of heaven for the both of us. Maybe being bound is not that bad? Maybe we can make this work?

I tug his sweater and shirt off and run my hands over his chest. The feeling of warmth sweeping over my own catches me by surprise and the breath leaves my lungs.

Oh, heavens.

"Sunshine, I don't know if I can do this."

I search his eyes as they darken from brown to black too quickly. I summon wind and slide it between us with just my mind, my hands still cupped around his face. "We can do this." The sensation caressing my jaw as I run my fingers over his is thrilling.

It's too much. It's everything.

His eyes slide closed.

His fangs descend.

"Bite me, Lew, please."

He lets his head fall back onto the door with a thud, a moan rumbles through his throat. I slide the belt from his jeans and undo the fasteners. He tenses. His fingers crawl through my hair as he huffs a laugh. He must have felt it, too.

I push the jeans from his hips, and he growls, low and breathy. He grips my hips, and the next thing I know, my back is against the door, my hands over my head, Lewis holds me against the hard surface. His weight is heavy despite the barrier of wind between us. I like the heaviness. I like him this close.

I brush my lips over his and nip his lip. The sting blooms on my own. I force shaky breaths in and out.

"Lewis," I rasp. The ache in my center is feeling the fire pooling low in my belly. I have far too many clothes on. "Too many clothes."

Rough hands tug the sweater and shirt off me. My breasts bounce with the movement and instantly he lays kisses on top of each, where they sit out of my lacy blue bra. He rips the zip on my jeans and shoves the jeans from my hips. I step out of them, pulling his head from my chest and crashing my mouth to his.

It is like nothing I have felt before. His hands are on my body. I feel every move he makes. Rough and soft. Urgent and slow. I circle a finger over his hard stomach and let it fall. His hard length is swollen, the tip glistens with need. The ghost of my fingers washes over my skin as they trace his.

"Sunshine," he chokes.

He nudges my neck, grazing the skin with his canines.

"Bite me," I utter, too breathless to make it sound like a command.

He stills for a moment, his eyes fully black now. His face twisted with desire and hunger. Still utterly gorgeous. I grip his hardness with one hand, and he rolls his head on his shoulders, closing his eyes with a growl.

"Bite me, Lew. Then fuck me."

"Manners, Sunshine." His voice is gravel.

He wants me to beg, and I absolutely will. "Please, Lewis."

His hand slides from my neck to my breast, his thumb sweeps over my nipple through the lace. I moan and arch into him. He slams me against the door harder. The wood groans.

I push more wind between us reluctantly. His hardness presses into my throbbing apex. His hand falls, and his fingers nudge past my panties and find my wet heat. I moan and open my legs, wanting more.

"Sunshine, I—"

"Please, Lew. Bite me or something, before I implode."

The door rattles behind me. "Lewis?"

Denver.

Really? Now??

"Busy," I choke out.

Lewis doesn't respond to Denver's call. Did he even hear

him? His head dips into my neck and the pang of sharp teeth into soft flesh hits my neck. I tilt my head to the side to give him what he needs. He sucks on my neck, one hand now on my hip, the other teases my aching center.

"Lewis. Please . . ." I whimper.

He breaks from my neck, meeting my gaze. Blood runs down his chin. My blood. Even feral, he is stunning. "Uh huh?"

"I'm burning up, Lew."

A cheeky smile flickers over his face. His eyes return to brown. He sinks two fingers into my core. I moan so loud; I am sure Denver would have heard it from the sawmill.

Somehow, I just know he's still on the other side of our door.

Lewis's focus slides to my left, resting on the door, before kissing me, hungry and hard. As if his brother being on the other side of the wall is fueling his need as much as it is mine.

Oh my god, Sammie.

His hand releases and snaps the hooks free on my bra. It falls to my feet. My breasts, heavy and aching, carry stiff peaks. All I can think of is his mouth on them. His teeth graze each nipple. I reaffirm my grip around his hardness and tug it toward me. I pump my hand until his eyes fade to black again.

"Sunshine."

"Your turn to beg," I whisper in his ear and nip it.

I swear something thumps on the other side of the wall to the left of the door.

"In a minute," Lewis rasps.

He drops his head and suckles and kisses his way around each breast, sending my aching apex throbbing. Every fiber of my being is lit up with the dire need for him to be inside me. Lewis sends me higher with every brush, flick, and sweep of his thumb over the bundle of nerves and my legs trembling. "Heavens above."

"Come for me, Sunshine."

The words vibrate around the nipple between his lips, sending me over the edge. I tighten around his fingers, sweet agony spilling through my core and through every limb. Cries pour from my parted lips.

"God, you're beautiful."

I slump against Lewis, and he removes his fingers, popping them into his mouth. He closes his eyes and groans. The second his fingers fall, I send my hands through his hair and pull him closer, kissing him, tasting my release on his lips, his tongue.

With a commanding touch, I grip his shoulders and turn him and push him against the door.

"Sammie."

"Your turn." I peck a kiss to the left corner of his lips and feel it on mine.

I trail both hands over his chest, down his stomach and lower to where his hard length stands waiting for my mouth. I drop to my knees. Instantly, his fingers are entwined between my curls. God, I love that feeling.

I take him into my mouth, only the tip. Sweeping my tongue over the slit. He fists my hair. It hurts a little, but it's a thrill. I take him in further and grip the base, pulling up in a long movement. Teasing with my tongue up the underside of his hard, velvety cock, I moan. Warmth surrounds my apex.

He tastes good. Heat rises and my apex throbs relentlessly. Unsure if it's because of what I'm doing to Lewis or just my reaction, I pause. His hands return to wandering through my hair.

I wonder?

I tweak my nipple. His jaw feathers. He felt it. I run my tongue up the underside of his length. I feel the brush of heat and softness on my entrance.

Holy shit.

I take him as deep as I can and suck with long, steady strokes up and down.

"Sunshine," he groans.

"Mhmm."

The vibration runs through me.

His legs tremble. I look up at him. His eyes are so dark, almost black.

Good.

I pick up the pace, intensifying the suction as I go. He bucks against the door. His hands fisted in my hair, he drives into my mouth. His face contorts with pleasure.

His canines descend fast.

Too fast.

Instantly, I am swept from my feet and against the door. It cracks before I can put more wind between us. The door gives way, and I land hard on top of its broken pieces in the hallway. Lewis pins me to the floor. His gorgeous face is pure feral animal. His hands slam around my throat as he rips my head to one side.

"No!" I choke, fingers grappling for purchase on his hard grip.

Peeling himself from the wall his forehead rests on, Denver's hands slide down the wall as he turns to face us. "Stop, Lewis," he chokes out.

Heat flushes my neck and face. Denver's eyes are almost as dark as his brother's. I meet his gaze. My wide eyes stay on his for a heartbeat before he rips his brother up and to his feet. I push up and off the door, hugging my arms around my bare breasts, putting space between Denver and me.

Lewis growls, low and hard. Denver slams him into the wall, and he struggles in his older brother's grip. Flailing like he's hellbent on getting to me. Desperate to take his fill.

He needs water. I drop my arms and raise my hands, palms up and twisting. Without taking my eyes from Denver's heated gaze, I pull water from the ensuite and drench Lewis.

I stand, chest heaving, eyes burning into Denver's.

He swallows. His Adam's apple bobs over and over.

His breaths are too short.

Mine burn, and I drop my focus to the splinted door at my feet. His drops to my chest.

Fuck.

His eyes turn black, and he loses a low moan, shaking his head. His eyes recover, the hazel irises I've grown to relish return.

I don't move to cover up. I don't know if I want to.

"Sammie?" Lewis's voice breaks.

I startle, snapping my gaze at Lewis. His face is pained. A sob flies past my lips. I hug my arms around myself and stagger into the bedroom. Looking around for a moment, the last few moments putting me in a daze. I pad to the bathroom and lock the door. I slide down the door and stare at the tiled wall opposite me.

Lewis's tortured face as he glanced between Denver and me.

Hot tears slide down my burning cheeks.

Dammit.

A pigeon that is not a pigeon coos outside my window of the second story of our London town house. My cue to tip toe outside and slip into Joseph's carriage. The sun is only now rising, but I can already hear Mother downstairs. Vials clinking, the soft thud of the fall of a heavy knife. The scratch and clunk of the mortar and pestle starts a moment later.

I tighten the laces on my corset and pull a shawl over my shoulders. I ship up my velvet bag, containing a few herbs, a handkerchief, a small vial of moon water and a key to the back door of the house in case Mother goes out while I'm gone. She should be busy all day, working to restock the supplies of the apothecary, but just in case. I will take the key.

I slide my wrist through the looped cord and poke my head from the bedroom door. The clunking of the mortar and pestle keeps its steady rhythm, so I duck down the stairs and head to the front door. Holding my breath, I crack the door and slip through, closing it softly behind me. The carriage waits across the street for me. Joseph jumps down when he sees me coming and disappears to the other side. I hurry across the cobbled street and round the carriage.

Joseph waits with the door open, a grin stretching his weathered face. "Good morning, Miss Serena. I trust you got away with no trouble?"

"Yes, she is preoccupied today. Restocking the shop."

"Let us not waste a second!" He climbs to the driver's bench, and the carriage pulls down the street, swaying with the cadence of Tender's gait.

Half an hour later, we slow as the road winds and ascends. The houses thin out, and green spans give way to farmland. Butterflies take flight, low in my belly, when Theo's home comes in to view around the next sweeping turn. Joseph calls to Tender, and she slows again. Trees line the gravel road.

White fences mark the boundaries and separate the fields. The large stone farmhouse sits beyond a round gravel entrance. Its thatched hip roof is dotted with chimneys losing smoke. In the center, a red door is flanked by multiple shuttered windows. The shutters are red, matching the door. Daisies and forget-me-nots grow wild around the base of the home.

"Woah, lassie," Jo coaxes, and the carriage halts.

I pick up my skirts, heart racing. The door opens, and I descend the carriage steps. Jo smiles at me before giving me a wink.

"I'll be back before sundown, Miss Serena. You enjoy your day, lass."

"I will," I gush, pecking a kiss to the old man's cheek. His smile blooms, and he steps back. I wave as I walk for the front door. The low, rowdy woof of Rufus is followed by footsteps. Then, Theo opens the door. "You made it!"

"Yes." I look at his riding boots, then at the pair of breaches and blouse in his hands. "Are those for me?"

"Come in. Before we go, Mother wants to say hello." He ushers me inside. Beth, Theo's little sister, rushes me, wrapping her arms around my waist.

"Hello, Beth." I squeeze her tight.

"Mother won't let me ride with you and Theo!"

"Oh, perhaps next time?" I offer.

"I am old enough, you know." She pouts, setting her fists to her hips. Her eight-year-old face screws up hilariously, and she huffs before walking to the drawing room and slumping onto a lounger.

"Is that you, Serena?" Mrs. Davies calls out.

"Yes, ma'am." I walk into the sitting room, and she pats the lounge beside her. I submit, resting my hands in my lap. She looks me over for a moment before smiling.

"I am unsure whether my son has told you this as yet or not. You are always welcome in our home." She pats my hands. "And so you know, this house is always a safe haven for those who need one." Studying my face, she tilts her head. How can she be so kind to me, yet my own mother so cruel?

"Thank you, Mrs. Davies. I am grateful for your kindness." I try to force a smile, but the feeling of being cared for overwhelms me and I struggle to keep my face composed.

Her hand cups my cheek. "My dear, you are so very precious to my Theo. Please come to us, if you ever feel the need. Promise me this."

I nod, and a tear runs down my cheek. My heart aches with hurt and love all at once. I steady my breaths. "Thank you."

"Nothing in this world lasts forever. It will get better, my girl."

I clap a hand over my mouth, and she pulls me into a hug, so tight, so warm, my heart almost cracks. A voice clears in the doorway and her soft arms release me. Theo stands, whip in hand, Rufus by his side, a smile so wide his eyes are lit up for days.

This is what family is supposed to be like.

Mrs. Davies rights herself, sitting back in the lounge and straightening her skirts. Her light brown hair and green eyes, like her son's, are so familiar. I rise from the seat and walk to where Theo waits. He stands taller than me and fills the doorway well. The clothes still rest in his hands, and I slide them into mine, our fingers brushing.

My heart flips in my chest, warmth spreading even with

his lightest touch. His smile falters, eyes darkening for a moment. "Follow me, Seri."

I follow down the hall to a quest room. By the bed are riding boots, a riding jacket made from fine navy velvet, and a matching vest.

"Oh, you have thought of everything, Thee."

He leans down, and his lips brush my ear. "Meet you in the stables."

His words touch my neck and then his warmth disappears, taking with it the last of my breath. I turn my head to reply, but he is already out the door, and his footsteps fade down the hall toward the back of the house.

I shut the bedroom door and place my bag on the bed with the clothes. I fumble with my laces for a moment before finally gripping the ends to release the bow. The second the tight boned encasement loosens, my lungs expand. No corsets needed here. I tug my dress down, dragging the skirts beneath it to the floor.

I stand only clad in undergarments for a moment and run my fingers across the rich navy velvet of the jacket. Its tails are adorned with silver thread. Vines and flowers making up the shimmering trim. My long hair tickles my shoulders. I guess I could ask for a ribbon to tie it up?

I slide the pants on. The blouse next, it fits me well. I ensure the laces at my decolletage are done up and tuck it into the pants before fastening them. The clothes are so light, and freeing, compared to the corset. This house, these people, this family are the riding clothes, welcoming and comfortable. My mother is like a corset. Restricting, harsh, and unbending. What I wouldn't give to leave the corset behind and live amongst the blouses and pants?

I giggle at the ridiculous notion and pluck up the vest. It covers the cream blouse easily and I do up the three silver buttons. It is soft and comfortable. I love it. Hanging over one side of the left boot are gray wool socks. I sit on the bed and pull on each one. I tuck the pants into the socks, the way I have seen Joseph do over the years and slide on the black riding boots. The supple leather is like an embrace on each leg.

I stand up and turn from side to side, inspecting my shape and the fit of the unfamiliar attire. With these clothes, I can see my curves. But I feel almost powerful in pants. I take the jacket from the bed. It slides on easily and I do up the buttons at my waist.

A mirror leans by the silky oak dresser on the other side of the canopy bed. I walk to it and check everything is done up and tucked in. My dark locks fall around my shoulders. Navy suits them well.

A soft knock lands on the bedroom door, and I walk over and open it. Beth hovers with a handful of ribbons. "Mama said you would need your hair up." She offers the ribbons. Her face is still pouty with disappointment.

"Would you be able to help me?"

She looks up as a smile floods her face. "Could I?"

"Absolutely! I have no idea about the hair requirements for horseback riding. You can do that for me."

She ushers me to the bed, and I sit side saddle so she can get to my hair. She plops on the bed behind me, gathering up my hair with her hands. "Are you and Theo going to get married?"

I still, huffing a small laugh at her directness. "I don't know. Would you want me for a sister?"

Her hands still.

I turn back to face her. Her face is lit up with excitement. "Yes!"

"Well, if he asks, I will be sure to say yes." I leave out the part where we have already talked about it. And the part where he tried to ask me and my mother interrupted. The part where I know in my heart, she will never allow it. That part hurts the most.

It scares me the most.

"Quickly, turn around so I can finish," Beth says.

I turn back and my face falls. Everything I want is under this roof. Everything I can't have. My chest tightens, and a stone lodges in my throat. Tears burn behind my eyes. I suck in a deep breath, willing them to disappear.

"All done!" Beth chirps.

I wipe my face, hoping to rid the tears and sorrowful thoughts in a few subtle motions. Beth dashes to the dresser and returns with a hand mirror. She holds it up so I can see. My hair is up, the ribbon delicately woven into my hair. Some strands are loose. It is as elegant as it is practical.

"Do you know where the stables are?" she asks.

"Thank you," I say, touching my hair before meeting her gaze. "I have an idea. Perhaps you can walk with me?"

She jumps on the spot, clasping her hands in front of her. "Yes!"

I crook my arm, offering it to her like her brother does for me. She giggles and loops hers through mine. We pad down the hall to the back door. Through the garden, growing all sorts of vegetables and herbs, along the gravel path, we walk. In step, arm in arm.

Rows of light fabric are propped up over the garden beds. Her father is bent over tending the garden, his large floppy hat obscuring his face. He rises, sinking a hand into his lower back before waving to us.

"Miss Serena! Theo mentioned you were visiting today."

"Hello, Mr. Davies."

Beth hurries me along, and we walk out the small white wooden gate nestled in the fence and turn right. The stables stand behind a row of ancient oaks. The red painted building is a stark contrast to its green surroundings. Theo waits by the open double doors of the stables, two horses stands either side of him, their reins in his left hand. One black. One dapple-gray.

Beth releases my arm and stops. Gravel skitters ahead of us with the movement.

"Beth?"

"On second thoughts, I'm sure my brother would like to see you alone." She walks backward, waving before turning and running back into the garden to her father.

I walk to Theo and his eyes lower to mine.

"What was that all about?" I ask.

"Beth is terrified of horses. She likes the idea of riding. However, the horses themselves give her quite the fright. You look magnificent, Seri."

Heat flushes my face, and I drop my attention to the polished black boots. I run my eye up the man before me, his black boots topped with brown leather. The pants hugging his legs. The dark riding jacket, cut slightly higher than his waist. The contrasting vest and the collar sitting up with a stiff peak. Above it, his angled jaw and cheeky smile. Lit up green eyes bore into me. His brown hair is ruffled, with some of it falling over his forehead. The pang from earlier returns. How can I lose him? How can I choose someone else over Theo?

He closes the distance between us. It's then I see the picnic basket on the gravel behind him. His hands find my face. I try to school my quivering chin and fail.

"Seri, look at me."

I can't. Every time I do, the pain intensifies.

He lifts my chin with a hand, the other takes one of mine. "No thinking. Let's ride. See where Mother Nature takes us."

I nod, still not meeting his gaze.

He drops something in my hands. I stare at two thin brown lines. Tracking my focus along them, I find the bridle of the black horse. A black horse for a shadow witch. How fitting.

"Dunstan here is an old hand at green riders. He will take care of you," Theo says.

I roll my eyes at him. Like it is the first time I have ridden. He whistles, and Rufus bounds down the gravel toward us. I bend down and greet him. He almost knocks me over with his enthusiastic and slobbery affections. Theo's hearty laugh echoes off the barn and my heart is set to burst.

"Good boy," I whisper to Rufus. We have a common goal, to make sure his master, my Theo, is happy. Loved. I want to be that for him more than anything.

Saddle leather creaks behind me and I turn to see Theo mounted. He is tying the basket to the back of the saddle with leather straps. I lift the reins over Dunstan's neck and grip the saddle. In one swift movement, I am up in the saddle. I thank the heavens above it is not one of those outdated sidesaddles and gather up the reins, copying Theo's hold on his horse. Joseph taught me to ride when I was a girl. But it has been years since I was astride, and Tender was a patient teacher.

"Where would you like to go, Seri? Fields or stream?"

The warm sunshine heats my neck and face as I glance around the pristine estate.

"Stream please."

Rufus barks. As if he understands the word. I laugh at him and Theo presses his horse forward. I do the same. Rufus trots in between the two horses as we walk out into the emerald-green field toward the forest.

Our riding coats hang over a low branch. The bubbles of water over stones and the constant splashing of Rufus snapping at the water as it tosses and turns its way past him lulls me into a doze. My head is on Theo's lap. He traces patterns over my forehead, down my temples, and around my cheeks. I breathe him in. His warmth. His scent.

This moment. Perfect.

His finger slows, brushing my lips. I resist the urge to bite him playfully.

"Seri?"

"Mhmm?" The sound is almost too quiet. I don't want to ruin this moment.

I hear him swallow.

I open my eyes. His are dark.

His face slackens as his chest heaves above me. I sit up and shuffle closer. "What is it?"

His hands wander to my neck, sweeping around the back before his fingers untangle the ribbons from my hair.

Oh . . .

My heart flings against my ribs. My breathing quickens as heat pools low in my belly. Rufus pauses his game, as if sensing something has shifted, but glances our way before snapping at the water in between barks.

"I know we're not supposed to—" he starts.

I press a finger to his lips and his breath falters. He swallows, his Adam's apple bobs and whispers my name. I close my eyes. That right there, my name in his whisper, is my undoing. I sit up onto my knees, heels under my seat, and run a hand through his hair. In the middle of nowhere, surrounded by countryside, nobody is going to see us here.

He closes his eyes with my touch. His hair is soft and luscious. I trail one hand around the back of his head and then toward his jaw, the other tracking over the bridge of his nose, descending to his lips. I trace each one, left to right. With the tip of my finger, I push his bottom lip down. The smile blooming over my face stretches it. He groans and my smile melts as my lips part. I dot a kiss to the tip of his nose.

It's too much.

We should stop.

I should stop.

Much further and I won't be able to keep myself from taking what I want. What I've always wanted. With the thought, I drop my hands to my lap. When my touch doesn't return, Theo opens his eyes. Searching my face, he takes my face in his hands, running a thumb over my lips.

"Heavens above, Seri."

"Thee, we can't—"

"Shhhh."

He pecks a kiss to my lips. Then hesitates, inches from my face. "Let me love you, Seri. Nothing else."

"Alright," I rasp. My body is on fire. I am sure the only cure is Theo. "I—"

He tracks kisses down my neck. Fingers tugging at the ties of my blouse, his hands push it aside as he goes. My chest heaves under his touch. Heat floods to my core. Every breath is too short.

"Thee—"

"Tell me to stop," he utters, pressing a kiss onto my skin above my now heavy, aching breasts.

I couldn't even if I wanted to. I can barely catch my breath. I cup his jaw with both hands and raise his head, allowing him to meet my gaze.

"Do you want me to stop, Seri?" he whispers.

I shake my head. No.

Please, God, never.

"Are you alright?" he asks.

"Yes," I whisper. "But I—"

"You can tell me."

I close my eyes. Drawing breath, like one draws courage. "I am not—I mean she won't—We can't—" Tears choke out the words in my throat. I hate this. I love Theo. I want Theo. Not some wealthy suitor to better my existence. I don't care about good standing in the inner circles of London. I want a life with the man in front of me. Be it a poor one or a wealthy one. A life without him would be the cruelest sentence.

"Leave your mother to me, I will make her see reason. It will be alright."

He has no idea what she is capable of. Nor how vicious she can be when her plans are not met. I shrug, not able to raise my eyes to his. He makes space between us, his face crumpling with concern and hurt, maybe confusion.

"She will never allow it. She will never allow us to be—" A sob steals the last of my words. A tear tracks down my cheek. I try to hold my composure. To not let him see my heartbreak. I close my eyes, hoping he will distance himself further.

It's better for him this way. Better for his family. I twist the now untucked blouse in my hands and the ache in my heart grows. The burn in my core fades with the pang lancing through my heart, with the notion I'm not able to have the very thing I am so desperate for.

Warm arms sweep me from the rug, and into his velvet coat, cotton shirt and muscled chest. I sit nestled in his hold on his lap. Folded in Theo's arms, I cannot stop the deluge of sobs choking from my throat. His hand strokes my hair. He hums something low and breathy as he rocks where he sits.

Wetness splashes onto my shoulder, soaking through my tunic and onto my skin. I gasp, lifting my head to find his face. It is bent back, his eyes are closed. Tears streak down his face. His wrecked face. I clasp a hand over my mouth, watching him breathe through waves of pain.

My pain. He is feeling what I feel, our skin touching.

He is absorbing my pain.

Taking it and healing it to save me from its intensity.

Oh Theo.

I settle my breath, squashing the thoughts of despair and longing for a life without him. It burns through my skin, pushing my ribs outward with every shallow inhale, and I force them longer, slower. His face twists. I groan and grip his hands in mine.

My breath slows, my heart following. I pull up every sweet moment we have ever had, until happiness washes the dark, heady agony from my mind. He lowers his head, brows furrowed. He swallows hard, eyes piercing. Once his face relaxes, I rest my hands on his shoulders, swiveling in his lap to face him square.

"I'm sorry, Thee."

"Never apologize for loving someone so deeply." His voice is gravel.

I huff a strained moan, not allowing myself to go back there. It's not helpful, and it does not keep him or his family safe.

"I felt it, you know, how much you care for me." His jaw feathers and the silver lining his eyes swells.

"So, you know why I can't let you talk to my mother. She will not accept this—us. I cannot put you in her sights, Theo. I will not." I straighten my vest and avoid his gaze. I know what it holds. If it is anything like the ruin I'm reeling in right now, it will be racked with devastation.

He stares at me and shifts on his seat. I slide from his lap and look toward the trees. I hate myself right now. For pushing him away. For being her daughter. For being the one to say no to what we have. Theo rises and wanders into the forest downstream.

I swallow back the torture of seeing him walk away from me. Rufus notices him winding off through the trees and lopes through the water toward his master. Rufus will always try to protect his master. I smile, but it fades. I lie on the rug as white fluffy clouds float past. The odd shaped parcels drift over the forest surrounding me. A bird sails by under the ceiling of floating white. The horses shuffle on their feet, tied to the trees behind me, chewing at their bits, nickering with contentment.

Rufus barks, loud and erratic from a distance.

I sit up and scan the woods for Theo's figure. Nothing.

I push from the rug. The midday sun warms my back. I toss the vest onto the rug and wander toward the forest. I follow the bank of the stream. Picking my way through the tufts of grass and stones. Rufus barks again, excited this time. I pick up the pace and slip into the forest at the tree line.

The shaded forest is cooler, and gooseflesh covers my arms. I hug my body, walking over the mossy ground. A few moments later, I find Theo leaning against a tree by the stream bank. He is tossing small stones into the water. Rufus is splashing about, hunting for them, fruitlessly.

I stop mere feet from him. He doesn't look at me.

"Thee, I'm sorry. I didn't mean for you to carry my burden."

He doesn't respond, tossing another stone into the turbulent water. Rufus barks, snapping at the water.

I close the space between us. His jaw is tense as it feathers.

I rest my hand on his upper arm. His eyes close.

"Theo?"

After a long moment, he opens his eyes and turns to face me. I drop my hand from his arm.

"I don't understand why you will not even consider trying, Serena."

Serena. Not Seri.

A lump rises in my throat.

"Of course I want to try. I am also acutely aware of what my mother is capable of. And I will not see you hurt or worse, because we got on the wrong side of her."

"You talk about me like I am helpless." He turns to face the stream again. I step in front of him, putting myself between him and the stream, forcing him to look at me.

"You are. Against her, you are. You do not know the things she's done. The people she has—"

I shove my hands through my hair, now flowing freely down my back and around my shoulders. Why won't he listen to me? I groan and meet his gaze. Now, it's turned to concern. "She will punish you, just for this, for today, should she find out."

His eyes widen and his lips part.

I step back and turn to walk away. His hand grabs my arm. I spin back. He is shaking his head, eyes pinched with worry. He closes the distance between us and takes my face in his hands. His mouth finds mine, hungry and urgent. I all but sob against his lips. Wanting him this much, and knowing I can never keep him, splits my heart in two. Like an axe to a weather-beaten stump. It shatters.

I break from the kiss and stalk back toward the picnic, the horses. I need to get away from him. The only way to keep him safe is to be nowhere near him. Until my mother is out of the picture, there is no Thee and Seri.

I bundle up the picnic and tie it onto the back of my horse, the way Theo did earlier. I toss my jacket over my shoulders and shove my left foot into the stirrup. I throw myself up into the saddle and pull the reins toward home, sinking my heels into Dunstan's sides.

He takes off over the fields. Tears, hot and rapid, stream across my temples and into my unbound hair. Wind whips my face as the horse underneath me thunders toward home. I scream, letting the agony of everything I love slipping through my fingers loose into the warm midday air. May the sun burn it before it reaches the ground.

The steady gait of my ride keeps pace with my heart. We reach the end of the fence, and I turn him, heading toward the red barn, now visible over the last of the shallow undulations of the field. Somewhere in the distance, I hear Rufus bark. I hope he stayed with Theo.

Pulling on the reins, I slow Dunstan as we close in on the barn. I swing down from the saddle and lead him inside. Tears still flowing, I fumble the girth with blurred, trembling fingers. The horse shifts on his feet, his muzzle brushes my leg as if he senses my pain. He knows the loss. I finally release the buckles on the girth and tug the tack from his back. Steam rises from his hot body. Tides of sweat outline where the saddle sat.

I turn back to drop the saddle onto the wooden bench in the stable area of the barn. Swift hands snatch it from me. Theo dumps the saddle into the straw by his feet and grips my shoulders, eyes burning. His horse wanders, reigns dragging over the ground outside the stable. Rufus trots around the gray horse, panting.

Thee walks me backward until I hit the timber wall of the barn. He is in my space a second later. His breath labors. He rode hard. His green eyes are dark and serious.

"Seri, we are not over because your mother disapproves." His voice is raw and his Adam's apple bobs.

"How can we be together, tell me how?" My words are harsh, too loud. I don't care.

I don't get to care. I don't get a say in my life.

"England isn't the only country in this godforsaken world. Run with me. We can go anywhere. Anywhere you want."

"But—"

He's right. If she can't find us, she can't hurt Theo.

Maybe it could work . . .

His finger presses against my lips. "No thinking. That simply gets you in trouble. We leave tonight. Go pack your things. Say you want a life with me as much as I want one with you, and we shall simply disappear." He grabs my face with both hands, rougher than he usually is. The second his hungry mouth finds mine, I know.

I can't live without him. I part my lips, and he claims my mouth. He deepens the kiss, and I melt against the barn wall. I press my hands to his chest and let them wander lower and lower. He groans into my mouth when I slip one hand under his shirt. His hardness presses against my center and I ache for more of him.

A voice clears by the front of the barn. Theo presses his forehead to my own before making space between us. Mr. Davies hovers in the doorway, Theo's horse's reigns in his hands, a crooked smile on his face. "How was the picnic, you two?"

Theo offers his hand, and I push off the wall and step beside him.

"It was good, thank you, Father."

"Did you enjoy the countryside, Miss Serena?"

"I did, thank you. It's beautiful," I manage breathlessly.

He nods and holds his hand out further. Theo steps over and takes the reins from them.

"If that brute eats any more of my silver beet, I'll flail the hide from your bones, young man." Mr. Davies glances between the gray horse and his son.

"Yes, sir," Theo says, trying to flatten a smile.

Mr. Davies waves and wanders back to his garden, shutting the small wooden gate firmly behind him. Theo walks his horse into a stable and I go back to Dunstan, rubbing him down with straw and removing his bridle, replacing it with the barn side ties on his leather halter.

"Where do you want to go, Seri?"

I smile. Where in the world? The prospect of starting over sparks excitement. "Anywhere you want. France?"

His head pops around the door of my stall. "You want to go to the land of our most recent enemy?"

"Well, they are not enemies now. Plus, wouldn't it be the last place an English woman would look for her lost daughter?"

Theo's smile, stretching his gorgeous face, is stuck on. "You may have a point there. It is supposed to be the most romantic city in the world. What better place to get married than Paris?"

My hands still on the bridle in my hands. I lift my gaze to his and he pads to where I stand. I stare, mouth agape. His smile widens and his hands relieve me of the bridle. He bends down, his lips by my ear. "I refuse to live without you. Marry me, Seri."

"I—" My heart flings against my ribs. The air long vanished from my lungs, I choke out a response but the words break.

He presses a kiss to my neck, his hands land on my hips, and his grip tightens. "I mean it, Serena." He whispers between kisses. I glance toward the garden where his father is bent over his vegetable patch.

"Theo Bartholomeus Davies," I utter, disbelief lines my tone, but wonder and delight fuels it.

He lifts his head and meets my gaze. "Yes? Is that a yes?"

For a heartbeat, uncertainty flashes through his eyes, followed by pure desperation. My heart skips a beat. Our hearts are so entangled. The notion of us being apart is unforgivable.

"Of course it's a yes, Thee. But I want to give you something first, the only thing I have to give . . . It has always been yours," I say, the last part a whisper.

"You don't have to give me a thing, Seri. Just you will always be all I will ever need."

I smile and grab his hand, dragging him to the ladder leading to the loft. "Up you go."

He plants a kiss on my forehead and throws me a quizzical glance before ascending the stairs. I follow him up. Every step higher, my heart thumps harder. I have thought about this since the day Theo told me he wanted us to be married one day.

We were so young.

Even then, I knew I wanted my soul to be his. My courses finished two days ago, so I have this window of time to do this for him. As I reach the top of the ladder, Theo is sitting amongst the hay, his coat lying beside him, his vest undone. His knees up and his hands on the hay at his sides. His focus never leaves me as I step over the last rung and walk to where he sits.

The angled ceiling of the barn is inches from my head. The air in the loft is warmer than below and outside. I pull the jacket from my shoulders and let it fall to the hay at my feet.

He swallows when my fingers release the buttons on my vest. His eyes wander over the skin showing up my neck, and then study my face. His green eyes darken, and his breathing quickens. I tug the boots from my feet. And step between his knees in just pants, blouse and socks. He holds up his hands and I take them.

"Kneel, Seri," he rasps.

I drop to my knees. Our faces are only inches apart, his fingers tremble as he undoes the ties on my blouse. I send my hands behind his neck and up into his hair. His mouth curves into a loving smile. He is perfect. So perfect. Sitting up taller, he presses kisses to my collarbones, then up my neck. I close my eyes, losing a soft moan. His fingers are still on the blouse and his forehead drops onto my chest.

"Thee?" I breathe.

"Mhmm."

I huff a heavy, strained laugh. "Please, I need to give you everything. I—we have waited so long."

"God, I know, Seri. I want it to be perfect."

I lift his head with both hands and brush my lips across his. "This is perfect, please, don't stop."

I kiss his mouth. His tongue parts my lips and I open for him. I trace my fingers over the curves of his chest under his shirt. I drop both hands to his pants and loosen them. He breaks from the kiss, and I tug at his pants. His warm, hard length strains against his undergarments when I run my fingers over it. The heat of it, even through the fabric, grows something similar low in my belly. With quick hands, my tunic is off and on the straw. Theo sends a thumb over each peaked, aching nipple and my breath stops.

I whimper a moan.

His hands pull my supports down, and his mouth is on

my nipple. Hungry, hot, and greedy. My center throbs for him. I palm his hard length, trying to shove his pants from his hips. He moves to his knees to allow me access and I push them down with his undergarments. His hard erection stands, the tip glistening. My heart beats against my ribs. Like any minute now, I will combust.

My skin is on fire.

My core molten.

My breath burns with each quick movement.

"Theo . . ."

"Let me love you, Seri."

He guides me onto the hay and makes quick work of my pants, undergarments, and socks until I lie bare in the hay. He runs his stare from my toes to my head. "God on earth, you are stunning."

Emotion closes over my throat. All I want is for us to be joined. To feel him. His weight on me. To be wrapped in his hold. He crawls over me and kisses my lips briefly. "Where would you like me to love you first?" The most beautiful smile stretches his cheeky face. His eyes are dark, one arm holding him over me, the other hand caresses my jaw.

"I just want you," I breathe.

He groans. "No, pick a spot, or I will choose."

"You chose then."

I can barely breathe, let alone make such choices at this moment.

Every set of eyes in the lecture theater has scanned Lewis and me, at least a few times. Heat prickles my neck. I shift in my seat and try to ignore them. Lewis continues his lecture as if they don't exist. Easy for him to do, they're not literally breathing down his neck from behind.

One girl snickers and whispers to her friend. I can't hear their conversation properly, but the words affair and extra-credit reach my ears. Ugh, what I wouldn't give to toss a fire ball over my head in this very moment.

"Did you hear what they were saying in his other classes? Apparently, they have been together for months. God, so gross," a girl whispers.

Lewis stills, looking up from his laptop, his hand frozen on the slide clicker.

Oh shit.

I try to meet his gaze, but his eyes burn into the girl's one row back to my left. Anger and frustration flood my veins. It's not mine.

"Something you would like to share with the class, Miss Howard?" Lewis snaps.

He never snaps. The last time he showed any sign of annoyance was when he called me out in class for the first time. Having your mortal enemy in your space would do that, I suppose. Then things turned much more complicated. Now, with this girl behind me insulting our bond, Lewis looks ready to break her in half.

"What's his problem?" a guy in the row in front of me utters to his friend.

Lewis closes his eyes. The plastic clicker in his fist cracks.

Heat flows through my veins. This time, it's all mine. I lean forward between their heads.

"Hey!" I whisper coarsely. "Shouldn't you be paying attention?"

They jerk away, but their widened eyes stare at me.

"Holy shit, she really is with him!" the girl from before hisses.

I turn back to see her face scrunched with disgust. My lungs heave through shallow breaths. Something animalistic snaps. How dare she attack Lewis?

My mate.

I stand and stalk down the row to the aisle. She laughs

at me. My hands curl to fists and warmth flickers across my palms.

"Well, this lecture just got interesting." A guy chuckles to his friend, she sits rigid beside him, her attention on my hands.

Fuck.

A hand touches my shoulder.

Instantly, the pent-up anger ebbs. I turn to find Lewis. He forces a smile but gestures for me to sit down in my chair. His body is tense. His eyes burn into me, as if he is merely holding himself together.

"Take a seat, Miss Williams," Lewis says. His voice is low, rough.

I nod, wiping my palms against my jeans. I walk back to my seat and slump into it. Closing my eyes, I run my hands through my hair before dragging them down my face. Why do people have to be so mean? Like it is any of their business what two consenting adults do off campus.

Lewis continues the lecture but wraps it up early. He dismisses the class, but one brunette girl hangs back. I make a show of packing up my things and listen as she approaches him. He's packing away his laptop and turning off the smart board when she reaches him, almost pinning him to the front wall of the lecture theater.

My grip around my notebook tightens. She adjusts the strap over her shoulder and tilts her head, one hand on her hip. "I could get you fired for interfering with a student, you know."

Annoyance floods my veins. His.

He leans down so his mouth is by her ear. I clench onto the notebook, heart thundering, bitterness squeezes my heart.

He whispers something to her, and she flinches, making distance between them. What did he say?

She lifts her chin and glances at me before huffing a laugh. "Is that supposed to be a threat?"

"It's whatever you decide it to be, Miss Howard. I don't want to see you in my class again. Transfer to another second-year subject, or I will do it for you."

She opens her mouth to retaliate, and he closes the distance between them and spins her on her feet to face the door. "Get out of my lecture theater, now!"

Her face crumples and her chin wobbles as she stalks through the door of the theater and into the dull sunshine. I finish packing my things and walk down the stairs to where he stands, leaning on the podium, watching me move closer. Arms crossed, his mouth pulls up into a lopsided smile. How can he be so calm?

"Lew, what did you do?"

"I simply reminded her of her place in the world. Nothing more."

"Oh, I don't want to know." I laugh.

"Would you like to know where yours is, Miss Williams?" he says, dropping his arms.

"I'm afraid to ask, but I'm guessing you are going to tell me, anyway."

He huffs a gravelly laugh and pulls me into my arms. "Your place is wherever I am. Mine is wherever you are, Sunshine."

Having Lewis this close, talking like that, floods me with want. His eyes light up. He felt that. Of course he did. His lips nip and kiss up my neck and over my jaw. His hands tangle between my blonde curls, pushing and pulling their way through. I rest my hands on his hard chest, short of breath. "I have to meet Serena for lunch."

"I think you are going to be late, Miss Williams."

He finds my mouth with his, and I open for him. He slides both hands under my bottom, and I am on his hips a second later. He deposits me on the lecture bench.

"God, Sunshine. I can feel everything you feel." His eyes have darkened.

"Me too," I breathe. The need flooding my body right now is overwhelming. Emotion chokes me up. He needs me that much? I close my eyes as a strangled laugh, sounding more like a sob, slips past my lips. "Lewis."

He pays me no heed.

I relent and lay my head back, arching into him. Giving him what he wants so desperately. His hand slides under my shirt and sweater and I moan. His canines descend, and I channel wind between us. I don't want to. I want nothing between us. No wind. No clothes. No nosy students.

Nothing.

The door to the lecture theater rattles under a knock. I tense up and grab Lewis's shoulders. He didn't hear it?

"Lewis, someone is at the door."

"Hmmm," he rumbles.

"Lew, the door."

He snaps his head up and his eyes fade to brown, his canines disappear upward. His phone vibrates in his bag. He grips it in one hand a second later; the screen lit up.

Dean.

The Dean?

Shit.

Lewis slides a finger across the screen and answers. "Hello."

I slide off the bench and wrap my arms around me, as if that can protect me from the Dean's wrath. Lewis is listening intently. He frowns. His hand rubs over his forehead and his hair falls over his face as he dips it, sighing. I hold my breath. What? What is it?

"I'll be there in five minutes."

He hangs up and forces a smile.

"What did he say?"

"The girl who was just here went straight to the Dean. I have to go, Sammie. I'll see you at home." He grabs his bag and presses a kiss to my forehead. My gut sinks. Something is off. My intuition is rarely wrong.

"Lewis? Do you want me to go with you?"

"I doubt it will help. It's okay Sammie, I'll see you at home." His gaze lingers on my face before he turns and walks through the door. We're busted, and it's all my fault. I should have ignored her. I never should have responded, let alone let myself get wound up. This bond is driving me crazy. Anything threatening Lewis has me seeing red. I barely have a scrap of control over it. I bury my head in my hands and scream.

Feeling somewhat defeated, I wander to the cafeteria. I push through the glass door to the communal eating area, and I swear every set of eyes in this place is on me. Serena sits at our usual table to the left of the door. I walk over and dump my bag on the seat, plopping into the one opposite her.

"You burn someone at the stake, bestie?" she whispers, as she scans the room.

"Something like that. Do they have to stare, really? What is this, high school?"

I roll my eyes and Serena laughs. "I guess they will grow up, eventually. Don't let them get to you, babes."

"How was class?" I ask.

"Great, very interesting. I can't believe I waited this long to study, I really enjoy it."

"Um, like, what was college like last century, anyhow? I think you started at the right time." I shake my coat off and hang it over the back of my chair. Serena pushes a tray of something savory and steaming over to me. I pluck the cutlery from the tray and dive into the hot, delicious goodness.

"Actually, study until now hasn't been an option, with all my family drama."

She says it so casually, but I know firsthand exactly what

family drama for Serena entails. I'm happy for her to finally be in a place where she can do something for herself for once. We eat fast and make our way to the library next. I have no other classes today, but Serena has an afternoon lecture. We kill an hour in the quiet space surrounded by the few occult texts the college has in their collection. Discussing the realities versus the text proffered information. Some are spot-on, but most are based on myth or haphazard guesses, I assume. Their take on vampires and witches is shallow at best.

My phone pings.

It's Denver.

I swipe the notification, and it opens.

> Hey Sammie, can you come home? Lewis just got here and something happened. He left the car for you. Keys are under the seat.

My stomach flips. Lewis went to the Dean's office.

> Be home in twenty.

"I have to go home, Rena. Something's happened with Lew. I'll see you later?"

"Shit, is he okay?"

"Yeah, I think it's about us, college. You know . . ."

She cringes and groans. "Hope everything is okay."

I wave goodbye and jog to the parking lot. The crisp day

turns each breath into a puff of smoke. But I don't feel cold. Only annoyance, frustration, and worry. All mine. Something that isn't mine crawls slowly through me, calm. How can he be calm? I fumble for the keys and drop into the driver's seat. Firing up the mustang, I shift the stick into reverse. She rumbles backward, and I slam the stick into drive and sink my foot, like I've seen Lewis do so many times.

Twenty minutes later, I am pulling into the garage. I kill the engine and rush inside. Denver sits on the sofa with Lewis. They're drinking their whiskey and laughing. What is going on?

"Lew?" I ask from the foyer, pulling my bag over my shoulder and dropping it onto the floor. I pull my coat off and shove it on the brass hook. He's in my space a beat later. Whiskey lines his breath. He kisses my lips, and I savor the taste of him. Worry floods my veins. His pleasant whiskey face is a facade.

"What is it?"

"Nothing really." He steps back and traces my face with his fingers. "I just . . . I won't be working at the university anymore."

"What?!" I grab the hand touching my face, as my eyes widen and search his.

"They didn't see a reason for me to stay after two reports of—"

"Reports of what?"

"The Howard girl, apparently it wasn't the first time she reported us to the Dean."

It wasn't. Serena followed her the first time. She was adamant the girl would drop it. She should have dropped it. I really made things worse. My breath quickens, and my heart slams into my ribs. Lewis shakes his head and moves closer. "Hey, it wasn't your fault, Sammie. None of this is your fault. Stop that thought right now."

I look away. "Serena saw her, the first time. We really thought she would let it go."

"It doesn't matter, Sunshine. As long as you're not affected and get to keep your place and scholarship, I am happy to take this one. It's not like I need the money, or the attitude." His face cracks with a cheeky smile. He's trying to be funny, to lighten the mood.

I push past him and stalk to where Denver now stands by the sofa. "Can we fix this? So Lewis gets his job back?"

"I don't think there is anything to fix, Sammie." Denver tilts his head in a sympathetic gesture.

"What, why not? They can't just take her word for it!"

"You heard what my brother said, Sammie. He doesn't want it, not if it means you lose your place at the college."

I spin back to Lewis. He's just shy of the foyer. "You had to choose your job or me?"

He swallows.

"Lewis, tell me you didn't have to choose," I whisper as I close the space between us. He studies my face for a moment. Love and adoration and a fraction of amusement weave their way into my core.

Dammit.

"I'd choose you every time, Sunshine."

Tears burn behind my eyes. I blow out a low breath. Of course he would. He won't even fight for the life he spent decades building. Because of me.

Denver's footsteps close in behind me. He's close, his scent tangles around me from behind. His breath drifts over my head. I almost feel him when he runs a hand through his hair and sighs. I spin back, my body inches from Den's.

Lewis moves in closer until I am pinned between the two of them.

I stare up at Denver. His hazel eyes are stunning, all grays, blues and greens with tiny nicks of yellow. His square jaw feathers. Desire and happiness chase the previous sensation of adoration in my veins. It's Lew's.

I rest a trembling hand tentatively on Denver's chest and lean back into Lewis. His lips drop beside my ear.

"I love you, Sunshine. You are worth every sacrifice."

I close my eyes. His hand slides around my stomach under my sweater. The other sweeps my hair from my neck and shoulders as he litters kisses over my neck, his teeth grazing my skin.

Denver's eyes darken, his body completely still and rigid, all but his heaving breaths. Want pools low in my belly as I search Denver's face, with Lewis behind me, touching my skin, kissing my neck.

The air in my lungs is too shallow.

Spots invade the sides of my vision and my hands tingle.

I push out from between the two brothers. I try to swallow back the stone in my throat, but emotion chokes me instead. I need to get out of here.

"I'm sorry." I pluck my coat from the hook and rush through the door and into the forest. I run, heaving through every burning breath. I run for what seems like an age. My legs burn. My lungs burn. My hands shake. I drop onto the damp, leafy forest floor and scream into my hands.

My mother once told me, our hearts stretch with every person we love, that it's infinite and not fixed. This is how a mother can love all of her children so deeply, so fiercely, she had told me. And maybe, how a woman can love more than one man. How a person can live a life rich in love and ties. Love is undeniable and the world's greatest force. It's courage, heart, and selflessness forged into one.

A stick snaps behind me. I wipe my face and push to my feet.

Denver's tortured eyes meet mine. I stay stuck to the spot. I don't know what to say to him. How to say all the things I want him to know? All the things I want him to understand. Lewis is my mate. I adore him. I love him with every fiber of my being. The instinct to protect him is overwhelming. But . . .

I know what Lewis wants. The three of us. Whether that's for my benefit or his brother's, I haven't figured out yet.

Knowing Lew, it's both.

Denver steps closer. "Sammie. I didn't mean to scare you."

"You didn't." It's the truth. He doesn't scare me, not at all. Despite him being the older, rougher brother, I have never felt scared in his presence. Vampire or not, Denver's always felt like more of a grounding force than anything else.

Dependable . . . Safe.

"Lewis chose you. You're his mate," he starts and clasps his hands behind his neck, staring through the trees. "But you're also much more than that. He loves you desperately. So much so he—" Den swallows.

"I know this, Denver."

He turns to face me, and his brows lower. "He wants you to be okay, even if he's not here."

He means if Lewis dies.

Lewis wants me to be okay if he dies. How would I ever be okay with that?

I grip my arms, swaying on my feet. "No. I would never be okay without him, Den."

He forces a smile, but his jaw clenches, and he groans, closing his eyes. "When Zah—"

He sucks in a breath and blows it out, slow. "When she was killed, it almost killed me. He's the only reason I am still here."

"He told me—" I can't finish the sentence.

"Losing your mate is worse than death. Lewis wants you to have someone with you if he ever . . ."

"You?"

He huffs a sharp laugh. "Apparently."

"Did you want someone else after Zahli?"

"I didn't want to breathe after Zahli, Sammie."

Heavens above.

"We broke the curse and the tether. What else could threaten Lewis?"

"The council will, they already know you two are together. One whiff of your mating bond and he is a dead man."

I stagger backward. I knew this. They both told me. But now, this deep into everything, it's a fresh blow. I sink to my knees. Breath leaves my lungs and doesn't return.

"Sammie?"

I clutch at my chest, willing air to return.

Spots fill my vision.

I gasp around air I can't manage to catch.

Denver's blurred figure drops to his knees in front of me.

"Sammie, breathe."

My throat tightens, and I claw at my neck.

"Fuck, Sammie."

Arms sweep me from the ground. Wind whips past me.

Sunshine blinds my already blurred vision until the comfort of home surrounds me and familiar hands find my face.

Lewis.

I turn toward the sound of his voice.

Air slips into my lungs.

Blond hair hangs so close. Something like paper closes over my mouth. Brown eyes search my face. A hand caresses my cheek. Lewis.

Lew.

"Lew?" I choke.

My shoulders snap up and down and the spots form again.

"Hey, I'm right here, Sunshine."

Lips, warm, soft and familiar, press to mine. My body relaxes instantly.

Denver paces back and forth by the fireplace, hands in his hair, arms flexing, a string of curse words splutter from his lips.

Lewis's face eclipses my view of his big brother. "I'm sorry, Sunshine."

No, not sorry. Please don't be sorry. I grab his face with both hands and pull him down to me. "D-don't you ever be sorry . . . for giving me everything," I rasp.

A wonky smile tugs at his lips, and his face sinks into my hair.

God, I love this man.

I love Denver.

How is it Lewis knows what I need before I do?

I love them both.

Theo dots kisses across my face, down my neck. I tilt my head to the side, and he nips my neck and descends to the peak of my left breast. He clamps it between his teeth and flicks it with his tongue. I arch my back off the straw. I need to be closer.

He lets the peak drag between his teeth before sucking it. Warmth floods my center, and the apex of my wet heat throbs. Heavens above. His free hand traces circles around the peak of my right breast and I moan, pushing my head back, closing my eyes.

God above, Theo Davies.

He removes his mouth from my breast and moves up over me.

Yes.

We need to be joined.

Now.

"Anywhere else you need my attention, Seri?" he rasps.

I open my eyes.

"Why did you stop?"

"We have all afternoon. I will not waste this moment by rushing it."

I smile and cup his jaw with both hands. I pull him into a kiss. Mouth open. Apex throbbing. I break the kiss, and he raises both eyebrows, as if to say well?

"You chose, Thee."

His mouth tilts to a cheeky smile. Heat flushes my neck and face. He crawls backward between my legs. I stare at the ceiling. Is he leaving?

I don't understand.

Strong arms slide under my knees. I snap my gaze between my legs. Theo is sitting on his heels, my legs hooked over the crook of his arms. "Theo, I don't—"

"Shhh. Wriggle a little closer, Seri."

I stare at him, heat flooding my face. He pulls me closer. My heart flings into my ribs. My core burns, and my apex throbs so badly I have no idea how to ease the ache. He pulls me closer, my legs spread, my wet center almost in his lap. I swallow and try to breathe.

"I want to hear you, Seri. Those sweet sounds you make. I love those."

He drops his head between my legs, and I squeak. Hands gripping the straw beside me. His tongue sweeps over my wetness and I almost die. The pleasure is too much. I moan, loud. Too loud, but I don't care.

"Good girl." His voice is gravel.

I adore it.

His tongue flickers over my throbbing apex and the ache turns to pure fire. I writhe on the bed of straw. One of his hands releases my leg and slides up to my breasts, cupping it. Another sweep of his tongue, this time deeper into my folds.

"Theo!"

"Again, Seri?"

"Yes. Please," I huff.

He chuckles. A beat later, his tongue sweeps through my folds and flickers over my apex before he suckles it. I moan continuously, arching off the straw. My grip around it burns.

More, I need more.

"Please, Thee, something—I feel set to—"

His fingers slide inside my core.

Oh, goddess above!

Sweeping around my apex, he flicks and sucks until I am writhing on the straw. Stuck in his hold, I am desperate for him to be inside me. He drags his fingers, and vibrations start everywhere in my body. Every part of me trembles. My legs shake around his hips.

"Do you want more, Seri?"

"Please, Thee."

He pumps his digits into my core, knuckles deep. Sucking and flicking my apex. His fingertips tweak my nipple and I explode around him. Courses of the most delicious agony I have ever felt start in my center and flood my body.

"Theo!" I release the straw and search for his hand. His fingers lace through mine instantly. He groans. The waves subside and I mourn the loss. I mourn his touch as he moves between my legs, taking his hands from my body, his mouth from where I want him.

I open my eyes and find his. I have never seen him look like this. He is almost ethereal. Not of this world. His eyes are dark green. His face is tense. His chest heaves. His hands gather me onto his lap. I ache to feel him inside me now.

"Come here, Seri."

I breathe through a soft, wobbly sound and rise to my knees.

"Now, my love. Now."

With his desperate words, I do as instructed and straddle his lap. I do not know what this will be like, but I know he needs me. All of me. I need to have him within me. We need to be joined. The ache that relented with the release from his mouth and fingers, builds once more.

As I breathe him in. He grips my hips and pulls me closer. His arms flex. His jaw is tight. I take his face in my palms and kiss his mouth. He guides me over him until the heat of the tip of his hard length pressing against my wet entrance.

"Are you sure, Serena?" he rasps.

"About you, Theo?"

He holds my gaze but nods.

"I am yours. I always have been. Take what you need."

He kisses me hard as his hands guide me down. I lower myself onto his swollen length. It's warm and the softest hardness I have ever felt. I sink a little lower. A sharp sting gives way to a stretch and burn. I halt, suspended halfway down.

His hands find my face, his all but wrecked.

I did that.

My heart aches with the swell that consumes it. I made this gorgeous man come undone. When the sting subsides, I lower a little further.

He groans, closing his eyes. "Seri. Oh, God."

I lower further, until every inch of him is buried deep inside me. His breathing is erratic. His grip on my hips tightens. His face transitions from wrecked to pure bliss. Heat pools low in my belly and I kiss his neck, moving in his lap with every kiss I dot on his skin. He grunts. I wriggle and he rubs against my core inside. I moan. Holy heavens, there is nothing that will ever compare to Theo moving inside me.

I wonder . . .

I rise ever so slowly until he is barely notched inside my entrance. The round head of him feels unbelievable as the last of the sting fades. I moan and he groans hard, his legs shaking underneath me. He moves, rolling slightly side to side, stretching his legs out. Every movement is like heaven.

I straddle him, still joined. He opens his eyes and searches my face for a minute. "Seri. I cannot take this much longer. You are heaven."

"You don't need to wait, Thee. Take what you need."

"I don't want to waste this moment, but you are driving me insane."

I wriggle my hips in the slightest, and he groans into the space between my breasts. "You sure know how to torture a man."

"I want to see that look on your face. Again and again."

He reaffirms his grip on my hips. "You mean this look?" He pushes me downward, slowly. I moan, breath leaving with every inch I descend. He closes his eyes, and there it is.

That wrecked face, pulled by pure bliss. I sink until the tip of him caresses my core and rise on my knees again until the round tip of his hardness is threatening to pop from my tight heat. I lower faster this time and rise to the very tip. Again.

He groans, his grip turning rough on my hips.

His body trembles.

"Seri, stop."

I don't want to. I want him to explode the way I did.

I rise and fall until he is groaning and saying my name with a low, gravel sound that sends heat to my core. Warmth pools and my apex throbs again.

I can't stop.

Theo's face changes. From bliss to agony. He clutches at his chest and his eyes snap open.

Oh, my heavens. What did I do?

No . . . Theo!

No, no, no, no.

"Theo!"

His breathing turns raspy, and I sink into his lap and still. I clasp a hand over my mouth, my other hunting his neck and face for the cause of his pain. Heavens, I broke him.

Goddess . . . No.

His pained face cracks into a tentative smile.

"What in the world?" I utter.

He relaxes and pulls me closer to him. He huffs a strained laugh into my hair.

"Thee, what happened? Did I hurt you?" I whimper.

He moans against my neck. "No, Seri."

After a moment, he pushes back and cups my face in his hands. "My bond snapped."

I shake my head.

What bond?

What is a bond?

"What does that mean?" I ask. If something snapped, is he injured?

"It means . . . I'm yours, forever."

I furrow my brows, but he simply kisses my lips, his hands wandering to my breasts. The second his fingers trace over each nipple, all thoughts of bonds and broken things disappear.

"Let me love you, Seri."

"You already do, Thee."

"Proper, please."

He thrusts, and the instant his soft tip caresses my core, I melt back into his lap.

"You must tell me of this bond I have harmed—" I desperately haul air into my lungs. "After . . ."

His teeth find my nipples, and I arch into him. He slides his hands under my bottom and lifts me up. His hardness fills my aching core is too much. My body trembles.

"God above, I love you, Serena."

"Thee, I love you too," I moan, the words breathy and hard.

He lets me fall. His tongue flicks over my nipples and warmth builds once more.

"I will love you until the end of the time, Seri."

He sucks my nipple, and his hand slides down my belly. His thumb sweeps over my apex as I rise on my knees again. I explode around him again. Crying out from the beautiful agony of release, I almost miss the twinge of lightning in my chest. I sink into his lap and something rough and vicious snaps over my heart.

"Ahhh. Thee!" I choke on my last inhale.

I grapple at the space around my left breast, whimpering through the waves of pain. His face alternates between happiness and concern. His eyes narrow as his face crumples. Tears swell in his green eyes, and he grips my face and kisses my mouth.

I sob, and a tear spills over, running down my heated cheek.

He chuckles against my lips, then breathes, "And now you are mine."

My bond snapped?

I don't understand.

He envelopes me in his warm embrace, and I huff through choked sobs as the release fades and the twang around my heart disappears.

Dressed and untangled, we lie on the straw and Theo explains the mating bond to me. Why my mother never told me of it, I will never know. Still, I am beyond thrilled mine snapped with Theo's. For a heartbeat, I think about what it would have meant if his had snapped with some other witch. The thought makes my stomach churn. Nausea climbs up my throat. I push it down and drown the thought along with it.

Theo's hand tracks patterns over my skin as we talk. Well, he talks, I listen. The mating bond means we are mated until one of us dies. I am his. And he is mine. There is no way I am letting my mother anywhere near him now.

When we finally give in to the hunger pains plaguing our stomachs, the sun has set and the aroma of stew wafts from the house coaxing us in. Theo checks my clothes and hair for straw before sliding his hand into my own. We walk back into the house. It's warm and cozy.

The harried, pacing figure of Joseph pulls me up short.

Oh no.

I had been so caught up in our plans and talking for hours, I completely forgot I was supposed to be home before dark.

I rush to the front of the house and hug Jo. He steps back and eyes me up and down, as if somehow he recognizes something is different.

"Joseph," Theo says, nodding.

"Mr. Davies, I must be getting Miss Serena home. We are past due." Jo walks outside, leaving me to my goodbyes.

I hate to leave. Especially now, but Joseph is right. As it is, Mother will be furious. I gather my belongings from the front room and bid goodbye to Theo's family. He walks me to the carriage, where an anxious Jo sits on the driver's bench. Tender fights with her bit, shaking her head. She knows too. Unease settles in my gut.

Theo rubs a thumb over the back of my hand as he helps me into the carriage. He shuts the door behind me and waves as Tender walks on and the carriage pulls down the driveway. I miss him already.

The lights are off when we get home, and Joseph's face is grim. I pluck my things from the seat and climb down from the carriage and walk inside. The lamps are off. The house is too quiet. I walk into the kitchen. The floor is littered with candles. In the middle, a pentagram is drawn up with salt.

Black candles sit at each of the five points of the star. They are almost burned down. It hasn't been too long since she did this.

Dark magic.

Heavens.

In the center sit four small dolls. Voodoo dolls. Thin needles stick from the chest and stomach of every doll. A small piece of paper adorns each doll, and a strand of hair is tied around its waist. I blow out the candles and break the salt circle with one foot. I drop to my knees and pluck up the first figure. My heart thunders, sending the blood in my veins roaring. I turn over the paper and read the name.

Beth.

My stomach turns.

I drop the doll as if it burned my hands. Cautiously, I sweep up the next one. The strand of hair is a match for Mrs. Davies.

Theresa.

I slump, staring at the remaining two dolls.

I grab the larger of the two dolls. The strand of hair is similar to Mr. Davies. I read the paper tied around its waist.

Bartholomeus.

My hands shake as I place the third one down. I don't want to pick up the last one. I already know whose name will be on it. I can't bring myself to look.

"Miss Serena? What is it?" Joseph asks softly.

"She—" I turn and lose my stomach to the floor.

Instantly, Jo's hand is on my shoulder. He steps into the

circle and picks up the last doll. His eyes go wide, and he removes his top hat and swallows.

"I'm so sorry, my girl."

I stare at the strand of hair that was in the last figure sits on the salted stone floor. It's dark. Too dark for Theo. "What does the paper say, Jo?"

I look up to meet his gaze.

"I'm so sorry, Miss Serena. It says Theo."

I snatch up the hair and roll it between my fingers. It is coarse and black. It's not Theo's, this strand belongs to Rufus. I stand and grab my bag. "Take me back now, Jo!"

We rush to the carriage. Joseph sends Tender flying along the cobblestone a moment later. My body burns, like something inside me is burning to ash, shriveling smaller and smaller with every minute that passes, and I clutch my sides. Every mile is too long. Every minute takes an hour. When the carriage wheels finally hit gravel outside Theo's house, I jump from the moving vehicle and fly through the front door, one hand clamped around the now dulled stitch in my side. The house is dark.

"Theo?!"

Rufus's bark doesn't follow this time.

My stomach plummets.

How could she do this? I will never forgive her. Our ties are severed. From this day forward, she is dead to me.

I run to Beth's room. She lies on her bed, unmoving. I pad closer. Her skin is gray. Her eyes are vacant. Her body is still. She's gone. I slap a hand over my mouth to stifle my cry. I turn and track to where Theo's parents' room is. Up the stairs and to the right.

I find them both in their bed, side by side. Both gray and unmoving. Both of them with vacant eyes. I extend a trembling hand and brush a fingertip over Mr. Davies' hand. The last of the dulled ache slips away. The bond is gone. A groan slips past my lips and I back away from their bed. I spin and run into Jo.

"Miss Serena. Let me check." Jo's hand lands on my arm.

"No," I sob and push past him. I rush to Theo's room. I turn the doorknob. It opens but doesn't budge very far. Something heavy is stopping it from opening.

"Jo," I rasp.

He walks over and helps me shove the door open. The black tail of Rufus curls around the door as it opens. Oh no. I drop to where he lies. His body is already stiff. His usually dark eyes are clouded white. I grip his black fur and whimper.

I can't breathe.

Somebody touches my shoulder. I look up to find Jo. He is staring at Theo. I can't look. I don't want to know.

Please, not my Thee.

"Miss Serena," Jo says.

I sob into my hands, sitting on the floor by Rufus.

I let the sobs pour from me. Pain crushes my heart, and I lose a strangled scream.

"Seri?" a croaky, sleep-riddled voice says.

Theo!!

I jump to my feet and rush to his bed. He sits, startled, in his bed. "What are you doing here? What happened?"

I slump to the floor by his bed, and he jumps down and crouches beside me. Torn between relief that he is alive and the next words needing to leave my mouth, I sit, suffocating through every shallow breath.

CHAPTER 25

SERENA

I clutch Theo's hand and run as fast as I can into the fields. I have to get him away from the house. Away from her reach. His heavy steps thunder behind me, as I drag him behind me, stunned. We crash through the forest, branches and bushes whipping past, leaving scratches and tears on my arms, face, and neck. I don't care. I am numb to it.

Theo groans behind me, his hand squeezing mine.

"Seri stop, please."

I slide to a halt and instantly the cool air of the winter night sinks into my trembling legs. Theo is in his sleeping attire. His loose pants, tied at the waist. His cream tunic is rumpled, the opening shows his bare chest, the sculpted muscle. His body is awash with goosebumps and tremors. The blow of seeing what happened to his family is taking its toll.

"I think I need to sit down, only for a moment." He lets go of my hand and bends to the side. He loses his stomach to the grass, sinking to his knees. His hands crawl through his hair. Ugly sobs spill from him as his shoulders shake.

"No. How could this happen?" he rasps.

I step around him and kneel on the ground at his side. His devastated eyes find mine. His jaw feathers and his chin wobbles. He sobs hard, and I cradle him into my shoulder. His arms wrap around me. For the first time since I saw the voodoo dolls lying on the floor with his family's names on them, I allow myself to comprehend what all this means.

She killed his family. She killed my family. My own mother murdered the people I love the most. A slither of worry runs through me for Jo. Will she punish him also when she finds out he has been helping me to see Theo all these years?

Theo goes still in my hold, and I push back, searching his face. He wavers on his knees, and I steady him with my hands on his arms. "Thee? We need to leave."

He swallows, and the tears that have run down his face and over his neck shine on his Adam's apple in the moon-light. My heart cracks at the sight of his shattered face. "Oh, Thee. I'm so sorry."

He shakes his head in a shallow movement. As if in disbelief.

I stand and take his hands. "We need to leave." My words are barely a whisper, but he looks up at me. Those stunning green eyes now swim beneath pools of tears. He clenches his jaw. I brush my fingers over it. He rises but hesitates.

I pull him further into the forest. Covered by the canopy and far enough in the depths of the forest, I stop and maneuver him onto a fallen tree. I pluck the pendant I have been practicing on for months and repeat the steps of time travel in my mind thrice before resting my fingers around his wrist.

I step between his legs.

His gaze meets mine.

"Do you trust me?" I choke.

"Always, Seri."

What I am about to do may or may not work, but I will not let my mother find him. Ever. I will keep him safe until the day she takes her last breath. For that moment, I will live for from this moment onward. We will be free when she is dead and buried.

I spin the center gold loop of the pendant and close my eyes, envisioning the place where she would never think to look. Where no sane Englishman would go.

France, 1722.

The ground slips from under my feet. My grip on Theo's wrist tightens. His eyes drill right through me.

"I love you, Thee."

His lips bloom into a sad smile.

Darkness swallows us.

The terrified French woman in front of me is throwing her hands around, repeating herself. She is scared.

So am I.

I spun the turner and took Theo's hand, and we ended up in provincial France, somewhere in the countryside. After a change of clothes, which we stole from some poor unsuspecting family's drying line. We stowed away on a hay cart to get to this out of the way farm and outside this tiny farmhouse.

Right now, all I want is sanctuary and somewhere for Theo to be safe. I am going back. She will not get away with this. How can I let her murder his entire family and get away with it? That will not happen.

"Maybe we should find somewhere else?" Theo says, his words weak, his stare almost as vacant as those of his dead family. My heart shatters every time I look at him. I am still reeling at how this happened. How did she even know where I was? What was going on?

I freeze.

Heavens. The bond. The one she, me, and Bartholomeus shared. She must have felt something when my bond snapped with Theo. Oh god, this is all my fault. I was the one who initiated the joining . . . I—

I swallow back the bile creeping up my throat and try to focus on the woman in front of me.

"S'il te plaît, nous avons besoin d'un endroit où rester," I beg.

My French is not perfect, but I hope the sentiment gets through, we need a place to stay. To hide.

"*Non, non!*" She glances between Theo and me, shaking her head. I notice a horseshoe nailed above her front door, upturned for good luck. She is superstitious then.

"I can tell you your future in exchange for somewhere to sleep?"

She shakes her head, waving us off.

No, we are not leaving. English or not, she is taking us in. I could persuade her to let us stay, but it would wear off in a few days and we would have the same situation on our hands. No, she needs to be convinced.

"*Je peux te dire ton avenir,*" I offer. Her future for our sanctuary.

Her mouth quiets to a thin line, and she glances into the house for a moment. "*Tu me parles de l'avenir de nos fils et tu peux rester, mais seulement une nuit.*"

One night for her *son's* future.

Deal.

"*Oui.*" It's the best we have, so I take it. I can convince her to let us stay, to let Theo stay for longer, after we get inside.

"What did she say, Seri?" Theo says.

I flinch, his voice is so strained. "She said we can stay the night. But I will convince her to let you stay longer. I have to go back." He moves his focus to the small farmhouse.

"Tell her I can do chores. Whatever work she needs done."

I relay the message to the woman. She forces a smile, nods and says, "*Je suis Marguerite. Maintenant, entrez avant que quiconque ne remarque deux Anglais devant ma porte.*"

Apparently, having two English folk outside her home for all the neighbors to see is a fate worse than most. We wander inside after her.

Warmth and the homely fragrance of bread baking and stew bubbling on the stove pull a stone from my stomach to my throat. For the first time in the last twenty-four hours, safety holds us in its soft embrace. And I am eternally grateful for it. I am grateful for Marguerite's kindness. For my magic. I grasp on to the tiny things giving me hope. Terrified if I let go of those thin strands, I will lose it all.

I have never seen Sammie so fragile before. I hate myself for putting her in that position. As if every-thing else she's been through because of me wasn't enough. I literally sent her spiraling into a panic attack over the university thing. I'm still not sure how she feels about Denver.

Part of me doesn't want to know. If things go south, I want her to be safe. I want them to stay safe and have each other. The two people I love most on this planet. I know he would take care of her. She isn't his mate nor he hers, but something deep down persistently gnaws away, telling me this is a good plan. That the day is coming when they will need this.

I listen as Denver tells Sammie the story of him and Zahli. It's heartbreaking every damn time. I pretend to clean the already spotless kitchen as he starts at the very beginning, back in the New Orleans days.

"Lew and I were hunting for jobs. We were on our third day of walking the streets, trying to find work, when we stopped in at a tiny cafe in the heart of the city. Zahli's pretty face was the first friendly one we'd seen all day. I was stunned. She smiled at me, probably thought I was a complete idiot."

"This was pretty recent, then?" Sammie asks.

"The 50s, so yeah, pretty recent in vampire terms." Denver clasps his hand together, resting his forearms on his knees as he takes a long inhale.

"I'm sorry," Sammie whispers.

"Tell her the rest of the story, brother," I say. The pained faces of my mate and my brother hush my words.

He nods and meets Sammie's gaze. "We found work eventually. And things started looking up, we hadn't seen Anjelica for years. I was hopeful she'd forgotten us. I frequented the cafe daily. Zahli would wait for me to take her lunch break. We explored the city. I knew I wasn't good for her. But I—"

Sammie's hand rests on his wrists, her fingers curl around it and then slip away.

"Vampires can't mate with humans. Not without significant risk of killing them during the joining. I found a witch and had myself bound. It was my greatest mistake. Maybe I shouldn't have let it go so far. But I couldn't stop myself. And Zahli paid the price for my selfishness in the end."

"You couldn't have known what would happen to her, Den." She brushes her palm across his jaw before dropping it into her lap.

His chin wobbles. My stoic, rugged brother is falling apart with Sammie's touch, her soft words. I can't blame him. I have done the same. She's pure sunshine.

Denver clears his throat. "We consummated our relationship. My scent was all over her. Anjelica arrived the week after. Her scouts had been scouring New Orleans, apparently. They found Zahli before they found Lewis or me. By then, our bond had snapped. She spent hours strung up to the ceiling of our little apartment before we found her. I tried to reason with Anjelica, my life for hers. She laughed in my face, the next thing I knew—"

He groans, and a tear slips down his cheek and over his stubbled jaw.

"Zahli survived long enough for Anjelica to haul us in. In the end . . ." I start, dragging my hands over my face, forcing the image of Sammie in Zahli's place from my mind. My gut churns. "She'd broken every bone in her body. We tried to kill the shadow witch that day. God knows we were desperate enough—" Air leaves my lungs, pushing a stone into my throat.

Sammie holds up a hand. "I can figure out the rest."

Den's cheeks are streaked with the tears still falling. He rubs his palms up and down his leaned thighs, over and over. Sammie stands and takes his hands in hers. She settles on his lap and pulls him into a hug. His head drops to her shoulders. He shudders through sobs as she tightens her hold, letting it all go. The storm absorbing the gift only sunshine brings. Her light chasing his ghosts. Her hands stroke his hair.

She whispers softly, letting him lose every last inch of baggage. He will never forget Zahli or forgive himself, but maybe Sammie can help him move on.

When Denver quiets, and Sammie releases him, pushing from his lap, I wander to the kitchen. The heat growing in my veins seeing them tangled together makes my throat burn. Coffee. Coffee will help. I fill the machine with beans and hit the power button. Instantly, the grinder hums and the scent of crushed beans infiltrates the air.

I pluck three mugs from the overhead cupboard and place them on the bench by the coffee machine. Sammie appears by my side. She leans against me and rests her head on my arm. I dot a kiss onto her golden curls, breathing her in, and close my eyes. I will never tire of having her around. I know I am absolutely blessed to have found my mate. And I will do anything to keep her safe.

The distinct tang of ash and smoke floods the living room, swirling its way across the marble floor and into the kitchen.

"What the hell?!" Denver shouts.

Sammie gasps. "Oh, no! Rena!"

I dash from the bench to the living room. On the rug

between the sofas lie two singed bodies. One moving, groaning. The other is still but breathing. Serena and a man around her age. His brown hair is still smoldering. Denver grabs the throw rug and swats out the last of the small flames dancing over their clothes.

Sammie drops to Serena's side, her hands frantically searching her friend for damage. I kneel by the head of the man. The shadow witch still clutches his hand in hers. Her pendant is lit up with a dull glow. Their clothes are old. Like renaissance old. He is wearing breaches, a long-sleeved tunic. She is in a layered gown with a corset. Wherever, or whenever, they were, they left in a hurry.

"Serena, can you hear me?" Denver asks, shaking her shoulder.

"Thee?" she whimpers and pushes halfway up on one hand. "Theo!"

She shuffles closer to the man lying unconscious on the rug. Her face twisted and breaths heaving, she searches his face with a trembling hand.

"He's still breathing," I offer.

She chokes through a sob.

"Rena, what happened?" Sammie asks.

"I went to check on him, in the farmhouse. Last time we were there, Marguerite told me about the scouts that had been. I was worried, so I went back again. When I got there, the whole house was up in flames. The family was nowhere to be found. They just left him there to burn!"

Anger and devastation turn her words into an angry, low growl.

Sammie moves beside Theo and searches for a pulse. She bends down and presses her ear to his chest. "His heartbeat is strong. Steady. He doesn't seem to be affected by whatever he went through."

Serena coughs, sending tears down her ash dusted cheeks. Her hair is singed. Ash mixes in with the dark tangles shrouding her face and sticking to her wet cheeks. Sammie comforts her friend and brushes away the matted hair and thumbs her cheeks dry.

"Let's wake him up," she says.

My stomach plummets. The last time she tried this, she almost died. But who am I to come between a mated pair? I haven't told her I know. Denver told me, eventually. These two keeping secrets is going to do my head in.

"No!" Denver snaps.

Sammie turns to him, her face torn between betrayal and hurt. "Yes, we are waking him up."

"Sammie, you don't have to d—"

She holds her hands over Theo and instantly a white light floods from her hands. She mutters something Latin under her breath, over and over. Serena shuffles closer to Theo's head. His jaw is smudged with ash. His shirt ripped and his chest bare down to the middle buttons. If I didn't know better, I'd say he's in sleeping attire.

She hovers by his head, whispering to him. As if soft

words and pleas will help him to come to. Sammie's words grow in temperance and volume. Her hands shake over Theo's body, and she pushes more light out. Saying each syllable with more gusto than the last. She groans and slams her eyes shut.

Serena grabs Theo's shoulders, shaking them. "Theo, wake up!"

I swear the shadow witch has lost it. Who could blame her . . .

Sammie's eyes open, her gaze finding mine.

The light from her hands disappears, and her eyes roll back in her head. She slumps to the floor, her head almost hits the floor, as Denver catches her and brings her to rest on his lap. Her heart beats fast, but strong. I wait for the rise and fall of her breath before turning back to Theo and Serena.

Groggy and disorientated, Theo moans and rolls over, eyes frantically searching the room. When they land on Serena, he cries out and pushes from the floor, crawling to where she sits instantly.

"Seri," he chokes. His palms are around her face in the next heartbeat. Sobs chug from her lips, and he caresses her cheeks with the backs of his hands, whispering to her softly. Dotting a kiss to her nose, he pulls her into his lap. She chuckles through a sob and clings to him, her arms around his neck, his face buried in her ash littered hair.

I'll never know how these two lived for centuries apart. That would be a new level of torture.

Sammie murmurs something, rolling out of Denver's lap. She sits up against the sofa, taking in her friend. A wobbly smile stretches her pretty face.

"Come here, Sunshine," I whisper.

She crawls to where I sit and drops into my lap. Denver watches her as she huddles against me and smiles with a laugh. He gets up and wanders toward his library. I hold Sammie close and train my gaze to Serena and Theo. After they have familiarized themselves with each other and he's planted kisses over her face and hands, he turns back to find Sammie and me.

"Thank you," he says. His English accent is crisp and dated, like not a day has passed since the year he was frozen in time.

Sammie sits up and removes herself from my lap, staring at Theo. He offers her a warm smile. Her face crumples with relief before she composes herself. Tears line her eyes as she says, "You must be Theo."

"Yes, madam," he replies, dipping his head.

Tears stream down Serena's cheeks again.

Sammie did it, she broke the spell, without needing Anjelica. Her powers are growing by the day. I can only imagine how powerful she will be after decades of homing them.

Sunshine will never cease to amaze me. Ever.

I stand and offer Theo my hand. He slaps his hand into my grip and pulls to his feet before turning back and helping Serena to hers. Her eyes don't drift from him for a second. As if just looking away for a moment would make him disappear.

A knock rattles our front door. A rapid heartbeat thumps on the other side. I dash to the foyer and rip the door open. A thoroughly rattled Jackson stands over the threshold. He shuffles from foot to foot, looking over his shoulder every few seconds. I pull him inside and shut the door. Sammie is in his space a second later. "Jackie, what is it? Why aren't you at school?"

He holds onto her for a long moment before holding her at arm's length. "I think someone is following me."

This sounds familiar.

"What? Who? Is it her, again?" I ask.

"Not sure, two guys, dark hoodies. Are always a block or two away. It's creeping me out. After last time, honestly, I don't want to go home and have them anywhere near Mom and Dad."

"You stay with us. I'll call Mom and tell her you're here." Sammie slides her phones from her pocket and taps the screen. The phone rings. It rings out. She tries another number. It rings out too.

She turns back to face her brother and me. "Nobody's picking up."

Serena walks to where we stand. Theo a step behind her.

"What's going on? Is she back, my mother?"

"We don't know," I say.

Her breath quickens, and she turns back to Theo. He

folds her into his arms. "Could we bother you for a change of clothes, Sullivan?" Theo says.

"Nice accent, bro," Jackson quips.

Everyone chuckles through pained laughs. Sammie slaps a hand over her mouth and strangles a sob before composing herself enough to say, "Jackson, this is Theo. He is from, well, 1837, London."

Jackson glances between Serena and Theo, who's still wrapped around her. Jackson swallows and nods. His heart races as he shoves his hands into his pockets, dropping his gaze to the floor.

Ah, now it makes sense.

Bad luck, Jackson, the shadow witch is already taken, buddy. Sammie reaches for Serena, and she takes her hand. "Come on, let's get you two changed."

"Then we are leaving. We can't stay here if my mother is anywhere nearby. Not with Theo."

"Where will you go?" Sammie asks as they walk down the hall toward my side of the manor.

"I have a little place in Italy."

"Oh, wow!"

"Yeah, kind of. Italy 1942."

"What is it with you and war zones, Seri?" Sammie laughs.

Serena rests her head on Theo's arm, and he slides it around her and tugs her closer. The heart of a battle is the last place someone wanting to survive would go.

Smart witch.

Sammie's phone vibrates. Her mom. I pick it up and answer.

"Lewis, how is my favorite nemesis?" the voice drawls.

My gut sinks as the blood drains from my face.

Jackson stares at me, his mouth agape.

Fuck.

Anjelica.

How do you tell the person you love most in this world their family is about to die? And it's all your fault. Sammie's face screws up with fear as her brother glances between the two of us.

The good news is Theo woke with no need for Anjelica's blood or magic. That makes her free game. Her lifespan just got a hell of a lot shorter.

Denver appears behind Sammie, arms crossed over his chest. As if my next words will inflict pain and suffering and he's ready to jump in and shield her from the hurt I'm about to cause her.

"Who was on the phone, Lewis," she breathes.

I tighten my grip around her phone and the screen cracks.

"Just tell us, man," Jackson breathes, shuffling closer to

his sister. His fists curl up and he exudes some sort of dark energy I have only felt around the shadow witches.

What on earth?

"Anjelica. She has your parents." I hold Sammie's gaze as her face crumples. My heart aches with every too-short breath she takes. She hugs herself. Denver folds himself around her and Jackson's eyes widen as he glances between them and me.

"She wants you and Serena in exchange for your folks," I utter. That is certainly not happening.

"I'll get Rena. We leave now," Sammie hisses and spins out of Den's hold and stalks down the hallway. "This ends today."

"Sammie, no!" I rush to the hall and block her path.

"Move, Lewis."

"Not happening, Sunshine."

"Move or I will make you!"

I reach for her, and she shoves past me.

"Serena!" she calls down the hallway, picking up her pace.

"Sammie, calm down, girl. I'm right here."

Serena appears through the doorway to the spare room she showed Theo to. Sammie grabs her and pulls her along toward the foyer.

"Babe, what on earth?" Serena mutters.

"Your mother has my parents."

Serena pulls out of her grip and halts in the hallway.

"Shit." She folds the cardigan she changed into, along with jeans and a T-shirt, around herself.

"Rena, this ends now. You have Theo. Lewis is safe. We end her now!" Sammie is pacing back and forth in front of Serena. The shadow witch watches her.

"I can't. I only just got Theo back. Please, Sammie, I can't risk it."

"Can't Theo heal you if something happens?" Sammie bites.

"In theory, yes. But he isn't a necromancer. He can't heal me if I'm dead. Sammie—" She steps back a step, shaking her head. "I have waited for centuries for this day. I can't, I'm sorry." Her chin wobbles, and she takes another step back from Sammie.

"You can't be serious! These are my parents we are talking about." Sammie curls her hands into fists. Flames burst from the center, engulfing her hands is heatless flame. Anger floods my veins, it's not mine.

Fuck.

I am in her space instantly, both hands cupping her face. "Sunshine, calm down. Please, we will work this out. You need to calm down."

She groans, sending a pang through my chest. The weight that's been crushing breath from my lungs the second Angelica announced she holds Sammie's parents hostage intensifies. Her anger and rage thunder through my veins. It's overwhelming.

Sammie stiffens in my hold. "She is a coward. Always taking people. Never confronting me head-on."

"Denver and I will go with you. Serena is right. This is not her fight, not anymore. This was aimed at you the second she endangered your family, taking Jackson. We will do this together, the three of us."

She melts in my hands, but her anger throbs through my veins. Jackson steps up behind me. I unfold Sammie from my embrace, and we both move to face him.

"I'm coming too." His face is stone.

"No, Jackie, stay here."

"Nope, not happening. Besides, I might be able to help."

Sammie shakes her head and opens her mouth to reply, and I step between them. "You will stay in the car. Anjelica isn't someone you want to interfere with," I say before Sammie can protest further. Denver's truck starts up outside. We make our way outside and Jackson gets in with Denver, Sammie and I file into the Mustang.

"Where did she take them?" she asks.

"Not far. Apparently, they're at a lake house west of Burlington.

"Water. She thinks my strength is fire. I'm half impressed. Too bad for her, she's wrong."

Den looks at me and forces a wry smile, but his eyes track back to the road. I stare out my window. Wishing Serena was with us. It's good to have her as backup, always. Her power would be comforting right now, not to mention the intimate knowledge she has on how her malicious mother operates. But I know how long she's waited, and what she's gone through to get Theo back. We can't blame her. I don't.

Sammie rubs the pendant between her fingers. My gut twists with every mile we travel closer to Burlington. I think back to all the tactics Anjelica's used before. To Sammie's strengths. Fireballs were always her favorite, even if they weren't always the easiest to control.

I just hope that this turns out to be elemental witch one, shadow witch none.

Fingers crossed.

CHAPTER 28

SAMMIE

The car park by the lake is deserted. The hour is late by the time we reach the spot Anjelica insisted we do the exchange. Unfortunately for her, there will be no exchange. I'm not in the habit of bowing down to bullies and especially not ones as evil and dark-hearted as this one.

I step out of the Mustang, and Lewis appears by my side. His hand slips into mine. His grip is firm and warm. He folds me into his hold, and I breathe him in. Reminding myself what we are fighting for.

"Please be careful, Sunshine," he rasps.

I run my hands behind his neck and nuzzle into his neck. "Always, Lew."

"I mean it. I will not lose you, no matter the cost."

"They are my parents, Lewis."

He closes his eyes and tightens his hold. "I know, Sammie."

He releases me. Denver walks over, nodding toward the lake. We track his gaze to a group of people standing by the lake north of the car park.

"Let's get this over and done with," Denver growls. Lewis gives him a look I don't fully understand. Something between knowing and pure fire.

I let go of Lewis and start the trek toward the group of people. As we close the distance, I see my parents. They are bound and gagged. Two of Anjelica's minions restrain each of them. Four more stand in pairs on either side of them and she moves in front, taking point. Her eyes narrow as we get closer. She's obviously noticed her daughter is missing.

"Hand them over AJ and nobody needs to get hurt," Denver says casually, running a hand through his messy hair.

AJ, that's a new one.

"Your humor is lost on me, blood sucker. Where is my traitorous daughter?"

"She's busy," I say, my hand landing on my hips and my brows lower.

"Too busy for her own mother, ungrateful little witch. Should have got rid of her the moment I had no use for her."

My heart thumps, fire growing in blood. How dare she talk about Serena like that?

"Release my parents, Anjelica," I snap.

"Or what, you will toss a fire ball at me, little witch? You forget I was honing my craft for centuries before you came along. Your power is no match for mine. Stop wasting my time. We will rendezvous when you are all present and accounted for. Not a second before, girl."

"Your funeral, you old hag," I say and curl my hands, pulling deep from the center well inside me.

"Uhhhhh," my mom growls around the gag, violently shaking her head.

Dad holds my stare, his eyes burning into me. They don't know I've been practicing my magic. As far as they know, the last time I used any element was the day I burned Jackson. And one teensy suspended tomato at the lunch table.

I inhale slowly and open my palms. A frigid wind rips over the entire lake. It cracks as it freezes over quickly. Mom's eyes boggle from her head. Dad gapes, stunned.

"I don't negotiate with lowlife, whose only motive is to hurt other people. Release them. Now!"

Anjelica flicks her wrists, and dark ribbons pour from her hands, soaring through the frozen air toward the three of us. Lewis pulls me out of the way as one swirls and darts toward us. Denver jumps out of the path of another, slipping on the ice beneath his feet. He lands with a crack. It breaks a little.

More ribbons, darker than the last, careen toward us and Anjelica walks forward cautiously on the ice. This time, I block her darkness with light. Exploding the dark ribbons to frayed threads as the bright white slices through them.

Lewis growls to my right and charges two of the shadow witches flanking my parents.

Denver follows his tactic to the left. Leaving me to face Anjelica head-on. She cackles something about lovesick pups and spins before slamming me to the ice with her silver lightning. Pain radiates through my body, and I cry out.

I push from the ice and stand. She wants fire. Fire is what she will get. I dig deep and curl my palms by my sides until the amber flames dance around each hand. I toss them at her, one after the other. The flames pour from my palms, and I pelt them toward her again and again. One misses and flies past my parents. Mom cries out. That was too close. I have to draw her away.

I track south, hoping she will follow.

Behind her, Lewis and Denver rip the shadow witches limb from limb. Red stains the ice where they stand, a united front back-to-back, as the witches attack. None of them last very long. Lewis is quick. Denver is strong. Their basic magic is barely enough to hold the boys off for more than a few seconds. On ice, Lewis and Denver are absolutely deadly as they use it to their advantage.

Anjelica closes the space between us.

She's inches from me. Her lip curls to a snarl like a rabid dog. If the shoe fits old woman. I smile at her like she's my favorite person in the entire world. "You can't win, Anjelica."

"You have no idea what I can and cannot do, you stupid bitch."

Ugh, really? Name calling now?

"Why can't you let this go? How long do you have to carry this vendetta around?"

"People think they can do whatever they want to women in this world. I educate them otherwise, girl."

"You're right on the first part. But there are better ways to solve your problems. Hurting innocent people is not one of them."

"Ha! Youth talking. People don't care about how nice you are. How much you sacrifice. They are only out for their pound of flesh. Well, I intend to take my share first. Nobody else in this lousy life will do it for you. You will learn that soon enough. Then what will you think of those two?" She tilts her head toward Lewis and Denver. One shadow witch remains. My parents are running cautiously across the ice.

"Just stop, Anjelica. Enough is enough."

"I will stop when every one of you is dead."

"Sorry, AJ. We won't be meeting death today. But you might be." I shove her backward and onto the hard, frozen surface with a quick wind, whipping her feet out from under her. She screams and is up and wielding her silver streaks in a heartbeat. One pierces my gut, and I groan, forcing myself to stay standing. She throws another and another. I block one and take another to the chest. This time, I cry out as the pain radiates with a crushing weight.

Lewis crumples in half across the frozen lake.

Anjelica rushes me.

Denver slides to a halt halfway to where I stand and slams a fist onto the ice. It cracks and splits with a thunderous boom. The crack skitters between Anjelica and I, inches from her still sliding feet. She scrambles to stop, arms windmilling around. Her feet slip over the edge of the ice, and she twists in the air as she plunges into the freezing water.

Lewis scrambles to his feet, grabbing at his chest. I look down at my own. Blood covers my sweater. The last blow must have been a direct hit. I collapse to my knees and clutch my sweater as the agony grows with the realization the injury is more than I bargained for.

We bargained for.

Denver slides to a halt beside me and holds me up by the shoulders. A broken gurgling sound from below the ice makes us all turn. Anjelica clambers from the water, hugging the jagged ice. She pulls herself up onto the ice and crouches. Her face is colorless, her lips blue. She shudders with the cold. Nobody moves to help her. Not even her last minion, who trembles behind Lewis, petrified.

I glance behind me to see my parents almost at the edge of the lake. A few more steps and they will be on solid ground.

"This is not over, girl." Anjelica rises on unsteady legs. She glances to the lake's edge. With the flick of both wrists, wind gushes and two thumps follow. Hugging myself, I turn on my knees. My parents fall to the ground, their necks bent at horrifying angles.

No!

No. No. No. No!

I moan and push to my feet.

Anjelica disappears.

Denver steadies me as I hobble toward them. Lewis is at my back a heartbeat later. I scramble over the lake's edge and drop beside my mom and dad. Their limp bodies lay still.

Lewis's bitten wrist appears at my mouth. He is trying to heal me. I push his wrist to my lips and take a few sips. The copper in his blood surges through my system and the pain subsides and the bleeding stops. I don't take my eyes off my mom the entire time.

Numbness covers my entire body. The air leaves my lungs and doesn't return. I choke through a sob and sink my head onto the grass beside Mom. I scream, clutching at the grass.

"No. Momma! Momma, please wake up!"

I shake her shoulders. Tears burn across my chilled cheeks and drop onto her sweater. Her hands are still bound, the gag rests on her coat. Lewis pries me from my mom and hugs me tight. I scream into his chest, sobbing, choking. Clinging to his navy sweater.

Movement rustles on the grass beside us. I don't leave the sanctuary of his arms. I can't. I can't look. If I do, this is real. It can't be. It just can't be.

I hear Jackson and bile rises in my throat.

Oh my god, my little brother.

I push from Lewis and turn to find my little brother. But something is off. He's not upset. He is kneeling by Dad, his hands hovering over Dad's face. My little brother closes his eyes and mumbles something in Latin. His head tilts slightly and his brows lower. His chin trembles and then he inhales.

And so does Dad.

What the hell?

Jackson wastes no time moving to Mom. He does the same, and a handful of heartbeats later, Mom gasps. Jolting up, eyes wide and searching. I wrap my arms around her, but my gaze doesn't leave Jackson's.

Not for a second.

"You going to tell me what the hell that was?" I snap at my little brother. I know I shouldn't be angry. I should be grateful. But the shock and surprise of seeing my brother bring our parents back to life ran off with my compassion.

He smiles sheepishly and runs a hand through his brown hair. His blue eyes study mine before he says, "I stumbled across my magic when I was ten. But it's dark, sis. Not like yours or Mom's. More like Serena's."

Is that why he was always so desperate to spend time with her? He wanted to learn from her? All this time, I thought he had a crush on her. Shadow witches aren't necromancers, but their magic is the closest thing to it. So many things make sense now.

"You have done this before, Jackie?"

"Yeah, I accidentally revived a rabbit once. After that, I worked on bigger game."

"That's incredible! Why didn't you tell me?"

"I don't know. You are like all sunshine and light. I didn't want to rain on your parade with my death tricks."

Lewis howls a laugh.

Denver joins in.

Sunshine. Apparently, Lewis is not the only one to see me that way. I'm not as amused. How did I not realize this? Why did Jackson not confide in me? After everything we went through with my powers, did he not trust me to know about this?

"Why didn't you tell me, Jackie?" I'm repeating myself, but I am desperate to know.

"I was afraid of what it would mean for our family if people found out. I thought maybe Serena could help me. But she is hard to keep tabs on most of the time."

As if Jackson talking about her had summoned her, Serena appears in the car park. Her hand still grasping the pendant as she weaves between the cars, heading for where we are huddled on the grass.

Noticing Mom and Dad, she rushes to us, dropping to the ground by my side. Her face is tortured with guilt and fear. "Sammie, what happened?"

"She killed them, Rena. They were almost out of reach, and she tossed around some wind and broke their necks. I didn't know she could do that . . ." My words fade to a whisper.

"Fuck. I should have been here. I'm so sorry. But how—"

My focus flicks to my little brother.

She jerks back and looks at Jackson. "You did this, Jackie?"

He blushes and drops his focus to the ground. "Yeah."

"Holy shit, little bro!" she says, her face lights up. "You're a necromancer. That is epic!"

"If you say so," Jackson mutters.

Mom clears her throat. "If it's okay with you guys. I really want to go home."

Dad nods, wrapping an arm around her shoulders. He says nothing, but his stare is constantly swinging between Jackson and me.

"Come on, I can get you all home fast," Serena says and rises, extending her hand to my mom.

"Thank you, Serena. It's much appreciated."

I take my best friend's hand, and she rolls the pendant between her fingers. "Hold on to each other."

Jackson hooks an arm through mine, and dad takes his other hand. A moment later, Mom slides her hand into Dad's and grips Serena's upper arm. Her gaze is weary, and I realize she has no idea what is about to happen.

A smile blooms on my face. My parents have discouraged magic for over a decade. Today, they have seen both of their children exhibit two very strong, very different powers.

Now, Serena is about to blow their minds.

·)·)·)·◐·(·(·((·

I pass the steaming, clean mug to Mom and she wipes it clean. After a thorough shower and an emotional moment upstairs in her bathroom. I have her showered, dressed and back to her normal routine. Washing up is always her go to when she's stressed, especially when I was a kid. Nothing has changed and we chat as I wash, and she dries.

Serena puts the items away, pottering around the house like she's lived here her entire life. Jackson is shut in his room, his music vibrating through the entire house. After today, nobody has the heart to tell him to turn it down.

"Are you girls looking forward to your term break?" Mom asks.

"Absolutely!" Serena says, offering her a megawatt smile. I remember Mom is still in the dark about Serena's extraordinarily long life and her real parentage. I smile to myself. Gosh, life can be complicated sometimes.

"I am looking forward to things going back to normal, school or no school. I have had quiet enough drama for one term," I say.

"Well, I was thinking about turning your room into a hobby room. You could always help me paint? Doesn't get any more mundane than watching paint dry, sweetheart." She winks at me, and I laugh.

"I'll pass, thanks, Mom. Plus, I'm hoping to spend some

downtime with Lewis. Now that he isn't working, there are a few things I want to do with him before the days heat up and the snow melts.

"Speaking of, you didn't tell me he's a vampire." Mom's face flattens under worry. Serena stops what she is doing, shutting the cupboard and turning to face Mom and me.

"I didn't really know how to tell you. Is it a big deal? I mean, supernatural things aside, we are—" Her hand rests on my arm and her face pulls to a wobbly smile.

"I am happy as long as my girl is happy."

"I am, Mom. Really happy," I breathe.

She pulls me into a hug. "Is Lewis who you were talking about when you came to talk about the mating bond?" she mutters into my hair.

I nod and she sighs. She knows the price of interspecies bonds; I gather. Mom's hold loosens, and I step back. "I can't lose him, Momma."

My breath turns short and my face crumples.

"We will figure it out, one day at a time, sweetheart." She squeezes my hands, and I nod.

My phone vibrates. I ignore it.

Serna lights up a second later. She grabs it and answers. "Denver."

She walks into the hall. Mom turns back to the sink, taking up the next item to wash. I pluck the tea towel from the bench.

"Woah, hold on. They what?"

I turn back to see her standing in the doorway to the kitchen, mouth agape, phone in her hand, still lit up.

"Sammie, we have to go." Her eyes narrow with devastation.

My gut flips. I toss the towel onto the bench and cross the kitchen in three strides. I search her face, and she swallows. "What is it, Rena?"

She shakes her head and grabs my hand.

The floor disappears.

·)))·◐·(((·

The shining marble floor of the manor floor rises to touch my feet. The front door is wide open. Three black suburban vehicles are parked in the driveway. Foreign voices, arguing a second ago, go quiet. Serena shakes my hand and turns me to face the living room.

Lewis and Denver stand, tense as hell, surrounded by six robed figures. At first glance, two vampires, two witches, and two demons. Their scents mingle but are still recognizable. Lew meets my gaze and instantly his chest heaves and his hands curl to fists.

Who are these people?

"You must be Samantha." The oldest of the men, a vampire, steps forward.

"What is going on?" Serena snaps.

He regards her no better than the dirt under his shoe, not even paying her a cursory glance.

"We have substantial evidence an interspecies mating bond has been acted upon. Between yourself," he waves at me, "and Lewis Sullivan. Do you have anything to add to this claim?"

My heart flings into my ribs. Fear prickles its way up my spine and a stone lodges in my throat, stealing my last parcel of air.

I open my mouth to respond. Only to find my mind and mouth are no longer connected.

"Just as I thought." He turns back and waves to his colleagues with a hand. Four sets of hands restrain Lewis. He doesn't struggle, nor put up a fight. His eyes burn into mine.

They will kill him.

They'll bind my magic for the rest of my life.

Anger and heat flood my veins. I heave through heavy, laden breaths and raise my hands. Fire bursts around my palms, and I stalk to where they stand. "Let. Him. Go!"

The old man tilts his head as his brows lower. "What do you plan to do, murder the head of the council?"

"If this is your idea of justice, I will burn you all." I seethe.

Denver's eyes go wide, and he shakes his head rapidly. I fling my palm to face the older man, and he counters with a block than knocks me backward. I stumble before finding my feet.

"Sammie, don't," Lewis begs.

"Why not? This isn't fair. If interspecies bonds are so horrendous, they wouldn't exist. Mother Nature does not make mistakes!"

"Unfortunately, Mother Nature is not coherent with modern civilization. Many have sacrificed to get to where we are now. And one elemental and one vampire will not change that. Nor will they even matter in the grand scheme of things. Go easy, lass. Or it will be harder for the both of you."

"No," I beg. "Please, you don't have to kill him. We can break the bond. I'm sure of it."

The old man lifts his chin. "You are not the first to have lived through this, and I am afraid you most likely won't be the last. There is no other option for a consummated mating bond. The vampire dies. Three hundred years is a fair life. Your magic will be bound. This is how it must be."

He gestures, and his posse walks Lewis toward the foyer. Denver collapses to his knees, gripping the sofa. He groans and screams.

No.

I chug through sobs, my body trembling with fear and heartbreak.

Lew looks over his shoulder at me. His dark brown eyes are full of love and adoration. His jaw works and he mutters, "I love you, Sunshine. I always have."

"No, Lew!" I scream.

Serena's hands slide around my arms. I summon wind

and slam it toward the older man as he goes to cross the threshold in front of the council members holding Lewis. It barely affects him. One witch turns back and whispers under her breath before holding both palms in front of her face, snapping them shut before flipping them toward me as they open. A dull sensation crawls over my skin. Serena curses and supports my weight as I struggle to stay on my feet.

Lewis groans, twisting in their hold. He is no match for the two vampires holding him. I choke on every too shallow breath. As my mate disappears over the threshold and down the steps, spots flood my vision and the ground sways beneath me.

I crash to the floor.

I can smell him all around me. The instant my mind is conscious, the last few events play on repeat. That's when I realize, although I can smell Lewis, he isn't here. I'm comfortable and warm. In bed.

Someone is beside me by the feel of the decline in the mattress on my right. The woodsy smell and slower breathing means it's Denver. My chest pangs.

"Sammie?"

A sob lodges in my throat.

I don't want this to be real.

I want my mate back.

A hand brushes mine and I force my eyes open. Denver sits on the bed, his back resting on the headboard. Boots off, in a fresh shirt and jeans, he meets my gaze before forcing a smile. "How are you feeling?"

Like I want to die.

Like everything worth living for, left with the council.

Like my heart will explode and kill me at any moment.

"I'm fine, Den."

I sit up and sweep the curls from my face. He studies me. Devastation crowds his rugged face. He runs a hand through his hair and slides an arm around me, pulling me into his side. "I'm so sorry, Sammie." His voice breaks with my name.

I turn, curling up at his side and he dots a kiss on my hair before his hand rubs my back. A deluge of sobs racks my body. I heave through every painful breath. Lewis is gone. My gorgeous, ethereal storm cloud is gone.

I don't feel anything apart from his emotions, but they're fainter as the hour drags on. I scratch my wrists, and the sting reminds me I'm alive. I dig my nails in until the skin breaks and the scent of copper floods the bedroom.

Denver stiffens beside me, but his hand comes to rest over the wound. "Sammie," he utters.

A sting scratches along my other wrists. I snap my stare at the reddened skin. I didn't do that.

Lewis.

Heavens . . . I can still feel him.

He can still feel me.

He's alive.

"Den, he's still alive!"

His face twists as he leans into me and whispers, "For fourteen more days . . ."

Need more of the Blood Fate Saga?
Pre-order the next book in the series, Bound Fate, now!

Bound Hate

Gracie Stone

ABOUT THE AUTHOR

The fantastical has always fascinated Gracie Stone. So much so, that she spends most of her days living in worlds other than our own.

She plays with mystical creatures, goes on journeys with imaginary people and loves places and people that will never exist.

As a reader, it is easy to escape to these places too. And it is Gracie's greatest wish to help a reader to be sucked into a place that doesn't exist. To befriend magical creatures and characters...

You too can find yourself in these pages, or you can disappear into them entirely.

That, friends, is up to you.